JFIC
AHM

Ahmadi, Arvin.

Down and across.

$17.99

DATE			

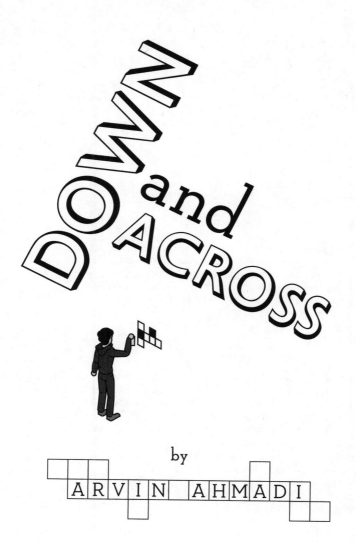

DOWN and ACROSS

and

by

ARVIN AHMADI

VIKING

VIKING
An imprint of Penguin Random House LLC
375 Hudson Street
New York, New York 10014

First published in the United States of America by Viking,
an imprint of Penguin Random House LLC, 2018

LIBRARY OF CONGRESS CATALOGING-IN-PUBLICATION DATA

Names: Ahmadi, Arvin.Title: Down and across / Arvin Ahmadi.
Description: New York : Viking, [2018]. | Summary: "Sixteen-year-old Scott
Ferdowsi's impromptu trip to a famous professor for advice about success
turns into a summer of freedom that brings him answers in unexpected
places"—Provided by publisher. Identifiers: LCCN 2017005389 | ISBN
9780425289877 (hardback) Subjects: | CYAC: Runaways—Fiction. |
Interpersonal relations—Fiction. | Self-actualization (Psychology)—Fiction. |
Iranian Americans—Fiction. | Washington (D.C.)—Fiction.
Classification: LCC PZ7.1.A343 Dow 2018 | DDC [Fic]—dc23
LC record available at https://lccn.loc.gov/2017005389

Printed in U.S.A   Set in Dante   Book design by Mariam Quraishi

10   9   8   7   6   5   4   3   2   1

I suppose I do have one unembarrassing passion—
I want to know what it feels like to care about
something passionately.

—Susan Orlean, *The Orchid Thief*

We as human beings seem to have a natural
compulsion to fill up empty spaces.

—Will Shortz

❑◻❑◻

PROLOGUE

EIGHT MORNINGS BEFORE running away, I found myself at McDonald's, wondering about the direction of my life. It was one of those moments that should have felt important. I should have said to myself: *Hey, Self! You're having a Pivotal Moment in a Sentimental Place.* On a scale of 1 to Serious, I should have rated this occasion at least a 9. But I didn't. My Serious Scale didn't even register. Not a single cell in my brain cared to define that morning in the grand scheme of things. Or in any scheme of things, really.

That morning I wondered about dirty tables. The one in front of me had almost certainly just been wiped down, still freshly wet and slippery. I imagined the motions the McDonald's employee made cleaning that surface: up, down, up, down. Left to right. Loop-de-flippin'-loop, like a drunk man on a Zamboni joyride. Still, the table reeked, so I knew they cleaned it with a dirty rag. This conundrum hijacked my focus. On one hand, sure, it was better for the environment to clean hard surfaces with a rag. But then, wasn't the rag just transferring gunk from one surface to another?

"Pay attention," he snapped. "I'm trying to understand what you want."

Right. My dad. He clenched his hands tight, the skin bunching up around his knuckles. I felt guilty. Not for anything I had actually done, but for what I wasn't doing.

We sat at our usual booth in the very back. It was like our boxing ring. In one corner: Me, Scott Ferdowsi, my lanky five-foot-ten frame slouched like a golden arch. Fighting to quit a summer internship that hadn't even begun yet. In the other corner: My dad. Fighting to keep me on the right track, any track, because I'd been known to derail.

"I know what I *don't* want," I said, stabbing my plastic fork into a rubbery glob of eggs. "I don't want to look at microscopic mouse poop for the rest of my life. Research is boring."

My dad chuckled. "What could be more exciting than mouse poop?"

I glanced over at the table next to us. A girl in a sparkly *Frozen* costume was stomping her My Little Pony toy into her hash browns.

"Horse poop," I said. "Perhaps I will become an equestrian."

Dad scrunched up his face. *"Saaket bash,"* he hissed. *Be quiet.*

"I am," I teased softly. My Iranian name is Saaket, which means "quiet" in Farsi. It's one of my best jokes: "Be quiet!" "That's my name!"

Dad didn't laugh.

"When are you going to get serious, Saaket? This is your life. You need to stop playing games and plan for your future."

Bingo. It would be his usual lecture. I rolled my eyes and slid lower into the tattered cushion to get comfortable. If there's one thing Iranian parents love more than chelo kebab and their children, it's making a point.

"You're all over the place," he said, waving his hands frantically. "Look at the opportunities you've already screwed up. High school! You get accepted to a very nice high school, but you hardly study. You're pulling lousy grades."

Jab.

"Last summer. I got you a job with Majid's law firm. You quit after three weeks."

Punch.

"And now, after I pulled every mediocre connection I have to get you an internship at the university lab, you're giving up before you even start."

Knockout.

He kept going, as if he hadn't just put me down over and over: "You know, I was reading a study the other day by a very famous professor at Georgetown . . . Cecily Mallard. She's a genius, Saaket. Really! They just gave her an award that is specifically for geniuses. The genius award, it's—"

"Okay, Dad," I moaned. "What did she say?"

My dad paused dramatically and pointed his finger upward, à la *eureka*. "Grit," he said. "She discovered that the best predictor of success isn't IQ or how wealthy your parents are, or even your grades. It's grit. Do you know what that is?"

"Nope, but I'm sure—"

"It's a person's ability to stick with something. To focus. To really follow through. *Tahammol*. It's treating everything you do like a marathon, not a sprint."

"Come on, Dad, a summer internship isn't a marathon. It's, like, the JV track meet that nobody watches. I don't need a participation ribbon for—"

"You're missing the point, Saaket."

"Scott," I said curtly. "It's Scott. I've been going by Scott since kindergarten."

"Sorry," he replied, only half-sincere. "*Scott*, you're missing the point. When you set your mind on something, you need to give it a shot and persist."

"Mouse poop."

"Yes, mouse poop," he said, gritting his teeth. "You were excited about it a few weeks ago. You were cracking jokes: 'poopular' this and 'micropoopic' that."

I buried my face in my hands, wondering if my dad was at all embarrassed by the words he had uttered in a public place. Probably not.

He sighed deeply, as if I were the one exhausting him and not the other way around.

"You're almost seventeen years old, Scott. In a few months you'll be a senior, filling out applications for college. What in the world do you care about? What do you want to do with the rest of your life?"

"I don't know, Dad."

"See? That's exactly the problem!" His eyes lit up. "*Pesaram.* My son. You need to start thinking about your future. You could study engineering, or you could go to medical school. Those are both respectable fields. I just"—he threw his hands up—"I just want you to *care* about something, Scott. I can't think of a single thing you're gritty about. I'm not calling you a failure, but I only wonder if we should have kept you more focused."

Clearly my dad *was* calling me a failure. I held my breath as a stream of shortcomings bogged down my mind. My grades. My SAT score. The Earth Club I let wither away like the ozone layer. The mystery novel I got bored with writing after three chapters. All those instruments I used to play.

"Are you paying attention?" he barked. "I need to know you'll take this internship seriously while your mother and I are away. This is important."

"Important for you or for me?"

His eyes jumped. "For you," he said, forcing the words out slowly. "You're almost an adult now."

"If I'm almost an adult, then why can't I go to Iran with you and Mom?"

"Here we go again. We'll take you one day, I promise, but

now isn't the right time. It's a critical summer for your future. And with everything going on with Baba Bozorg . . ."

We both got quiet. Dad broke the silence with two taps on the table.

"This is the right plan. You stay home and do your internship. We deal with Baba Bozorg's health." His voice cracked, and he forced a smile. "Don't you always say we should trust you more? Well, here's your trust. One month!"

"One month," I repeated.

"June fourteenth to July fourteenth. *Precisely* one month. I asked the travel agent what kind of discount we would get for such a nice coincidence—"

"Dad, you're so lame."

"We're coming back on your birthday! I believe that is the opposite of lame."

"Uh-huh."

"In fact, your mother and I are very cool. We suspect you might throw a birthday party with your fellow interns, and we are *cool* with that."

"I'm the only intern. And I'm sure you'll be calling twenty-four/seven."

Dad dropped his buddy act. "One phone call a week, that's all. Look, we're trying to meet you halfway. Please, focus on your internship."

I didn't have it in me to keep arguing, so as usual, I gave up. "Okay, Dad. I'll do the stupid internship."

We sat there silently for the rest of breakfast like boxers with their foreheads pressed together, dripping sweat, too tired to throw the last punch. I didn't finish my eggs. Instead, I imagined my parents in the airplane to Iran, gazing out the pressurized window at the chalky sky and everything beyond it—stars and galaxies and dark matter–type craziness. I imagined the big bang, which created our scattered universe: scattered, but acceptable. Indefinitely incomplete.

I wondered: Why aren't I allowed to be indefinitely incomplete, too?

The next morning, I hugged my parents goodbye in the kitchen. Once again I didn't finish my breakfast. I left a few flakes of Raisin Bran in the bowl, dumped it in the sink, and took off to catch the bus to my internship in Philly.

Exactly one week later, I boarded a different bus to Washington, DC.

Everything happened so quickly. I drew a blank as soon as I stepped onto the Greyhound. Technically I was running away. I knew that. The stream of gut-punching, sweat-inducing adrenaline made that much clear, even if it would only be for two days. But for a brief moment I couldn't recall why I was doing it, like I'd stumbled into the kitchen in the middle of the night but forgotten what exactly I wanted. The reason was escaping me.

Then the bus jolted forward, and I remembered.

Fucking grit.

WEEK ONE

CHAPTER 1

I INHALED DEEPLY, then exhaled. *This is happening*, I whispered under my breath as I drifted down the aisle.

The bus smelled cheap. It didn't reek, but it had a sterile stench that was on par with the cleaned-by-a-rag whiff of a McDonald's table. I lifted my chin up to look around. Virtually every seat was filled with strangers, and for the first time in my life, I saw an extra layer of meaning in that word. Not that there's anything inherently *strange* about a man in a business suit drinking wine straight from the bottle, or an all-girls punk rock band, or a person with teardrops tattooed on his face, but when you put these unique individuals together inside a moving box . . . voilà. Strangers. Noah Webster must have ridden this very bus when he wrote the definition. But who was I to judge? I was the token teen with a half-baked plan, so I suppose I added to the strange vibe.

I made it to the back of the bus and found two seats by the bathroom, which added a truly special touch to the smell situation. Strategically, I plopped my backpack down in one seat and myself into the other. First I would pretend to be asleep to ward off potential seatmates. They would have no choice but to assume the backpack belonged to someone else. Then, when everyone was seated, I would sprawl out across both seats and sleep like a king. It was a foolproof plan.

Seconds after I closed my eyes, though, I felt a tap on my shoulder.

"Is anyone sitting there?"

I opened my eyes and rubbed them pathetically, gazing up like a lost puppy. A remarkably pretty girl towered over me. She had wispy blonde hair and the kind of deep blue eyes that suck you right in. No high cheekbones or sharp jawline or anything—her face was confidently undefined. Round, but in a sweet way. Her lips, on the other hand, were inhumanly voluminous, and she pursed them while she asked. She knew no one was sitting there. She was totally onto me.

"Yeah, someone's sitting there," I lied. I wasn't going to let an attractive girl distract me from my plan. "They're, uh, in the bathroom."

She scanned the packed bus and pointed at the bathroom, smirking.

"Do they know they left the door open?"

Ugh. I never get away with anything. I pushed my backpack to the ground, and the girl took a seat without missing a beat.

She turned her head and looked up at me with those eyes. They had this intense nonchalance that I couldn't bear to look at, so I lowered my gaze, which meant staring at the arch formed by the small of her back, which was her ass. I shot my attention back upward. Eye contact with her chin would have to do.

"I'm Fiora," she said. The words flowed from her mouth like waves, rhythmic and decisive. "Did you really think you'd get away with that imaginary friend stunt?"

My mouth dropped. I couldn't find any words.

"I don't blame you," Fiora said. "You'd think it would be emptier on a Monday morning. Who travels to DC on a Monday?"

Still no words, but I furrowed my brows this time, because, well . . .

"Right. Us. Normally I leave Philly on Sundays. But last night was my mom's birthday, and it's been . . . Oh. You're a complete stranger."

"That's correct," I finally said.

"And I'm talking your ear off."

"Yes."

Confident as she was, there was something desperate about Fiora's expression. Her lips quivered like the words were scratching to escape. Maybe she had wild stories from the weekend. Maybe it was family drama. Whatever her situation, I had my own story to figure out, so I decided to stage an exit.

"It's nice to meet you, Fiora. I'm really tired and . . . Well, I'm going to take a nap, if that's all right."

She chuckled. "Your choice, pal."

Fate had placed a beautiful and friendly girl in the seat next to me, but grit demanded that I stay focused on the task at hand. I put in earbuds and shut my eyes. In a matter of hours, I would be standing face-to-face with the leading expert on this subject I had become so obsessed with.

◻◻◻◻

When I first heard about Professor Cecily Mallard, I thought she was full of shit—another motivational speaker-thinker-quack my dad thought could save my potential or whatever. Grit sounded like a self-help guide for parents with kids like me.

On Monday when my parents left for Iran, I started my internship, which was actually full of shit. Approximately 98 percent of my job involved collecting feces from lab rats and preparing them for various tests. It stank. It *reeked*— even more than all of those poop puns. I recognize that fecal research is tied to natural pathogens and pulmonary symptoms and other virtuous science-y things. But it's still poop. I was squinting at it for eight hours a day and taking notes on its density and hue in a lab notebook. Most of the time I wanted to stab my head with a micropipette.

That first night after work, I showered and popped one of my mom's Lean Cuisines into the microwave. I was ready to surf the web. It was going to be a long and lonely summer without my best friends, Jack and Kevin, who were away on a highly selective teen tour of Southeast Asia. In the absence of friends, parents, or a car—sore subject—our family PC was my only portal to the outside world.

One link led to another, and eventually I found myself on Professor Mallard's Wikipedia page. She sounded legit, and her lecture on YouTube had about a zillion views:

> **CECILY MALLARD:** It's not students with the highest IQ who consistently succeed. It's not the best-looking ones or the ones from wealthy families. It's the grittiest. The ones who keep trying, even when they fail. The single most reliable predictor of success is grit.

When my dad talked about grit, I hated it. I was convinced he was using it to put me down. But Professor Mallard wasn't putting me down; she was telling me there was still hope. That I could still be successful—with grit.

By the end of the week, I had grown obsessed. Grit became my magic potion: the cure to my constantly side-tracked train of thought. It was the gigantic anvil that would squash my insecurities and pave the way for the rest of my life. I watched all of Professor Mallard's lecture videos, read all of her interviews, and absorbed as much as I could from her psychological studies. I even checked out a copy of her book from the Union Library.

Sunday night, I took her online evaluation, the Grit Quiz, which asked me to value how much I identified with a series of statements:

> #1: *New ideas and projects distract me from previous ones.*

If grit was distracting me from my internship, didn't that mean . . . Never mind. Too meta. I was stuck between "Very much like me" and "Mostly like me," which sounded like the same answer. These options were sketchily subjective. [Mostly like me.]

> #2: *Setbacks don't discourage me.*

The double negative threw me off, so I simplified the statement: *Setbacks encourage me.* That sounded even weirder. I picked the neutral option. [Somewhat like me.]

> #3: *I have been obsessed with a certain idea or project for a short time but later lost interest.*

Wasn't this just the first question worded differently? For variety's sake, I stepped up my answer. [Very much like me.]

The assessment went on like this for a few more questions.

Calculating your grit . . .
Your grit score is: 2.63. You are grittier than 10% of the US population.

I flunked. At first I wasn't surprised. The Grit Quiz was just confirming what I already knew about myself. But then it hit me—the heavy hand of failure—and boy, did it sting. Suddenly I was back in that godforsaken boxing ring. *When are you going to get serious?* Jab. *You're all over the place!* Punch. *Stop playing games. You're almost an adult. What in the world do you care about?* Knockout.

Grit was supposed to be this equal-access path to success, but what if I was just lost? What if I kept stumbling down all the wrong paths until it was too late? If I couldn't get gritty about something on my own terms, then I would no doubt get forced into one of my dad's "practical" career paths. There were plenty of people who wanted to become engineers and doctors. I wasn't one of them.

The Grit Quiz left a giant, bleeding stain in my mind that I couldn't wash off. What it didn't leave was a how-to guide. If I wanted to be gritty, I needed a passion—that much was obvious. But as far as I could tell, Professor Mallard's site didn't offer a BuzzFeed-style quiz for *that*. Instead it linked to her bio, which noted her summer office hours: Mondays 2–4 p.m. and Wednesdays 8–10 a.m.

If I was going to take control of my life, I had to prove this diagnosis wrong. The first step would be showing up at Professor Mallard's office on Monday. No one was better equipped to reverse my track record than the expert herself. Since her website wouldn't tell me how to improve my grit score, I would solicit her guidance in person. I had no choice but to get gritty about grit.

🔲🔳🔲🔳

I woke up about an hour into the bus ride. I could hear Fiora riffling through a newspaper, folding it, and scribbling with a pen before I had even opened my eyes.

"You know you were snoring," Fiora said. She was curled up in the fetal position, her legs digging into the seat in front of her.

"Well . . . you're scribbling in a newspaper," I muttered back.

"I'm not scribbling, asshole, I'm doing a crossword." I'd known Fiora for less than an hour and she had already called my bluff, endured my snoring, and dubbed me an asshole. And I wonder why I'm still a virgin.

"Sorry, I didn't mean to offend you. I'm in a weird place right now. I'm kind of discombobulated from my nap and from life and—"

"Discombobulated from life?" She looked up quickly and

tilted her face sideways in an attempt to read mine. I froze. "Join the club."

Again with the words behind her lips. This girl had a story. *May I continue?*

"I like that word," she continued. *"Discombobulated.* It's exactly fifteen letters. Fits perfectly into a standard grid. I take it you're not a cruciverbalist?"

"A cruci-what?"

Fiora pointed at her newspaper. "A cruciverbalist. Someone who's into crossword puzzles. Like when you have a bunch of boxes going across and down, and you have to fill them with . . ."

"I know what a crossword puzzle is."

"Do you solve them?"

"I don't," I said. Fiora shrugged and went back to her crossword. This should have been my cue to take another nap—or better yet, think about what I'd say to Professor Mallard—but all I wanted was to keep talking to Fiora. There was this relentless force whirling between us, magnetic but not quite two-sided. It was more like a hurricane, sucking me into the eye of the storm. Her eyes. God. They were turned away, yet I could still feel their pull.

Before I could come to my senses about Fiora, the bus hit a bump in the road, and it was as if one of my friends had pushed me into her at a school dance.

"I don't think I've ever done a crossword puzzle in my life," I blurted.

No reaction.

"Maybe I've done one or two . . ."

Fiora looked at me like I was a crazy person. A sharp pang of humiliation twisted my stomach. Quickly I resorted to sarcasm.

"Aw, shucks. I guess this means we can't be seatmates. You could try switching seats with someone up front, although I recommend steering clear of the Asian guy with dreads. I'm suspicious of anyone that culturally juxtaposed."

Fiora held back her laughter. Success.

"Good try," she said. "I'll stay right here, if you don't mind. Unless your friend decides to come back from the bathroom. He must really be struggling in there."

"Very funny, Fiora. Maybe I should go and look for my friend, it could take—"

"Also, culturally juxtaposed? Really?"

"It was a joke," I mumbled. Fine, it was a stupid joke. I kicked at my backpack—in part because it was cramping my legroom, but also to relieve myself of our conversation's awkward turn.

"The joke wasn't going anywhere," Fiora said. "That's not the nature of our relationship, anyway."

"What relationship? I've known you for all of, like, five waking minutes."

Fiora lifted her knees from the seat back and bent down to reach her bag. She popped back up with a pack of Twizzlers, which she promptly shared.

"Our bus friendship. The one where we're the kind of people taking a Monday-morning bus to get away from their . . . *discombobulated* circumstances."

"Would you like to talk about it?" I asked.

"Nah. Not anymore."

"You must be itching to get back to that crossword puzzle."

Fiora rolled her eyes, smiling. "Why are you going to DC, anyhow?"

"To meet a Georgetown professor," I said, biting off another chunk of Twizzler. In an attempt to sound cooler, I added, "I'm kind of running away from home."

Fiora simply replied: "Cool."

While I wasn't going to let my microcrush on Fiora distract me from my real business in DC, I couldn't help feeling a little turned on by her nonchalant reaction. *Cool.* No prying, no eyes-growing-wide with a side of "Oh my God!" She started taking these colorful bracelets off her wrist, two by two, and I swear, the casualness of it all gave me goose bumps.

"Well, I'm getting tired myself." Fiora bent over to pack the wristbands, Twizzlers, and newspaper into her bag. "It's been super chatting . . ."

"Scott," I said, filling in her implied blank.

Fiora had barely closed her eyes when we hit another bump. A series of bumps, actually. She let out a theatrical groan.

"Is that your real name?" I blurted again. "Fiora?"

"Is your real name Scott?"

"Of course."

"Don't look Scottish to me. Unless you're culturally, what was it? Juxtaposed?"

I shook my head, glaring at the back of the seat in front of me.

"What's *your* real name?" she asked.

Ah, the uphill battle with my real name. First days of school were always a nightmare. Every roll call went the same way: *Suh . . . Suh-keet? SAY-kit?* "It's Scott," I'd say, staring at the podium to avoid eye contact. They'd cross out my Iranian name and scribble down my "American" one. Kids used to tease me about it in elementary school, calling me every variation of "Suck It" imaginable. (Philadelphia might be the City of Brotherly Love, but second-grade classrooms are all the same.) High school was better because I got into Tesla, our local magnet school, and my classmates morphed from mostly white to mostly Asian and Indian. I was surrounded by other kids who shared my name woes. Like Kevin—that's his real name, but his last name is Ho. Sophomore year I won a bet and now he has to name his firstborn after me. Saaket Ho. That poor kid will never hear the end of it.

"Saaket Ferdowsi," I told Fiora.

"I like it. Saaket Ferdowsi," she said perfectly, like she was the first person ever to utter my name. "Well, it's been super chatting, Saaket."

Before I could react, Fiora turned her head to rest. Her eyes slipped effortlessly back into the hospitality of their spheres. Then she turned again to face me directly.

What a tease.

I stared out the bus window as we passed hazy fields and concrete walls, the highway blurring in a streak of gray. I relished this extra-fictional turn of events. People weren't supposed to meet like this in real life. But, then again, people weren't supposed to ditch their summer jobs to run away and confront world-class professors. I couldn't resist imagining my life as one of those coming-of-age movies—and Fiora as the quirky, two-dimensional female character, written in solely to help me discover my full potential. The idea was nice. It smoothed over a good fifteen minutes of bumpy road time.

But that wasn't Fiora's job. I was counting on a real genius to help me out. For the rest of the bus ride, I told myself over and over that I would not let Fiora or anyone else distract me. I had to stay gritty. Otherwise, I'd never make it to Professor Mallard's.

CHAPTER 2

WE STEPPED OFF the bus an hour later at Dupont Circle. I said goodbye to Fiora, but then we did that awkward thing where we started walking in the same direction. I looked over and smiled politely before turning around. I thought Fiora would keep moving along, so I stopped to pull up directions to the hostel I had found online the night before.

Fiora tapped me on the shoulder. "You don't know where you're going, do you?"

I opened my last Google search. "The . . . Hanover Hostel?"

It turned out she knew exactly where that was. My hostel was on the way to Fiora's apartment, so she insisted on walking me there. "Blame it on my Southern hospitality," she said, though her eyes flickered with sarcasm.

Dupont Circle was many things: bustling traffic circle,

commercial hub, sprawling park with kids running around carelessly and a gushing fountain in the middle. From there we moved down New Hampshire Avenue. The street was packed tight with town houses, all glowing majestically under the early-afternoon sun. I cupped a hand over my eyes and followed Fiora's lead. The skin of her hips jutted out above the waistline of her ripped jeans, rocking with a seductive rhythm as she moved.

"So how'd you do it?" Fiora asked. "The old note on the pillow?"

"Even easier," I said. "My parents are out of the country for a while. They flew to Iran last week and don't get back until July fourteenth."

"*Le quatorze juillet!*" Fiora twirled her hand in a faux-snooty way. "Pardon my French. That's Bastille Day. My boyfriend is French."

Her boyfriend. Of course this Twizzler-carrying crossword girl had a boyfriend. Not that I was interested in Fiora. I had my own mission.

"Does he live in Philly?"

"No, he lives here. I live here, too, sort of."

"Sort of?"

"I'm a student at George Washington, but I grew up in Charleston."

Almost like she sensed that I would ask about Charleston, or that I'd pry into why she had spent the weekend in Philly and what made it so discombobulated, Fiora quickly added:

"What's the deal with this professor you're seeing?"

"It's a long story."

"We've got two blocks," she said.

"Ehhh . . ."

"Come on! Don't be shady. Give me the short version."

I took a deep breath and picked up the pace. "So this professor, Cecily Mallard. She's literally a genius—like, they gave her one of those awards for geniuses, the MacArthur Grant. Her whole thing is grit. How if you choose a path and work hard and persist, even in the face of setbacks and fire-breathing dragons, you'll succeed. I took a quiz on her website, the Grit Quiz, and I failed miserably. I'm not gritty. My parents are obsessed with me growing up and becoming a successful *something*, and if I can't figure it out myself, then they'll force me into a career that I hate. So I need to talk to Professor Mallard."

"Ballsy."

"Thanks," I said, sweaty and breathless. That's what I got for yapping about fire-breathing dragons.

"How long are you here for?" Fiora asked.

I took a second to catch my breath again and cool down. I shook my T-shirt. I could feel the individual letters sticking to my body: TESLA MODEL UN on one side, CRISIS AVERTED on the other. Crisis most definitely *not* averted.

"Well, I'm meeting Professor Mallard this afternoon," I finally said. "And my bus back is tomorrow morning."

Fiora scowled. "Why would you leave so soon?"

"To go home and actually get grittier," I said. "Write a novel, learn to code . . . whatever this genius tells me I should be doing. I've already quit my summer internship for this. I need to focus on the rest of my life."

"Aren't you already focused?"

"What do you mean?"

"I'm saying you had the balls to come here. Why don't you 'get grittier,'" she said, using air quotes, "in DC? That's what a real runaway would do."

I shrugged. "I dunno. Going home just makes sense."

Apparently that wasn't the right answer.

"Saaket. I know we just met, but trust me. You're too young to be preoccupied with making *sense*." Fiora spat the last word out like a mosquito had flown into her mouth. "Rational thinking moves us forward, sure, but only in big steps. Industrial revolutions and shit. That's how humans evolve: they set goals and chase them, make families and protect them . . . But people like us? It's not our job. Not yet. We're still figuring things out. So we take smaller steps and enjoy them irrationally."

"What are you saying?"

"I'm saying you should stay for two weeks! Two months! Anything longer than two days."

"Why should it matter to you?"

"Because!" Fiora sighed, running her fingers along the reflective glass of an office building. "I—I don't know. For a second there, when you said you were running away, I felt relieved. I thought I wasn't the only crazy one."

"Thanks . . . ?"

"I'm joking," she said half-heartedly. "But seriously. Don't chicken out. You'll find pockets of excitement here."

"How would you know that?"

Fiora smiled, her eyes growing wide. "Last winter break! I spent a month in Spain by myself, selling pocket warmers. *Literal* pockets of excitement. The kind you snap and shake vigorously to make heat." She gave a demonstration, flicking her wrists—delicate and thin, but not so thin that you could see bone—and shaking the imaginary pocket warmer before slipping both hands back into her real pockets. "It was right when things with my mom got complicated, and I'd just flunked my Spanish final. I bought the flight at the last minute and found the job through a friend of a friend of a distant cousin. Best month of my life, and now my Spanish is a lot better."

There was something endearing about Fiora's satisfaction with the little things when I had set out to confront something bigger. I should have brushed off her Spain story—distractions were my *problem*, not my fix—but instead, I simply shrugged. Fiora took this as a small victory and shot back a cocky smile.

We arrived at the Hanover Hostel on the corner of 21st and New Hampshire. It was a quiet brick town house with large bay windows and a deck overlooking the front yard. There was a fenced-off lawn that tapered into the street corner—perfect for Slip 'N Slide in the intense summer heat. Fiora turned around and placed a hand on my shoulder.

"Stay right here," she said. Her tone was urgent, like I was being assigned to a special mission. "I have something for you. I'll be back in two seconds."

Twenty minutes later, Fiora came riding back on an outrageous lime-green bicycle with razor-thin wheels and 1920s-style curved handlebars. Even with its wear and tear, it was the kind of bike that screamed for attention.

"What do you think?" Fiora said. "It's brand spankin' new. A work of modern, vehicular, two-wheeled innovation."

"It's a bike, Fiora, and there's no way it's new. Maybe like a decade old."

"Well, do you want it? This bike is your access to DC, your *manifest destiny*."

Fiora would have made a great salesperson, because instead of questioning her use of "manifest destiny" or telling her I didn't need a bike, I asked: "How much does it cost?"

She said nothing. Literally, it would cost me nothing.

"Nothing?"

"Nothing. My housewarming gift to you."

"Seriously, Fiora, I'd love a free bike, but don't you need it to get around to classes or your job or . . . whatever it is you do?"

"What are you, my academic advisor?" She rolled her eyes. "I'm taking a summer class at GW. Sociology. Easy A."

Separately, I noticed she didn't bring a helmet. I thought

about my mother, who would kill me if she caught me riding without a helmet, because in her mind a helmetless death is not a matter of "if" but "when," and her catching me was still distinctly possible from halfway around the world. Helicopter Moms are capable of exceptional feats.

"Anyway," Fiora said, "you're the one who ran away to do big things."

Before I could respond, Fiora leaned the bike against the fence and took off down New Hampshire, waving goodbye from behind.

"Hey!" I yelled.

Fiora swiveled around like a ninja, narrowing her eyes.

"May I ask you a question, Saaket?"

I gawked. Wasn't she just running away from me?

"Um, sure."

"What does the grit lady say about distractions? What if you don't *want* to focus on the persistent and serious things in your life?"

I cleared my throat and surprised myself with a quick answer.

"Find new things, I guess."

CHAPTER 3

THE HANOVER HOSTEL was smaller than it looked in the pictures online. The velvet armchairs and wooden tables in the lobby were more worn down than I had imagined, and the lighting much less charming. I walked over to the front desk.

"One night, please," I said.

The hostel employee hardly looked up, his nose buried in a copy of *Atlas Shrugged*.

"There's a two-night minimum," he said.

"Oh. Okay." I pulled out my wallet to pay in cash. Thankfully, I'd brought more than enough money.

"ID?"

Crap. There must have been a minimum age, too. I really should've spent less time looking at pictures on their website and more time reading the fine print.

I made up an excuse on the spot, stumbling over my words as I explained how I'd lost my ID in Maryland and didn't have anywhere else to stay for the night. The front-desk guy, who couldn't have been much older than me, was clearly itching to get back to his Ayn Rand novel. He took my name and payment in cash for two nights, no questions asked.

My room in the hostel was remarkably plain, with linoleum floor tiles and four empty bunk beds. Each bed had its own special flavor of stains: scarlet speckles, dusty brown blotches, even a large mustard island on one of the pillows. There was no winning with any of them.

I picked the one with the pillow stain, comforting myself with the fact that I would only be in DC for one night, despite Fiora's best efforts to keep me around. Not to mention I could just flip the pillow. I threw my backpack on the bed, changed into a blue polo shirt and corduroys, took a quick look in the mirror, and took off for Georgetown.

Stepping outside and lingering in the shade of the small front porch, I could feel the heat waves looming on the other side. I whipped out my phone to pull up walking directions to Georgetown, specifically Professor Mallard's office. Her office hours started in half an hour, and I wanted to arrive before any of her students.

There was a small problem. Apparently, Georgetown the *school* was over a mile farther than Georgetown the *neighborhood*. So much for my "hostels near georgetown" Google search. Not only was I cutting it close on time, but it had to be nearly a hundred degrees outside. If I walked to her office, I would be late. If I ran, I'd show up looking like I had run a marathon—and not the metaphorical grit kind.

I looked down from the porch; Fiora's bike was still parked by the chain-link fence. I made an impulse decision to hop on and ride to campus. Fight *and* flight—how about that for psychology? The bike ride filled me with a kind of sugary upbeatness straight out of a Kidz Bop commercial. I floated past blocks of short, brightly colored town houses on M Street that lined up like candies on display in a boutique treat shop. The people were preppy and happy. Georgetown-the-school was a more majestic scene; I navigated one gargantuan Gothic building after another. Each building was made of thick gray slabs of stone. They soared into the sky, crowned with pointed roofs and wooden crosses that reminded me of the university's Catholic ties. By the time I reached Cecily Mallard's building, White-Gravenor Hall, I had considered converting at least three times.

I threw my bike on the grass outside the building and made it to Professor Mallard's office with a few minutes to spare. I stood outside her door catching my breath. I wanted to run through exactly what I would say to her, sentence by sentence. Instead, my brain did that thing where it explodes and freaks out with a million thoughts, all stepping on one another's toes, fighting for my attention. Why was I the only person there? Didn't Professor Mallard teach summer classes? Was her website outdated? Could I be at the wrong office? Maybe she had canceled office hours that day? How crazy was I *really* to try meeting this psychology professor who had no obligation to help me?

I took a breath and pulled the brakes on my brain. I was stalling. I thought about the irony of having a mental breakdown in the Georgetown Psychology Department, which made me smile and calmed my nerves a bit. I took another breath, deeper, and opened the door.

"What! The! Ffff— Damn it!" I jumped back as Professor Mallard shrieked and spattered coffee off her lips. I must have opened the door right into her and knocked the coffee out of her hands. She stood there drenched and, more noticeably, pissed. The Queen of Grit had become the Wicked Witch of Georgetown, except instead of melting into a puddle, she erupted like Vesuvius.

"Oh my God. I'm so sorry," I said, offering my shaky hands as if they were paper towels and not the useless limbs that caused this disaster. "Are you okay? Is that hot?"

"I'm fine," the professor snapped. "I was just stepping out to reheat it." She took a moment to collect herself as a tall Sikh student walked up, his mouth slightly agape. Professor Mallard looked at him apologetically. "I'll be with you in a minute, Mandeep." She looked back at me. "You're here for office hours, I suppose? Come inside. Just . . . give me a moment to clean up."

Professor Mallard marched over to her desk, which sat at

the end of a long and narrow office. Floor-to-ceiling book-cases lined both walls, packed tight with nonfiction titles like *Handbook of Child and Adolescent Sexuality* and *Do Hard Things: A Teenage Rebellion Against Low Expectations*. Her desk, in stark contrast to the rest of the office, was unclut-tered, with a picture frame and an abacus occupying the corners. The abacus had all the beads slid to one side, and the picture was your classic couple's shot, showing Profes-sor Mallard giving a piggyback ride to an older man.

I sat silently across from the desk. Professor Mallard dabbed her blouse with a stack of napkins, digging in and rubbing firmly with each dab like she'd done this a million times before—head bent down, intensely focused. Locks of charcoal-black hair covered most of her face, though I could still make out a few soft freckles on her olive cheeks.

"Ahem," she said, head still down.

"Oh! Hello, Professor. My, um, name is Scott Ferdowsi. Again, I'm so, so sorry about what just happened. I prom-ise—"

"Good afternoon, Scott. You must be in my summer course, yes?" Professor Mallard looked more petite in real life than I had imagined. This did not make her any less intimi-dating.

"Yes?" she repeated.

"I—No, I'm actually not." I straightened my back and scooted to the edge of my seat.

"Pardon?"

"I'm not in your class."

Professor Mallard lifted her face. I could finally see her eyes—piercing teal lasers that shot me down instantly.

"I'm afraid I have to ask you to leave, Scott. Office hours are for current students only."

I started to feel dizzy.

"I'm going to be a senior in high school, and I took your Grit Quiz last week—"

Professor Mallard raised her hand. "Scott, I'm sorry, but my time is limited. Feel free to email me, and I'll do my best to respond."

Everything around me started to spin. I felt the rug pulled from under my feet, and now my vision was rumbling and spinning out of control. I wanted to throw up. I needed to leave.

"S-sorry," I said, trying my best to stand up and exit coolly.

A small crowd had formed outside Professor Mallard's office. I leaned against the closed door for a moment to collect myself, gasping for air. Then I ran. I shot past the cluster of students, down the halls and stairs of White-Gravenor until I was out of that damned psychology building. I collapsed on a bench, burying my face in my hands. Hyperventilating. The vertigo came rumbling back, and I hurled into a trash bin.

❑❑❑❑

Wasted time.

Wasted money.

Wasted energy.

Most of all—wasted hope.

◻◻◻◻

I never thought I'd go on a "walk of shame" before college, but leaving Professor Mallard's office after getting rejected sure felt like one. I tried my hardest not to think any more about our brief encounter. The disappointment would go away eventually—it always did. Something else would distract me soon enough.

As I was biking through Georgetown-the-neighborhood, I stopped to watch a young man playing the violin at a street corner. He wore a tuxedo with bright red sneakers and was playing Justin Timberlake's "Mirrors." His music filled the busy corner with liveliness, but my eyes were focused on the violin nuzzled between his shoulder and neck. An old memory flashed across my mind.

"Play it again."

I was eleven years old. Practically chained to a folding chair in the corner of my bedroom. My legs were crossed, and a clunky Persian guitar, the *tar*, rested on my lap. It had a long, delicate neck carved out of mulberry wood, and the sound came out of a hollow chamber shaped like a figure eight. I'd been playing *tar* for a few years, but that night I held the instrument like a baby that wasn't mine.

"Play it . . . again," he repeated, sending shivers down my spine.

My dad stood over my shoulders, the drill sergeant of my last-minute practice session. We'd been going for hours that night. It was the eve of Nowruz, the Iranian New Year, and while I had known for months that I was performing in our local celebration, I'd waited until the night before to learn the song.

My eyes shifted jerkily between the flimsy sheet music and my fingers as I plucked at the *tar* and sang along with the melody: *"Mikham . . . beram . . . kooh."*

I choked on the *kh* sound. My eyes quivered, and I held back tears. I hated this instrument. I hated Iranian music. Most of the time, the ancient lyrics meant nothing to me, but for once I understood them and could even relate.

I want . . . to escape . . . to the mountain.

"Relax. Relax, damn it." Now my dad was hunched in his chair, massaging his temples. He wanted me to relax physically, not mentally. Everything about my posture was tight. My legs were crossed tight. My fingers pressed tightly into the neck of the *tar*. I even held the wax-covered pick tightly, "shaping the wax like kebab," as my dad would say.

I sang the next line without understanding the meaning, or why I was subjecting myself to this nightmarish practice session. I broke down.

My father cursed in Farsi. I stormed out of the room, leaving my *tar* turned over sideways on the carpet. I locked myself in our small upstairs bathroom, still clenching the pick in my sweaty palms. I threw my head over the sink and sobbed loudly. You could say I was being overdramatic, but I preferred choosing my own performances.

Eventually I looked up, confronting my reflection in the mirror. Pathetic. Confused. I was filled with anger toward my dad, but I couldn't even empathize with myself. I began assessing my face, feature by feature, channeling my anger to my physical shortcomings. I hated my bushy eyebrows—unyielding caterpillars that lurked over my watery black eyes. My Mr. Potato Head nose, sniffling, looking wider than usual. Most of all, I glared at my mouth: not just for the fuzzy mustache that was beginning to grow over it, or the squashed M shape of my upper lip—but for the words that slipped out of it. A language I didn't care to speak. Song lyrics I didn't care to sing. Names of exotic food I was too embarrassed to bring to school lunches. Words that held me back from fitting in.

I carried myself to my room and continued crying softly in the corner of my bed, curled into a ball, when I heard something fly over my head and smash into the wall. It was the miniature violin I kept on my desk, and it had shattered into a million little wooden shards. Dad stood by the door.

"It's not worth it," he yelled, fists clenched at his sides. "You're lazy, and you'll never practice. Keep up this habit and you won't ever amount to anything."

I brushed the splinters off my bed and cried myself to

sleep. I probably dreamed of botching my performance—which I did.

I never officially quit the *tar*. I just stopped playing. One skipped lesson turned into another, and then I was out of commission for three weeks with the chicken pox. This closed the musical chapter of my life for good. Every few months or so, my dad would suggest I take out my old *tar* and play some chords. My dad and I lived in our own fantasy worlds where I'd pretend my failures never existed and he, after some time, believed that I never failed but simply pressed pause. One of our fictions had to be true.

I hopped off my bike to drop a dollar into the violin player's case, watching the crisp bill swim in the air on its way down.

I buried my latest disappointment in the ground with all the others.

I hopped back on my bike and rode away.

CHAPTER 4

I HAD ALMOST reached the hostel when I noticed a bald, bearded man riding very close behind me on a neon-orange bike. He looked at least thirty and was wearing a tattered shirt. To be safe, I rode past the Hanover Hostel and made a right on a small road called Sunderland Place. The man also turned. He was following me.

Fuck fuck fuck this isn't good, I thought. Also not good: Sunderland Place wasn't a real road. It was about one hundred yards long—one of those chode roads they use for drug deals and gang violence and now my impending death. I thought about making a sharp right at the end of Sunderland, but the guy was right behind me, practically breathing down my neck. There was no way I'd lose him with another turn.

"Hey," he said. I jumped in my seat. In my imagination,

this man had a gun and would shoot if I even acknowledged his presence. We reached the end of Sunderland, and I made a spontaneous move—I veered into a sudden U-turn. My bike bounced off the curb and onto the road, brushing past the stranger's bike. He stumbled and yelled: "Hey, what the hell, man? I'm trying to talk to you!"

All right, I had temporarily paralyzed him. This time I jetted down Sunderland in what felt like a microsecond before turning left onto New Hampshire. I raced down the street, my face straight ahead. I was almost back at the hostel when I heard his voice getting louder from the other end of the block: *"Hey! Kid! Hold the fuck up."*

God. Damn. It. If I stopped at the hostel, he'd find me inside, or at least he would know where I was staying, so I kept speeding down New Hampshire. I turned right on L Street—now I was going against traffic—then made a sharp left, shooting past backpacked college students who ducked out of my way. . . . *Kind of badass*, I thought to myself, *right? Wait, focus.* I couldn't hear his voice anymore, but I didn't want to turn around, so I kept biking and turning onto random streets to lose He Who Must Be Right Behind Me.

"Hey, kid . . ."

Ah, shoot. Somehow he'd caught up fast. I pedaled faster, faster—

"Hey! Stop!"

Pedal, pedal, PEDAAALLLLLL—

Whack.

My face was covered in blood. I must have lost control of the bike and steered straight into a phone booth. I could feel stinging wounds all across my cheeks. My arms and legs were pretty messed up, too.

I managed to lift up my head and assess my surroundings. There were signs for K Street and 22nd down the block. Then I froze. In front of me, there was a man's shadow. Slowly I looked up and breathed a sigh of relief; this man was neither bald nor scruffy.

"I tried yelling at you to stop"—the stranger chuckled—"but you were heading straight for that telephone booth. Like, you were impressively determined to take it down, so props for that, but honestly? You never had a chance."

"I—I don't know what I was doing . . . I was running away from this guy who was chasing me and lost control and I guess just kept biking. And then—I . . ."

"No worries, man," he said. He grabbed my arm and helped me up. "Let's get you cleaned up. I saw the health services building a block or two that way."

"What?" I must have wound up on another campus. "Oh, I'm not a student here."

"Really?"

"Yeah. Don't worry, I'll be—" I tried standing up and fell over pathetically. "Fine."

"No, no way." The stranger extended his hand to help me

up. He thought for a moment, then spoke: "Here, I've got a plan. I'm Trent, by the way."

"I'm Scott," I said. "Thanks for helping."

Trent hoisted my arm over his shoulder, and we limped together down the block. Normally I wouldn't accept help from a stranger, but I was desperate—not to mention the only thing threatening about Trent was his good looks. He towered over me with an athletic build, dirty-blond hair, and a jawline so sharp it put other faces to shame. Trent wore a kelly-green polo with khakis and boat shoes. Unless he had plans to strangle me with an argyle sweater, I was pretty confident this stranger wasn't going to kill me.

We stepped into the health services building at George Washington University and approached the reception desk. Trent placed one elbow on the desk. "Hello," he said, coming on strong to the receptionist. "My friend Carlos Zambrano here just suffered a horrible biking accident and requires immediate attention from a health services professional. He can't seem to locate his wallet or phone, and his memory seems to have suffered somewhat, but you can look him up in the student database."

"I'm sorry, but we're closing early today," the receptionist said.

Trent pouted his lower lip ever so slightly. His eyes were kind and patient, and they stayed fixed on the receptionist.

"One moment," she said, shuffling to the back.

"Carlos Zambrano? For real?" I whispered. "I'm not even Hispanic."

"Whatever, your face looks rough enough that it should work," he said. "Carlos goes to school here. We work together over at—"

We heard the receptionist coming back. "All right, Mr. Zambrano, there's no need for your student ID. I found your file and informed our after-hours nurse of your circumstance. She'll see you right away. Follow me."

Trent winked as I walked off with the receptionist. True to my made-up brain injury, I was dumbfounded. Who was this guy?

❑❑❑❑

The nurse cleaned me up quickly without asking too many questions, wrapping my wounds with Band-Aids and medical tape, and the receptionist referred me to a neurologist in case my memory had actually suffered. As soon as I left the building, I crumpled the referral and chucked it into the trash. Trent was waiting by the door.

"You're looking a lot better," he said.

"Thanks," I said. The word lingered on my tongue for a second. "For everything. You didn't have to do that, you know."

"Come on, you think I was gonna let a kid like you sit

there and suffer after an accident like that? It was the least I could do."

It struck me that Trent wasn't just a kind stranger; he embodied the Mount Everest of moral high grounds. He could have walked by the pay phone, but he stopped to help me up. He could have called 911, but he brought me to the health services building. He could have left me there, but he made up a story to get me admitted. And he could have left right after, but he stood outside and waited. I felt further comforted by his slight Southern drawl, which drew out words like *"suhhh*fer" and accented his sincere manners with a layer of hospitality.

We walked slowly to the phone booth. Trent bent over to pick up what was left of my bike—a mangled clump of aluminum, chain, and wheels.

"So how the hell did you drive this thing into a phone booth, anyway?"

I laughed nervously.

"Well, I just got into DC today," I said.

"No kidding. That makes two newbies in town!" Trent said, slapping me on the back. "I moved here last month. Just graduated from College of Charleston. What brought you?"

I explained my story to Trent—my track record of failure and how it manifested itself as this failed quest to meet Professor Mallard. I even told him about the peculiar blonde girl who gave me her bike just a few hours earlier.

"Well, she wasn't that peculiar," I said. "She was insanely

pretty. And nice, like you. Fiora, that was her—"

"Fiora Buchanan!" Trent bellowed. "She's been up in Philly a lot lately."

"You know her?"

"Abso-freakin'-lutely. She's about the only person I know in DC. We were best friends growing up. Fiora's a couple of years younger than me, but our fathers did business together back in Charleston. Paper business." Trent froze. "Wait a minute."

"What?"

He shook his head and started to laugh.

"What?" I said louder, my voice cracking. This only intensified Trent's laughter.

"You must have biked through Washington Circle, didn't you? It's smack in the middle of Georgetown and GW, with a big ol' statue of George Washington, a bunch of students hanging out on the benches. Philosophy types . . ."

"I was coming from Georgetown, so, probably?"

"You, my accident-prone friend, were riding around on a stolen bike."

"Huh? No way."

"Yessir," he said. "She's always challenging herself like that, Fiora. . . . Doing risky shit for the hell of it. Last week she told me she was stealing her TA's bike to teach *him* a lesson. They, um, have a rocky relationship." Trent let out a sigh. "I used to try and talk Fiora out of these things when we were kids, you know? But she's stubborn."

If I had any interest in Fiora before as a cute girl, a stranger who briefly distracted me from the stakes of my running away—God damn it. I couldn't believe the man who chased me was her teacher. I couldn't believe I was riding his stolen bike. I was furious. I breathed heavily, clenching the bike's battered handlebar before throwing it to the ground.

"Do you think she was trying to screw me over or something?"

"Absolutely not," Trent said. He looked simultaneously stern and sympathetic. "You need to know something, Scott. Fiora's life these days is about as messed up as a bunch of lawmakers trying to do their damn jobs. She's going through some big changes with her family. Lord knows she's not the kind of girl to let the world get away with giving her a kick, so sometimes, she'll kick back. Stealing that bike, giving it away—these things give her a necessary thrill. Does that make sense?"

"It's still messed up," I said. "But whatever."

We dumped the remains of my bike into a garbage can, the aluminum frame and rubber wheels overflowing the top. Not to be outdone by Fiora, Trent insisted on walking me back to my hostel. The sun was glistening off the DC skyline, a fiery blitz of rays dancing along the shiny glass buildings around us. We passed important government agencies whose names were too convoluted to bother reading in full: *The International Something Policy Something, the Federal Mediation and Something Else Center*, among others.

"What's your background?" Trent asked.

"Persian," I said. "I mean, my parents are. I was born here."

"Is that the same thing as Iranian?"

I gulped, reminding myself that Trent grew up in the Deep South. My parents said that people there still think of Iran as an Axis of Evil, no thanks to President Bush.

"Yeah," I mumbled.

"Dude, that's awesome! I didn't grow up around a lot of, um, diversity," Trent said. *Diversity* was one of those buzzwords that always annoyed me, but Trent made it sound like an exciting taboo. Something otherworldly. "I did know a Middle Eastern guy in college. Afghan, I think. Do they speak the same language? Arabic?"

I smiled for a couple of reasons. The way he said words like *diversity* and *Middle Eastern*, *Afghan* and *Arabic*—Trent might as well have been speaking a foreign language. The juxtaposition of those words with his accent was like nothing I'd heard before. More important, though, his interest was genuine. Trent was looking to me as an expert, not an alien, and that felt uniquely special.

"Iranians and Afghans speak the same language, Farsi."

"*Farsi,*" Trent said fondly. "Right. My friend taught me to say something in Farsi. Um . . . *Basanam dard meekoneh?* Something like that?"

I stopped in my place and fell to the ground laughing. I told Trent that the phrase his friend had taught him translated into

"My butt hurts." He crossed his arms and grumbled, saying, "After that fall, I bet yours does, too . . ."

Then he helped me up.

I asked Trent what he was doing in DC, and the rest of our walk home took the form of an episode of *The West Wing*, guest-starring future US Senator Trent Worthington.

"I've been obsessed since I was a kid," he gushed. "It's been my dream for as long as I can remember to get elected to Congress."

Trent's hopeful gaze melted into reluctant cynicism when I asked him how a person gets into politics in the first place. He complained that it was impossible to land a job in DC without the right connections—like being the daughter of a Kennedy, or roommates with the second cousin of a slimy oil magnate. He sounded like a megaphone-equipped activist standing on a soapbox in the town square.

"It's not like I've got nothing," Trent said, wiping a bead of sweat from his forehead. "Between Fiora's dad and mine, I could have gotten a job with at least half a dozen Republicans in this city. But my politics are particular."

"How so?" I asked.

"I'm no fan of the Republican Party," Trent said, "but I'm no liberal, either. There's only one man in the US Senate right now whose views line up with mine. Renault Cohen. He's an Independent. Open-minded on immigration and gay marriage, but he's patriotic as hell and has all the right views on the economy. I applied for a job in his office right before I moved here but haven't heard anything yet." Trent sighed, his eyes tired but undeterred—the kind of expression that would go on a billboard for grit. "We'll see if I can find the right connections in the meantime. Every day's a new opportunity to network in this city."

We exchanged numbers at the steps of the hostel. I thanked Trent endlessly for coming to my rescue today—no problem, no worries, don't sweat it, he kept repeating—and I told him to text me if he ever found himself in Philly.

CHAPTER 5

I MISSED THE bus to Philly.

I went to bed exhausted Monday night, and I was expecting to wake up feeling equal parts refreshed and displaced. I did not get that luxury. The hostel roomed me with a trio of French backpackers who were shuffling around noisily at the crack of dawn. One of them opened the curtains, inviting a flood of premature sunlight into the room. I pulled the sheets over my face, but light still managed to slip through, not to mention I could hear the sound of their footsteps. This went on for two hours, from about six until eight in the morning.

After they left, I fell back asleep and snoozed through my alarm. I woke up three hours later. My 9:30 a.m. bus was long gone.

I also saw that Trent had texted me.

Hey man, how much longer are you in town for?

I texted him back.

Funny that you ask. I missed my bus this morning.

He replied almost instantly.

Aw I'm sorry man, that's pretty shitty. When do you think you'll leave now?

Good question, Trent. I put on my thinking cap and ran through my situation. I'd already prepaid for two nights at the hostel. I didn't have a grit assignment or an internship to jump into back home. I was feeling exhausted. Verdict: I was in no rush to leave.

I guess I'm stuck here till I can get another ticket.

Trent replied fifteen minutes later:

Free for a goodbye drink tonight then?

Ha. Part of me wanted to say, "What the hell, sure!" and make the most of my last night as a runaway. The logical part reminded me that I'd literally met Trent yesterday. He was a nice guy who helped me out—but still a complete stranger. I played the underage card:

You know I'm not 21, right?

Kevin and Jack wanted to wait until college to drink. They said it would be less risky when we were on a college campus, and there weren't many parties at Tesla, anyway. So none of us drank. I tried convincing Jack to throw a party once when his parents were out of town, but he was too afraid of getting arrested. Fiora would have probably said getting arrested was part of the adventure.

Yeah that's fine. Let's meet at Thomas Foolery.
It's angry hour from 4-7.

If my age wasn't going to be an issue . . . *What the hell, sure.* I looked up Thomas Foolery on Google Maps. It was on P Street, which stemmed out of Dupont Circle, so it wasn't even far. Actually, it struck me that there were a lot of streets coming out of Dupont Circle. Ten, to be exact. If you stared at the circle and its surrounding streets, it vaguely resembled a sun—the kind I used to draw as a kid, with a circle and some lines coming out of it.

All right, see you at 5.

Instead of getting out of bed, I scrolled lazily through

my Facebook newsfeed. I was surprised to see Kevin had posted a picture in the middle of the night. He and Jack were jumping in the air outside a massive Chinese pagoda. Caption: *WE FOUND WIFI IN WUHAN! And a 2000-year-old tower! Mixing up that old and new. #win #hotasballs #chinasoven #SEAsiaYouthLeadersTour*

I'd almost forgotten my best friends were off exploring a new continent together, meeting other like-minded kids from around the world. Kevin the aspiring economist and Jack the aspiring diplomat. Compared to them, I felt like an aspiring nothing.

It was hard to believe the three of us met in the same globalization seminar freshman year. I never understood how those lessons had such a profound impact on them yet did so little for me. It might have had something to do with Peggy Zuckerman, the wackiest teacher in a school full of wacky kids. On the first day of class, Mrs. Zuckerman placed an inflatable globe about the size of a basketball on her wooden podium, only to squash it with a thick textbook. "The world is flat," she said crisply.

Most of the class exchanged skeptical looks, but Kevin, Jack, and I were sold. We spent our lunch breaks studying for her Human Rights Violations (pop quizzes) and guessing what antics she would pull next. We relished her peculiar simulations, like the gummy bear arms race. Who would have thought you could demonstrate cultural hegemony *and* strengthen your friendship with seventy-five packs of Haribo gummy bears? The three of us appreciated Mrs. Zuckerman's class for different reasons; I found her lessons amusing, while Kevin and Jack were genuinely inspired. Early on, this didn't matter. But lately, as their passions solidified and mine didn't, I've felt us drifting. As if it wasn't enough dealing with my own future, I've been having doubts about our future as friends, too.

Suddenly I felt restless. I jumped down from my bunk and threw on my shorts and T-shirt, still damp from yesterday's sweat shower. I didn't want to sit around and keep moping about Professor Mallard or the bus or my friends, so I stepped outside to explore this sun-of-a-neighborhood. First, I wandered into a bookshop off Dupont Circle called Kramerbooks. It was cramped and smelled of burnt rubber, but the books were stacked high and wide, so I stuck around. I picked up a Steve Jobs biography and skimmed the first few chapters. I found it fascinating that the guy dropped out of college, backpacked his way through India, and still managed to build one of the biggest companies in the world. It made me wonder if success was less about grit and more about the journey.

I left Kramerbooks and walked around the corner to a café called Afterwords. Exhausted, I found a table and whipped out my phone. In an effort to exist in a pretend state of stability, I opened a news app called Flipboard. Not because the world was a particularly stable place, but because reading the news was something that stable, levelheaded people did.

Flip. *The situation in the Middle East is bleak. A small terrorist organization funded by a larger terrorist organization tore through a village in Syria, killing 290 civilians. Sixty-six were children. Flip. It's worse than I thought. Shit's going down between Israel and Palestine. Flip. Amanda Bynes . . . Shia LaBeouf . . . I can't keep track of all these former child stars getting arrested. Flip. Speculation about who's running for president. Flip. Democrat hints she's running for president. Flip. Republican criticizes said Democrat's economic policies. Flip. 12 Adorably Teeny Animals That Will Make Your Day. Flip. Flip. Flip.*

Cecily Mallard Explains Why Grit Matters More Than Talent.

I flipped out and knocked over my cup of iced tea.

"God damn it," I grumbled. Fortunately, there weren't more than a few sips left, and the man sitting next to me jumped in with a stack of napkins.

"Thanks," I said, smiling half-heartedly.

"No problem," he said, wiping away at the liquid. The man appeared to be in his forties, wearing a tank top and in better physical shape than me.

"I just saw something that triggered me on this app and freaked out."

"Really? What app?"

"Have you heard of Flipboard? It's one of those apps where you swipe through—"

The man smiled. "Oh yeah. I know all about those swiping apps."

"Well, I was swiping, and I saw this professor I got rejected by the other day and . . . Yeah. It was awkward, so I guess I spilled my tea."

"Happens to the best of us," he said with a delicate lisp. He smiled at me again, and I smiled back. We finished wiping down the table, bumping hands twice.

"I'm Arnold," the man said. "Can I buy you another coffee?"

I pondered for a second.

"That's very—um—"

"Are you . . . ?"

Arnold looked at me like I had misled him somehow, and immediately, I realized what was going on. I shook my head intensely.

"No. No, sorry."

He rolled his eyes, strutted back to his table, gathered his things, and left. I was pretty aware of what just happened. I stared blankly ahead as the man made a dramatic exit. When he was gone, I pulled my phone back out. *Flip.*

❑❑❑❑

I'd never been hit on by an older person before. He probably thought I was a college student, so I couldn't totally blame him. But it still felt weird. Maybe it felt that way because the man was gay. Believe it or not, I didn't know anyone gay personally. My parents' only friends were other Iranian parents, and they were all straight. At Tesla, there were seven or eight "out" students who were members of the Gay-Straight Alliance, but they usually kept to themselves in the physics hallway.

My dad used to say people were full of surprises. As I

walked over to meet Trent at the bar, I wondered about every person I passed. Is this woman gay? Is this man a violin prodigy? What if I have a surprise in me? By the time I reached Thomas Foolery, I realized I'd go crazy if I kept thinking like this.

That is, unless I'd already gone crazy. I stepped into the bar, and the city's chaotic soundtrack faded out, replaced by a familiar '90s tune: "I Want It That Way." The Backstreet Boys. It wasn't just the playlist. I looked around and realized I had entered a literal playground. To my left, a wall covered in Etch A Sketch pads. To my right, an entire corner dedicated to Mario Kart—leaderboard and all. There were pinball machines, dartboards, and, directly under my feet, a hopscotch court. I kind of felt bad for walking right over it.

There was no way I was in the right spot. I took a hop and a few steps back outside to double-check the awning. Sure enough, it said Thomas Foolery. I went back inside, hesitant, and took a seat at one of the Etch A Sketch tables.

I should have known from the name, Thomas *Foolery*, that it would be a silly establishment, but I thought adults were subtler about these things. I figured they'd just serve fun drinks, and the bartenders would wear striped bowties or something. Instead, this place had more Etch A Sketches than I could count. I grabbed the one at my table and shook it clean. I turned the right knob and just like magic, a horizontal black line appeared on the gray screen. Then I turned the left knob and a vertical line appeared. I turned the knob the other way and it drew back over the line I had just drawn. This was so cool. Why didn't my childhood involve more Etch A Sketches? What if I was on the verge of creating an Etch A Sketch masterpiece? This might have been my calling all along—the reason I felt an impulse to run away to DC and befriend Trent and end up in this kids-themed bar.

Right as I was figuring out how to make diagonal lines, I heard a jingle from the front door. I looked up and it was not Trent.

"Saaket?"

It was Fiora.

"Fiora?" is what I should have said. Instead, I said nothing. I looked down at my Etch A Sketch and made another diagonal line.

She came up and tapped me on the shoulder. "Uh, hello. What are you doing here?"

I looked up slowly. Fiora was wearing a black tank top and camouflage parachute pants. At least half her forearm was covered in bracelets—multicolored, beaded, gold, spiked, eccentric—and they jingled as she waved her hand in front of my dazed and confused face.

"I'm waiting for Trent," I finally said. I was trying my hardest to act calm. "Who speaks very highly of you." I couldn't help that part. "What are you doing here?"

"I'm here to see Trent, too," Fiora said.

"That's a weird coincidence."

For a second we were both puzzled, looking around the

bar for an eight ball or something with an answer. Then, out of nowhere, Fiora started to laugh uncontrollably.

"What?" I asked, kind of annoyed. "What's so funny?"

Fiora kept laughing, bending over to catch her breath.

"I never thought Trent had the balls to do something like this," she said.

"Ah. Hm. I think I see what's happening . . ."

"So for what do I have the honor of this blind setup? How'd you even meet Trent?" Fiora suddenly grimaced. "Wait, are you in *love* with me?" I rolled my eyes. "Oh my God, you're in love with me, so you tracked down my friend and convinced him to set us up on a date! Saaket, this is getting out of hand."

"You remember my name," I said.

Fiora looked at me with puppy-dog eyes and mouthed an *awww*. I shook my head furiously. "Wait, no. I'm totally not, not, not in love with you," I said, making sure to use an odd number of *not*s in case she felt like twisting my words.

"So what is it, then? Why are we here?" she asked, taking a seat at the table.

"You really can't figure it out, can you?"

"Nope. I'm stumped. Why did Trent feel the need to trick the two of us into meeting?"

"Because, *Fiora*." I emphasized her name because I was about to be blunt, and I wasn't typically a blunt person. "You tricked me. Obviously Trent set up this meeting so you could apologize to me."

"Oh, come on, Saaket, don't be dramatic."

"No, seriously. Do you see the cuts on my arms and face?" I showed her my arms and turned my chin to show off the full extent of my injuries. "I got them from the guy you stole that bike from. He chased me all around the city, and I was biking ridiculously, dangerously fast to lose him, since I had no fucking clue who he was or why he was after me. And then I finally lost him, but I kept biking and ran into a phone booth, which is where Trent found me in a pool of blood—"

Fiora gave me a look.

"Fine, maybe it wasn't a pool of blood. But I was covered in blood and cuts and bruises," I said. "That's when Trent found me and helped me get cleaned up."

"Well, you're welcome," Fiora said smugly.

"What?"

"I gave you your first adventure in DC. You're welcome."

I should have known Fiora would twist my catastrophe into an initiation, what with her free-spirited, life-is-an-adventure-so-carpe-freaking-diem perspective. But it still killed me that she didn't feel even an ounce of remorse.

"You're *welcome*?" I repeated.

"Yes, you're welcome. It sounds like I gave you one heck of a joyride. So what happened to the bike?"

"I don't care about the bike, Fiora!" I burst out. There was a couple sitting at the bar, and you could tell they were trying their hardest not to stare. "You stole it. Do you know what that means? You took something from someone—your teacher, of all goddamn people—and gave it to someone else. That's worse than stealing. That's conning."

"Technically he's my boyfriend."

"You're dating your . . ." She nodded. "Wow, Fiora. I'm past my limit." I leaned in closer and whispered, "What's *wrong* with you?"

"Saaket, I didn't mean to—"

"Don't call me that. It's Scott. I don't like it when people call me Saaket. Not my friends, not my parents, and especially not you."

My words were sharp daggers, catching even myself off guard. I could see them tearing into Fiora's skin with punishing force.

"You were fine with it earlier," she muttered. "I . . ." Her words trailed off.

Fiora, the stranger who could always play it cool and make everything larger than life, had shrunk before my eyes. And you know what? I didn't know what to say, because her shrinking didn't make me feel any bigger. I shouldn't have cared if she used my real name. So we sat in silence for a few seconds and forgot how big or small we were in this world, and especially to each other. The entire bar went quiet. I reached for the Etch A Sketch and fumbled around with its knobs to make a diagonal line.

Then Fiora spoke: "Look, I can walk out of this bar and forget we ever met. The ball's in your court. Alternatively, you can accept me for who I am, baggage and all, and how that might rub off on you or bruise you or whatever, and we can get a drink—"

"We?"

"*I* can get a drink," she corrected. "We can sit here and catch up like sane people."

I didn't say anything, but I didn't pick up and leave, either. So Fiora, in all her presumptuousness, got out of her seat and walked over to the bar.

"Hey, douchebag," she yelled at the bartender. "Give me a fucking gin and tonic, and a goddamn root beer for my freak of a friend over here."

"Fiora? Are you all right?"

"It's angry hour, Scott. You get a dollar off drinks if you order with your finest angry voice."

I giggled the way you're supposed to giggle at a kids-themed bar. It didn't strike me when Trent mentioned "angry hour" that it would actually be a thing.

"Fiora?" I said.

"Yeah?"

"You can use my real name if you want."

"Sure thing, Saaket."

CHAPTER 6

THOMAS FOOLERY'S BUSINESS model was simple. Nostalgia. It linked fond memories of childhood to an adult world without rules. You could raise your voice without getting punished! Sketch your night away and erase it with a few shakes or shots! Play pinball on a buzz. Hop some scotch and drink it, too.

For better or worse, that strategy was never going to work on me. My childhood sucked. Thomas Foolery brought me back to my worst days, when the playground was a war zone. Like any post-trauma victim, I had blocked most of the memories but I remembered bits and pieces. The name-calling, for instance. "Suck It" was by far the most popular. "Sucker Punch" was a close second. There were plenty of other names. Nerd, wimp, immigrant, terrorist, bookworm, teacher's pet, Goody Two-shoes. I got made fun of for listen-ing to different music, eating different snacks. I got pushed off the jungle gym by Jack Vance in the third grade. I scraped the mulch off my bleeding arms and legs and looked up at his crew as they snickered, feeling nothing because I'd come to expect it all.

I could try erasing my failures, but I couldn't erase my insecurities. Places like Thomas Foolery brought them back in powerful snippets. Just like the flakes of Raisin Bran I leave at the bottom of the bowl, the shitty parts of my past were always going to stay with me.

My life was a cluster-fuck of remainders.

"I like this place," Fiora said, walking back from the bar with our drinks. She handed me my root beer and took a prolonged sip of her gin and tonic. "Because it's all games."

Fiora leaned in. Her hands were clasped and her fingers interlocked, uncommittedly so, like I could unknot them if I wanted to.

"Huh?" I was paying more attention to Fiora's body language than her actual language.

"Because it's all games," she repeated. "Tom's Foolery is exactly the kind of bar this town needs."

"And why is that, Fiora?"

"People in DC treat life so *seriously*," Fiora moaned. "Every day they pretend to make an impact with their entry-level job on Capitol Hill or at a think tank, when in reality they're just pushing paper. Or worse, they're running the whole fucking office, so they're actually creating more bullshit in the world."

"So . . . politicians?"

"Not just politicians. Lobbyists, lawyers, quote-unquote think tanks. Men!" she said, slamming her glass down. "Let's be honest, they're all men. They create bullshit at work, and then, after work, they make dinner plans and brag about the law they passed or the pamphlet they wrote—the one only four people will ever read."

I thought about Jack and Kevin, who wanted nothing more than to pass those laws or write those pamphlets. If only they could have met Fiora.

"When they're at work," she continued, "they can't wait for dinner. When they're at dinner, they can't wait to get away and go home. And you know what they do at home? This human being who used to read books and play board games and maybe even build model airplanes? They watch the news. The *news*. They finally have a few hours away from the bullshit of DC, and they *choose* to consume the world's bullshit before going to bed and hitting repeat on this whole cycle."

Fiora took another sip of her drink. She fiddled with my Etch A Sketch's knob and sighed. "That's why I like this place. It doesn't take itself too seriously."

"Okay," I said, smiling. "But isn't that what college is for? Being a real person without all the seriousness of the real world?"

"Clearly you haven't spent any time at GW, Saaket. There are two types of people at this school." She tapped two of her fingers on the table. I noticed the bartender watching out of the side of his eye, entertaining himself with the Fiora Show. "First, you have your future dick-heads of America. The political science majors doing Capitol Hill internships, the premeds spending all their time in GelHell."

"GelHell?"

"Gelman Library. Second, you have your sorority girls and frat bros, who are even worse. At least the future dick-heads stress over crap that matters to the outside world. The latest uproar in the Greek community was over a Kappa who wore lime-green flats to a Sigma Chi formal. I'm serious. Not-figurative-but-*literal* shoes. You've got to give them credit, though, because the almighty Panhellenic Council got involved and promptly squashed the controversy before the Greeks could claim any human casualties. Thank God for authority, right?"

"Sounds pretty dumb," I said.

Fiora nodded slowly—a bow for her spontaneous monologue. Brava.

"How am I supposed to pretend like nothing matters, though?" I pleaded. "These days it feels like every step I take is setting me up for the rest of my life."

Fiora smiled and bounced out of her seat, making her way to the chalkboard. She picked up a piece of chalk and drew a long, horizontal rectangle on one end of the board, dividing it into eight squares.

"See this row?" she said. "This is me."

I walked up to the chalkboard, picked up a piece of chalk, and drew something else:

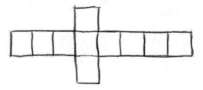

"This is you," I said.

"Okay, smart-ass. Just listen, I'm trying to make a point. Pretend this long row of squares contains all of Fiora Buchanan—who I am, what I was born with, my brain, my hair, my lips, eyes, everything."

Fiora drew two more squares onto the row:

"This new column, the one with three boxes? That's my parents. They were the first intersection, or rather, the first piece of baggage life threw into my grid." She kept adding new rows and columns, each one intersecting the last. "This one is their divorce. These are all my dad's new wives. This one's summer camp, and here's the junior counselor I ended up kissing there. This one's Trent—a handsome row of squares . . ." She went on and on with even more squares until half the chalkboard was sufficiently gridded.

On the opposite end of the board, Fiora drew another long rectangle and divided it into seven squares. "This guy is you, Saaket."

"You have parents, right?" Fiora asked.

My eyes leapt. She might as well have asked if they were dead or alive.

"Um, yeah," I said.

"Okay, good. Here's your parents," she said, drawing another row that intersected the first one like a cross—

—followed by a bunch more rows and columns that intersected. "And this is all the other shit in your life."

Fiora drew one last row of squares to connect the two clusters. "And this, my friend, is where our paths intersected on that bus yesterday."

"You drew a crossword puzzle."

"Precisely," she replied.

"Fiora, the cruciverbalist, conveys the *profound* metaphor that life is a puzzle," I said, using my finest sarcastic voice. Did Thomas Foolery have Sarcasm Hour? I deserved a drink special.

"No, Saaket, I'm just explaining why I don't have my panties in an existential bunch like you." She moved from the chalkboard back to the table. "Our lives aren't so different from a crossword puzzle, sure. But the thing about life is we don't get to draw the grid; we take the rows and columns we're given. Our bodies, parents, mental health issues, all that. What we *do* get to do is fill the cells. And rather than filling mine with anxiety over medical school or Greek politics—instead of feeling trapped by my circumstance—I fill them with arbitrary words. An eight-letter word for 'snowstorm' or a three-letter word for 'soda.' Silly shit that's true but doesn't mean anything. I can live with my downs and acrosses; I accept the larger truths of my life. But I don't take the cells so seriously."

I accepted Fiora's analysis, even if I wasn't convinced the content of my cells didn't mean anything. We went up to the bar, and Fiora persuaded the couple to join us in a game of Cards Against Humanity. She played some alarmingly disrespectful cards, like the one with Oprah crying into a Lean Cuisine. I had a few drinks, too, because the bartender got involved and turned it into a drinking game. Then we left.

"Cobble," I slurred. We were back on the street where my bike chase had happened the day before, and I chuckled. "Sunderland Place is very cobbley."

"It's not cobble. It's brick," Fiora said.

My first alcoholic drink ever. And my second, and my third. I couldn't believe how it happened, where it happened, with *whom* it happened. It was dark outside; the shades of black and gray and dusky charcoal spun before my eyes. Nighttime befuddled my senses. My feet were floating along. I was too buzzed to feel anything but good.

"It's cobble!" I asserted.

"Brick, Saaket. Cobble is a sedimentary rock you find in pebble form."

"Cobble," I repeated. "Cobble, cobble, cobble."

Fiora laughed. "Now it just sounds funny. The more you say it, the funnier it sounds."

"Funny!" That was a pretty funny word. I wanted to say it again. "Funny, funny, funny. Funnnnyyyy . . ."

"Stop it! You're stealing all the words!"

We reached the end of the street. Instead of turning, Fiora grabbed me by the shoulders and looked me straight in the eyes.

"Saaket," she said in a very play-serious tone. "I think you're drunk."

I always thought my first time getting drunk would feel momentous, like I would savor every sip and wear a permanent grin from ear to ear. In fact, yes, I was grinning, but I think that was from the alcohol, not the fact that I just *drank* alcohol for the first time. The actual drinking part had been weirdly casual. I didn't think much of it, and I certainly wasn't thinking that a few drinks would get me plastered.

"So what's your plan?" Fiora asked.

"Well, Fiora, it's funny that you should ask. I'm going hooowwwme tomorrow." I tripped over my own ankle somehow and nose-planted into Fiora's shoulder. I shouldn't be allowed to get drunk, ever.

"What happened with that grit professor?"

"Pfffaw," I said, unleashing a spray of spit. "She wouldn't even talk to me. I'll never be gritty. No grit material here. Grit. Shit. Maybe if I say it enough times, I'll ruin that word, too. Grit, grit, griiii—"

Fiora cupped her hand over my mouth.

"Shush. This is the most ironic wimp-out ever. Tell me, what exactly is grit?"

I sobered up a little. "Perseverance and passion for long-term goals."

"Exactly. So go back! Don't let one pathetic no push you away from something you care about. Believe me, if I did, I wouldn't be writing crossword puzzles or still in a relationship or . . ." Fiora's words trailed off. "That's the whole point of grit, right?"

I stared past Fiora at a red, hexagonal sign that said STOP. (Yes, I was so drunk that it took me a few seconds to piece together the color, shape, and letters of a regular old stop sign.) Everything around me was spinning, again, for the second time that day. I whispered to the sign, "Fuck you." *I'm not stopping.*

"What?" Fiora said.

"No, not you, I was talking to . . . What time is it?"

"I dunno, like midnight?"

"Shut up."

Fiora pulled out her phone.

"What? Look. It's twelve twenty-three a.m."

"Let me see that." I snatched the phone from her hand. She was wrong.

12:24 a.m.

It was Wednesday. Professor Mallard held office hours on Wednesdays from 8 to 10 a.m. I had to stay gritty about grit— that was the point. I'd do exactly what she wanted me to do, even if it was the opposite of what she told me in her office.

The reality of my recklessness hit me like a ton of bricks. Fiora had distracted me. I handed her the phone back and took off without so much as a goodbye. I shouted far too many expletives far too loudly and publicly as I sprinted down New Hampshire and back to the hostel and made it into my bed, somehow, because it was all a blur after 12:24 a.m.

CHAPTER 7

THIS TIME, I knocked first.

"Come in," she said. Her voice sounded distant—thank God, since one cup of spilled coffee was enough. I took a second to check my breath. It wasn't so bad anymore. I woke up that morning with a throbbing headache and some nausea, but the worst offender was the foul stench that had taken over the inside of my mouth.

"Ahem. Come in," she repeated. I twisted the doorknob and pushed before I had the chance to second-guess myself.

Professor Mallard was wearing another white blouse, clearly unfazed by Monday's accident. This one even had ruffles. We stood face-to-face, with ten feet of narrow office space between us, and her expression immediately dropped. I could feel everything from our last encounter stirring inside me—along with the hangover—but I held my ground. I ignored the stop signs. I locked eyes with her.

She raised a finger to speak, but I beat her to the first word.

"Hear me out," I said. "I came all the way down from Philadelphia to speak with you. This is important."

Professor Mallard crossed her arms and really looked at me. She lifted her chin slowly and assessed my face. I could pinpoint the exact moment when she noticed the fresh cuts under my left eye and against the side of my jaw.

"Remind me of your name . . . ?"

"Scott Ferdowsi."

"And why, Scott, must you speak with me?"

"I took your Grit Quiz and failed miserably. I give up a lot. I'm sixteen. I have no passions. I guess what I'm trying to say is . . . I need your help, you know, to get gritty."

Knowing I had a problem was one thing, but admitting it out loud was another. I couldn't bear to look at Professor Mallard as I rattled off my list, so I let my eyes scan her desk in a spontaneous game of "Spot the difference!" The abacus beads had been spread out, and the picture frame with her husband was facedown today.

"Have you read my research, Scott?"

"I practically devoured it last week," I blurted. "I'm a bit obsessed with your work."

Professor Mallard leaned back in her chair. She took a

moment to tie her hair into a tight but ultimately messy bun. Slowly she faked a smile.

"Then you should be the first to know that a person doesn't get gritty overnight," she said. "I admire you for making the journey to Washington, and I'm glad you've taken comfort in my findings around grit. But I'm a psychology professor, not a psychologist. I can't help you."

"You *can*," I begged. "I'm passionate about grit. I'm desperately passionate. Doesn't that mean something?"

Professor Mallard gave me a thumbs-up. "That's wonderful. Call me in a decade when you have your PhD."

"But I failed the Grit Quiz. What if that doesn't work out—"

"Scott, have you heard of a growth mindset?"

"You've talked about it in a few of your interviews, yeah. It's the idea that failure isn't a permanent state."

"Precisely. Why would you get hung up over that silly Grit Quiz? Or anything else you might have failed at? Everybody fails. We deal with failure and disappointment and other feelings that are far more damaging. That's how you grow. Don't go thinking my research will make you grittier. All I've done is prove a few hypotheses: There is no correlation between natural ability and grit. There's a *strong* correlation between grit and success." Professor Mallard set the picture frame upright, then immediately picked it up absentmindedly. "What you need is thicker skin, Scott. Get over your failures and . . . I don't know. Go live your life."

I looked down at Professor Mallard's fingers, which were clutched tightly around the frame in her lap. Something was off. I decided it would be best for me to leave.

"Thanks for your time," I said. Before stepping out I added, "I'm sorry if I bothered you. I hope everything is all right."

◻◻◻◻

Back at the hostel, I found the door to my room slightly ajar. I opened it slowly and heard the sound of turning pages from the top bunk—not mine, but the other one. I could make out a female of the blonde species lying in the bed, probably one of my French roommates, her face buried in a book.

"*Bonjour?*" I said with hesitation.

"Ah, Saaket! You never mentioned you spoke French. *T'as bien dormi?*"

Fiora.

"Uh, no, my French is pretty crappy . . . ?" My words slurred and trailed off and generally conveyed a *What the fuck are you doing here?* kind of tone. But the more perplexing question, which I actually asked, was, "How the fuck did you get in here?"

"Eh, it was a breeze," Fiora said. "I complimented the front-desk guy on his Ron Paul shirt and chatted him up about some laissez-faire shit. Then I told him I was your sister, and he gave me your room number. Your roommates let me in, the French ones. Real friendly folks. Totally not snobby at all . . . But I convinced them I was your *half* sister, since they actually know you look ethnic-ish, and they let me chill here. Those guys are checked out now, so it's just you and me. I came over to wake up your hungover ass and give you a wet willy or something but—"

"Hey. Hey. Fiora?" I climbed up to my own bunk and sat crisscross. "This is creepy."

"Chill out, dude. I just wanted to make sure you were still alive after your first night getting *plastered*."

"You know, Fiora, I'm starting to think *you* might be the one with the crush on *me*."

"All right, Saaket. You got me." Fiora jumped down from the other bunk and ran up to mine, craning her neck over the rail guard. "I have a *massive* crush on you, the sun is actually a huge-ass dandelion, and you, my love—you really kept it together last night."

Crap. My memory of Tom's Foolery wasn't exactly perfect. "How bad was I . . . ?"

"Let's just say I had to help you hopscotch your way out," she said.

"Uggghhhh." I fell over sideways like someone had yelled timber, my legs still crisscrossed and arms covering my mortified face.

Out of nowhere, I laughed. "You know, Fiora, people aren't like this."

"Like what?"

I sat up, clutching a pillow between my arms.

"Like . . . you. Real people don't give free bikes to strangers and get them drunk and surprise them in their hostel room," I said. "You're a caricature of a real person."

"Do *not* mansplain me," Fiora snapped. "So what? I'm a bunch of different caricatures. You're a bunch of caricatures. This is the one I am right now. You didn't see me in Spain over winter break. You didn't see me last summer when I wrote puzzles obsessively. Every day—sometimes multiple puzzles a day! I didn't stop until the *Times* finally accepted one."

"I didn't mean it like—"

"I know you didn't," she said, her eyes weary. "No one does. I've got my shit, and you've got yours. We've got our own grids, remember? And just because I don't fit into this perfectly themed grid you have in mind for me . . . it doesn't mean I'm not real."

"Well, for a girl who's only taking one class this summer—" I said. Fiora's eyes turned fiercely hostile. "You definitely just schooled me."

Her expression lit up, and we both giggled.

"So how'd you spend your first ever hangover day?" Fiora asked.

"Don't you remember?"

"Remember what?"

"Professor Mallard. I saw her today," I said. "That's why I ran off at the end of last night."

"No way," Fiora said, her eyes wide in disbelief. "There's no way you weren't painfully hungover this morning."

I shrugged, and Fiora gave me a different look. The best way I could describe it was with an equation:

$$Look = (Okay\ WOW + Okay + Okay\ fine) = Okay$$
$$x\ (WOW + 1 + Fine) \approx Unexpected\ Surprise\ with$$
$$Eventual\ Acceptance$$

"And you thought *I* wasn't real," she said. "So, how'd it go?"

"Not good. She doesn't want to help me. I think Professor Mallard has some personal shit going on, because she went off on a rant and told me to 'live my life.' I don't want to be an asshole and keep bugging her."

Fiora smiled. "Why do you even care about grit, anyway?"

I cracked my knuckles and let my eyes wander to the corner of the room, right above where Fiora had been sitting a few minutes ago. A wire stuck out at the edge where both walls met the ceiling.

"I don't know," I said, staring at that wire, "I just do. Everyone cares about random stuff. Like, why do you care about crossword puzzles?"

"Easy. I'm desperate."

"Well, that's not the best way to promote yourself . . ."

"Not what I mean," Fiora said, rolling her eyes before focusing intensely on the floor between her two feet. "My grandmother used to live in Virginia Beach. We'd drive up from Charleston and visit her when I was really, really little—just me and my dad. Grams lived right off the beach, which was funny because I was terrified of sand. Like, absolutely scared shirtless—I mean, shitless. Ha. Words. Speaking of . . ."

Without realizing it, I zoned out and followed the torn wire around the edges of the ceiling. I wondered what would happen if I touched it. How much charge would be emitted through my body? I wondered if the sloppy coat of white paint on the outside of the wire would protect me, or if I'd blow into a million smithereens, my ashes—I stopped myself. I was being rude to Fiora. I tuned her back in.

". . . every morning. It was insane. *They* were insane. They started each day with a pen and a copy of the *New York Times*, and five minutes later they had a grid full of answers. I always perched my head over the edge of the breakfast table to sneak a peek, so freaking fascinated by their teamwork—counting boxes together, passing the pen back and forth. Eventually they let me join when I was six or seven, but I wasn't so good. Not as good as them."

"Are you better now?" I asked.

"Not really. I'm still only a decent solver," Fiora said. "But I'm really fucking good at constructing them."

"That's so cool," I said. "I never realized that people actually, you know . . ."

"What? That there were people who took the time to come up with grids and clues for something as trivial as a crossword puzzle?"

"I guess you could say I'm a bit . . . puzzled," I said, smiling.

Fiora got up and bolted for the door.

"I'm sorry! Sorry!" I giggled. "Bad pun."

"Don't pretend you wouldn't love it if I walked out right now."

"Oh, come on," I said, shaking my head the way you do in an unreal situation. "Anyway, how does all of this make you desperate?"

"Isn't it obvious?" Her voice crumbled to something more vulnerable. "I'm desperate for answers. Desperate for a connection to my dead grandma. To my dad who fucking sucks now. For complexity with some clarity at the end. For clues." Fiora went silent. I couldn't even see her anymore. I realized she was sitting directly beneath me, on the bottom bunk, when I heard the mattress springs creaking with every breath she took.

"A lot of things changed after my grandma passed away," she said, almost whispering. "My dad got depressed. My mom's drug problems got worse. Turns out all those trips to Virginia Beach were to distract me whenever Mom was 'visiting her sister.' After Grams died, well . . . You know how these stories go. My therapist keeps trying to connect the dots, but I don't really care. All I know is for some reason or another, I'm desperate to keep doing puzzles—solve them, build them—until the day I die."

I lay on my back and gazed at the ceiling, daydreaming about my parents, who were less complicated but who would love it if I felt so desperately about anything.

"Maybe that's what it takes, Saaket," Fiora said. "Some massive, life-shifting event to force you into your passion."

"Boy, do I hope this is the one."

"And if it isn't?"

"Then I'm screwed. My parents will keep pushing me to study medicine or engineering or another 'safe-enough' field I have no real interest in."

Fiora began to say something, but she stopped herself at "I."

Smithereens. If I touched the wire, I'd blow into a million smithereens. My ashes would scatter along the walls and the ceiling and the floor—the downs and acrosses of this room I existed in.

CHAPTER 8

"ONE MORE NIGHT, please."

After Fiora left, I went downstairs to pay for another night at the hostel. The lobby was eerily quiet, and the floor creaked as I approached the front desk. Behind it sat the same guy who had checked me in on Monday. He was wearing a fisherman's hat, and his messy brown curls slipped out from underneath.

"Just one?"

"Um, yeah."

Fiora had convinced me stay in DC a little longer. We agreed to meet later that night at Tonic, a restaurant on GW's campus where Trent worked as a bartender. She promised we would concoct the perfect plan to get Professor Mallard to talk to me and help me get grittier.

Personally, I wasn't convinced that Fiora and I would come

up with anything game-changing, but what else was I going to do? I couldn't give up in front of her or I'd look like a loser. Besides, I had already quit my internship back home, and without any specific direction from Professor Mallard, I'd have nothing to do around an empty house.

"What's your name again?" the front-desk guy asked.

"Scott Ferdowsi."

His laptop was turned slightly toward me, and I could see him open an Excel file. There were four entries on the entire spreadsheet. Makes sense, I thought. Other than my French roommates, I'd never encountered another soul in that hostel.

"That'll be thirty-five bucks," he said.

I pulled out my wallet, handing him my second-to-last hundred. He reached under the desk for a tin box and snapped it open.

"My name's Scott, too," he mumbled, counting my change.

"Cool," I said. He thumbed through the bills with intense precision. I stood there tapping my heel. What was one Scott supposed to say to another? "Nice shirt," I said, because apparently that worked for Fiora. His tight gray V-neck had a massive cartoon of Ron Paul's face with the quote *There is only one kind of freedom and that's individual liberty.*

Scott perked up. "You a fan of Ron?"

He handed me sixty-five dollars, and I lingered for a moment.

"I'm a fan of individual liberty."

□⊐⊔⊐

Tonic looked like every college bar you see in movies, with a long row of wooden bar stools and flat-screen TVs playing ESPN and a female bouncer at the door who politely asked for my ID. Yes, my under-21, 20, 19, 18 . . . ID. I froze. Not only because I was embarrassingly underage, but because she was hot. She had wavy strawberry-blonde hair, with locks draped over her freckled boobs—which were super visible through the low-cut tank top she was wearing. Did I mention that I froze? Fortunately, seconds later, Trent appeared out of nowhere and latched onto my shoulders from behind.

"Scott-ayyyyy!"

He smelled like a combination of Abercrombie and pot.

"Hey, Charlotte, this guy is with me," Trent told the hot bouncer. We stumbled to the bar, Trent's arms wrapped around my chest and his chin resting on my shoulder from behind like we were old pals. "I always show up exactly when you need me, man."

Trent gestured at an empty bar stool right before sliding under the bar top. I took a seat between a gaggle of girls and a middle-aged man drinking by himself.

"Nice shirt," Trent said from across the bar. I looked down. I was wearing the same Model UN shirt that I had sweated through the other day. I should have felt more embarrassed, but I saw this coming. I'd only packed two outfits with me to

DC, and I wasn't going to risk spilling on my polo and corduroys if there was a chance I might see Professor Mallard tomorrow. I had already hand-washed them once after my bike accident.

I shrugged.

"All right, buddy," Trent began. "What are you having? And where's Fiora? She's always late, but it's a Wednesday and happy hour is all night. The earlier she gets here, the more drinks she can guilt me into pouring for free. You know that girl loves her G and Ts."

Trent would have kept going if I didn't stop him to say, "Wait, Trent, are you—"

"High?" He shoved a dirty glass into the sink's cleaning contraption and wiped it dry with a rag. "Yep, my man, I am high as a *drone*. And we both know the Democrats are gonna be all over those gizmos to creep on our every friggin' move. Say goodbye to what little privacy you have left, amigo. Unless my man Renault Cohen does something about it ASAP, liberal America is makin' moves, and it's making 'em fast."

"That sounds—I mean. Yeah, frickin' drones," I said. I couldn't believe Trent was bartending high, but who was I to judge?

"Anyway, man, what have you been up to?" Trent asked.

Before I could answer, Fiora marched up and slammed her hands on the bar.

"Oh. My. *God*," she gushed, squeezing herself between the middle-aged man and me.

He shot her a look.

"You won't believe what just happened to me on the corner of F and 21st. This homeless woman came up to my face and pointed her finger, like, an inch from my nose and goes, 'You're *shit*. D'ya know that?' And I'm like, 'What?' And she squints her eyes and kinda sways and goes off! 'You albino white-haired piece of shit. All of ya. You're shittier than shit. You're *piss*.' And then the traffic light changed to walk and I bolted past her, but not without saying, 'Well, at least I don't smell like piss.' Then I walked away. Anyway, how are you?"

"Honestly, just kind of in awe."

"Awesome. That's only the beginning, Saaket. I've been thinking a lot this afternoon about your predicament, and boy, do I have the answer you're looking for."

Trent stuck his head in between us from the bar. "Missus Crossword Queen with the answers," he said, grinning. "You got a clue? She's got an answer."

Fiora pushed his face away.

"Trent puts the *merry* in *marijuana*," she said.

"So what's my answer?" I blurted out. I was tapping my right foot quickly. Four or five taps per second.

"Specificity," Fiora said. She leaned into me like she was divulging one of the secrets of the universe. "You need to be specific."

"How?"

"I don't specifically know *how* . . . but you need to go into this professor's office and make a specific demand."

"I've already asked her to help me twice," I said.

"She doesn't even know how to help you."

I raised one eyebrow. "But she's the grit expert."

"Correction: she doesn't *want* to help you. And why should she? You're just a random sixteen-year-old who popped into her office. You've got to be specific with your demand—give her no choice but to say, 'Okay, we can do that.' Can you do that?"

Trent was busy mixing drinks behind the bar, but that didn't stop him from eavesdropping on our conversation.

"You know, buddy," Trent said, his attention squarely focused on the liquor bottles, glasses, and cocktail shakers he was juggling. "Right after I saved your ass the other day, I went home and read up on Iran. It's amazing, the kinds of people you meet when you get out of the Deep South. Anyway, I was just surfin' Wikipedia. Your country's got some insane history—like that poet, the famous one who wrote the epic stories . . ."

"Ferdowsi!" I exclaimed.

"Isn't that your last name, Saaket?" Fiora asked. I nodded.

I never cared to learn about my family's namesake, but I knew his stories. Epic tales from *Shahnameh*, the Persian book of kings that my dad would bring to life at bedtime when I was a kid. He never read them out of books—it was all from memory. These were the stories he grew up with in Iran. Tales of Rostam, the mighty warrior who unknowingly killed his son Sohrab in battle; Zal, the albino king who was banished at birth and raised by a phoenix; and Rudabeh, the Persian Empire's own Rapunzel, who let down her hair for Zal and fell madly in love with him. These stories were fascinating to me at the time, but I always told myself I would read American stories like *Clifford* and *The Cat in the Hat* to my own kids. I never thought I'd hear a word about *Shahnameh* again.

"No kidding!" Trent said. "Well, Ferdowsi was a *boss*. Spent thirty years slaving away on that book just to get duped by the sultan. If you're talking grit, he's your man."

I was amazed that Trent had taken such an interest in my background. Fiora must have been, too, because she'd already pulled up Ferdowsi's Wikipedia page on her phone.

"It says here the king had promised to pay Ferdowsi a piece of gold for every couplet that he wrote," Fiora said, her eyes laser-focused on her screen.

"Right. I remember the story now," I said. "The sultan's messenger replaced the gold pieces with silver. Somehow he made Ferdowsi look like the bad guy and got him exiled for life. You know the craziest part?"

Trent and Fiora shook their heads.

"Eventually the sultan found out his messenger was a two-timing jackass, and he tried sending Ferdowsi the gold again, but it was too late. The gold arrived on the day of his funeral."

Fiora's jaw dropped ever so slightly.

"Saaket," she said slowly. "This is it. Specificity. You need stories."

"I don't get it."

"This poet, Ferdowsi. He was gritty," she stressed. "That's just one historic example. Marina Abramović. She's endured all sorts of shit for decades for her performance art. Gritty. Nelson Mandela. Thrown in prison over and over for what he believed in. Gritty."

"Professor Mallard studies kids, though," I said.

"Who grow up into adults, Saaket. Here's your proposal: 'Professor, I think I can be of assistance to you. I would like to investigate *Grit throughout History*. You keep studying children in your brilliant, academic way, and I, Saaket Ferdowsi, will dig up facts about the most ambitious and gritty minds of our past.' It's a project, Saaket. There's no effort on her part, and it's obviously valuable for you. She might even get a research lead out of it."

I liked the idea of learning about important people who found ways to be gritty. Doesn't everyone like a good success story? Maybe I would learn a thing or two from their example. Fiora and I agreed there was a fifty-fifty chance that Professor Mallard would bite. But we also agreed there was a hundred percent chance that I had nothing to lose. She'd already turned me down twice.

We were only halfway through our drinks, and my plan was all set. Fiora was drinking a gin and tonic, and I was nursing a Coke. (I didn't want to be hungover again if I was seeing Professor Mallard tomorrow.) An awkward silence and two sips later, I asked: "So . . . if you're so good at constructing crosswords, could you make one right now?"

Fiora smiled. Without saying a word, she pulled a pen out of her purse and reached over the bar for a napkin. She tapped the pen against her cheek a few times, then began scribbling furiously. Five minutes later, she took another napkin. Her eyes ping-ponged between the two as she transferred an empty grid and came up with clues. She slid the second napkin down to me:

Across:

1. Position on grid
4. Feeling that everyone's having fun without you
5. Scrutinize
6. Scott is high on ____
7. Hurricane center

Down:

1. "It's _____ for!"
2. Leave out
3. Trent is high on ___, slang
4. Anger
5. 21+ to drink, e.g.

"It's pretty sloppy, even for a five-by-five," Fiora warned shyly, "but I didn't want to keep you waiting too long."

I went straight to work. A few minutes later I slid the napkin back in her direction. She compared it against the solution while I held my breath. Thumbs-up. I breathed a sigh of relief, then giggled.

"That was weirdly fun," I said. "Satisfying."

"Welcome to my world." Fiora smirked.

I gazed at her as if she'd just done a triple backflip. "How'd you even—"

"I started with *grit* and *pot*, and then I liked the inverseness of *pot* and *top*, so I made it all work. Broke some construction rules, but whatever. I figured you would appreciate the personalization."

"Incredible." I imagined what it might look like inside of Fiora's mind. An alphabet soup with letters floating into place? Or an assembly line with pulleys and levers and conveyer belts manufacturing the puzzle in its rightful order? Whatever was going on in there, I couldn't contain my astonishment.

"Would you show me how to make one?" I blurted out.

Fiora had already finished her drink, but she kept sipping through the tiny red straw, making a slurpy, air-sucking sound. "Tell you what," she said. "You come back here tomorrow with a grit update, and I'll share a thing or two about how I construct these puzzles."

Before I could get more than a nod in, Fiora stepped away from the bar. I figured she was going to the bathroom, so I waited. She didn't come back in five minutes, and she didn't come back in ten, and finally fifteen minutes later Trent came around the bar and put his hand on my shoulder, telling me she was long gone. Honestly, I wasn't hurt. I wasn't even confused. It all made sense in a strange Fiora way.

I stuck around until Trent had shut down the bar, and we left together. It was a balmy summer night, made bearable by a whistling breeze that kept teasing us. The streets of DC were empty, dark, and wide.

Trent and I bonded on our walk about Fiora's elusiveness and her other quirks, like how fidgety she would get sometimes, or how she would bend straws into halves and quarters and eighths. I asked Trent if he ever had a crush on Fiora growing up, and he clarified that no, never, they were only friends and didn't have any sexual history. She wasn't his type, he assured me, which I thought was absurd. But then I reasoned that Southern Gentlemen like Trent were destined to marry Southern Belles with proper etiquette who cooked nice meals and went to church and carried small talk.

Fiora didn't give two shits about any of those things. She was a crossword girl, and there was more beneath her surface than nice meals and small talk.

"Her parents divorced when she was a kid," Trent explained. "That's when Fiora got crazy obsessed with crosswords. Her mom left and her dad didn't want to talk about it; he just kept her in the dark till she stopped caring."

We crossed at a red light. There were no cars in sight, but I still looked both ways.

"What exactly is her mom's deal?" I asked.

"It's a slippery pickle."

"I don't speak Southern . . ."

"It's complicated," Trent said, elbowing me hard. "Lucy

Buchanan's Oxy addiction was no secret. Everyone in town knew. When she went AWOL after the divorce, no one asked questions. My folks were friends with Fiora's dad, and they knew he was still struggling with the divorce on top of his mom's death, so they told me, 'Play nice with that Fiora girl, bless her heart. She's got it tough.' So I did. That's when we became friends.

"Fiora never heard from her mom until a couple years ago. She started getting these letters saying she'd gotten clean, got married, even had a baby on the way. But Fiora didn't want anything to do with her new family. That all changed this year, God knows why. It's why she goes to Philly so much; she's visited three times just since I moved here. And you know what? The minute she steps off that bus, it's the last thing she wants to talk about. She'd rather preoccupy herself with more . . ."

"More what?"

Trent pursed his lips, searching for the right explanation. "Have you ever heard that saying, *the personal is political*?"

"Sure."

"Fiora's the opposite of that. She hates politics, and she avoids the personal." Trent bit his lower lip. "The impersonal is Fiora."

Fiora was a crossword girl. A beautiful, slippery-pickle crossword girl.

That night in bed, I felt something tugging at my insides, restless and optimistic. That feeling where your heart swells and your arms go limp, and a tickling spirit gallops through your veins, Paul Revere-ing at the top of its lungs: *An adventure is coming! An adventure is coming!* My lungs tightened from excitement. Tomorrow, I would follow through on my most important project yet. I would confront the genius who could help with my problem. The finish line felt so close. I could see myself crossing it, tearing through the ribbon, determined never to fail again.

CHAPTER 9

SPOILER ALERT: Professor Mallard didn't hate the idea.

I wasn't sure she'd be in her office, since she didn't technically hold office hours on Thursdays. And if she was, I'd be catching her even more off guard than usual. But Professor Mallard wasn't angry. In fact, she looked more chipper than the last time. I caught a smile flicker across her face when I walked in, and that threw *me* off guard. Before I had the chance to pitch her on the grit study, she put one hand up. I held my breath, almost certain I was getting kicked out again.

"I need to apologize," she began, and we simultaneously took a deep breath, "for my erratic behavior the last two times you visited my office. I gave it some serious thought last night. Professors are not celebrities, and I should be flattered that you care enough about my research to travel all the way down from Philadelphia. I'm glad you came back."

And so, with newfound confidence, I accepted her apology and immediately dove into my quasi-research proposal, starting with *I had a specific idea* . . . and sprinkled with *it could benefit both of us* and *you don't have to say yes*. I didn't bring up my parental situation. I was on a roll—a surge of blind faith rippled down my neck—and I convinced myself that I could make DC work all summer. My parents would be angry, sure, but a research internship with a famous Georgetown professor? True grit? My dad would be beyond impressed.

Professor Mallard didn't accept the idea right away, but she didn't wrinkle her nose and reject it, either. As I rambled on about important people who had discovered their passion later in life, she nodded absently, like her eyes were on me but her mind was somewhere else.

When I finished, Professor Mallard nodded one more time, half smiling. "I am actually writing a new book about—well, you can guess the subject. In it, I depict many firsthand cases of grit in sports teams, classrooms, fields like entrepreneurship and politics. But I must admit, I am intrigued by the direction you're going with historic grit. . . . My book is almost finished, but perhaps your findings could be of some use. We can always learn from the past. I have a feeling you can, too."

I took a seat in the same chair where I choked that first morning, my muscles tense from the nostalgia, as Professor Mallard laid out a few ground rules:

⇨ I would begin the project on Monday. I could come in every day if I wished, but no less than every other day. (This would give me nearly three weeks to legitimize my quasi-internship before Mom and Dad got home on my birthday.)

⇨ I would work out of the empty room next to hers. It was another professor's office, but he was out on sabbatical for the year.

⇨ I shouldn't expect my research to end up in Professor Mallard's book. In fact, it most likely wouldn't. She was a psychology professor, not a historian. And I was in no way an official researcher.

As she explained how she was *interested* in my historical grit research but didn't necessarily *need* it, I had to wonder why Professor Mallard was really going through with this. Did she feel bad for me? Maybe my persistence was finally paying off. Three visits could have easily turned into seven or fifteen or fifty, and before we knew it I'd be sitting in her classroom as a Georgetown freshman—

"Last condition," she said, her face gravely serious. "Let me make myself abundantly clear: our relationship will not afford you any competitive edge for admission into Georgetown. I'm sorry, but that's my firm stance. I only take bribes from immediate family members and people with lots of money."

It took a moment for me to realize that Professor Mallard—the MacArthur Grant "genius" with bestselling books, groundbreaking studies, and viral YouTube videos under her belt—had actually cracked a joke. My neck and shoulder muscles relaxed, and a wiry smile slid across my face. Professor Mallard's uproarious laughter filled the rest of the room.

I made a triumphant exit through the wooden doors of White-Gravenor Hall, the sun shining in my face as I marched down the steps and across the lawn. It was the opposite of a walk of shame. It was a walk of *game*. Stride of pride. Pace of Ace.

Suddenly it occurred to me that without realizing it, I had decided to stay in DC. I was already feeling at home in this new city. Independence was one of those things I never had growing up with strict immigrant parents. They always wanted the best for me, but what if that meant giving me space? As a kid, I begged my parents to send me to summer camp. I had an impulse to get away and discover myself—not some mom-and-dad-monitored version of myself. Where better than the great outdoors?

"We don't know anything about summer camps," Mom would say in her high-pitched Farsi accent. "Maybe when you're older, we'll all go camping together."

After begging didn't work, I tried a different tactic: PowerPoint presentations. I put together slides with photos of campers hiking the Appalachian Trail, roasting marshmallows, and trust-falling into each other's arms. I researched five reputable camps in the Northeast, comparing activities and fees. My slides were impeccable. They had graphics. They had music. They had custom animations! I presented to my parents in front of the PC, their eyes beaming with pride as I recited my rehearsed lines. I was convinced they would say yes.

"So?" I clicked the mouse, and a colorful THE END zoomed into my last slide.

Dad looked to Mom.

"Well," she said. "That was a wonderful performance." *It's not a performance, Mom. This is serious.* "But, um, Scott . . . I'm not sure how safe it is in the woods."

"They have counselors," I blurted immediately.

"Right, but how many? How can one counselor keep track of so many kids?" Mom said, her voice shaky. "Why don't you take summer classes here instead? Amir's mom says they have a very nice pre-algebra course at Drexel."

Undeterred, I shifted my focus. I looked for summer programs that were more educational, like the ones at Harvard and Johns Hopkins. These "camps" for middle and high school students offered a full catalog of classes ranging from pre-algebra to archaeology. I redid my slides with pictures of Ivy League campuses, complete with bullet points about the academic merits of each program. I emphasized dorm safety. Once again, I presented to my parents, even more confident than the last time.

Again, Dad turned to Mom.

"It's like college, right?" she said, twisting her face desperately. "You'll go to college when you're eighteen. Why are you in such a hurry to grow up?"

I never made it to summer camp, but I'd made it to Washington. And if I was going to stay here, then I would set my own rules.

RULE #1: Money was real. And I was running out of it. My parents had left $800 of emergency funds—along with food and a SEPTA pass—and I had brought half of that with me to DC. I should have taken the whole stash. My expenses were stacking up: Greyhound ticket, hostel fees, meals. And drinking! I must have thrown down at least fifty bucks at Tom's Foolery. Running away wasn't cheap, and even if I stretched my budget, I could only make it a few more days. I'd have to get creative.

RULE #2: Thou shalt not smell like a homeless person. I couldn't afford new clothes, but maybe I'd borrow some shirts from Trent.

RULE #3: Don't fall for the girl. Fiora. *Come back tomorrow*, she said at Tonic, and I'd agreed. I'd go, but I wouldn't give in. Because even if I was beginning to like her—even if my heart turned into a twisty ball of rubber bands whenever she opened those unearthly lips—even if

Fiora painted one self-portrait with her staggering beauty and another with her unwavering strength, and I wanted the entire gallery—she was in college and had a boyfriend. It was a harsh reality, but also a blessing in disguise because I had business to take care of in DC.

Fiora was filling her grid with distractions; I was filling mine with grit. I promised myself that I would not, under any circumstance, fall for her.

CHAPTER 10

AT THE STREET corner opposite my hostel, four crosswalks created a narrow baseball diamond. The space between the bases was striped like Abbey Road. I stood on the home plate and checked my phone when I realized there was one rule I had forgotten:

MOM AND DAD—IRAN
MISSED CALLS (4)

My eyes bulged at the phone screen. *Do I call them back?* I could feel my heart rate going haywire. I had just talked to my parents on Sunday and wasn't expecting them to call again until the weekend. I took a deep breath and ran through some calculations. It was ten in the morning in the United States, so it had to be around six in the evening over there. They were probably eating dinner with my grandfather. No, that wasn't possible. No one eats dinner before ten in Iran. Perhaps they'd just left Baba Bozorg with his caretaker and were relaxing in his apartment, sipping tea, thinking about me.

Were my parents suspicious, or were they simply checking up?

A Metrobus screeched to a halt just down the block. On one hand, I felt caught, but on the other hand, I knew I was fine. My parents would have left a voice mail if it was anything serious. They had no way of knowing I was in DC; I'd covered all my bases. Even my excuse for quitting the internship was airtight. Dr. Mehta would never email my dad about *that*. Mom and Dad were supposed to trust me while they were gone, and until my face was plastered on milk cartons across the country, I would milk their trust.

I took another deep breath, and I decided to hop on the bus. The doors slid open, and I boarded from the middle, shuffling past the fare machine. The driver wasn't paying attention, anyway. The digital display read *D6*. Destination: unknown.

We drove around the corner where I crashed my bike, and I chuckled to myself. I had already forgotten about that incident with Fiora. It felt like ages ago.

A family of four tourists boarded the bus at Ford's Theatre—the matching "Proud to be an American" T-shirts gave them away. The dad was in the middle of describing

Abraham Lincoln's assassination in great detail. He must have been a history teacher, judging from his thick-rimmed glasses and his ability to ignore an apathetic audience. His two teenage daughters spent most of the bus ride scrolling through Instagram, "uh-huh"-ing their dad's every word. I discreetly paid attention. After Lincoln he talked about the International Spy Museum—with its exhibit on celebrity spies like Julia Child and Josephine Baker—and Union Station, the city's main transportation hub. His wife snapped pictures of these landmarks with her disposable camera. They hopped off shortly after Union Station, and from there, the bus passed run-down blocks with saloons, chicken joints, hair salons, and people of all colors and sizes.

I hopped off at the last stop, Stadium-Armory. It wasn't a particularly nice neighborhood. The streets smelled of urine, and it took me all of two minutes to find a prison next to a cemetery. I immediately hopped on another bus, and somehow, after transferring twice, found my way back to Dupont Circle.

I had barely made it two steps into the Hanover Hostel when I heard my name.

"Scott," the front-desk guy called. We met eyes and raised our chins slowly, cautiously, as if doubting the reality of this Scott-ception. It was the meta experience of facing your namesake—accepting the loss of a small fraction of your identity. "You were supposed to check out three hours ago."

"Right. About that . . . I'm going to need another—" How

much longer would I be staying at the hostel? Weeks, at least, but I couldn't afford that. "Listen, Scott. My plans have changed, and it looks like I'll be in DC for a while."

He went to pull up the Excel spreadsheet.

"How many nights?"

I didn't know. Maybe just one or two more, if I could find somewhere cheaper to stay. What was cheaper than thirty-five bucks a night? My only other option was to ask Fiora or Trent if I could crash with them—but I'd only known them for three days. Realistically, how much could I expect these new friends to help me?

I pulled out my wallet to check how much cash I had left. There was a hundred and some smaller bills. "I'd like to stay at least one more night."

"Just one?"

"Look, Scott—" I hesitated. "Isn't it weird when I call you that?"

"Not really. It's my name."

"Right. I'm Scott and you're Scott, and there are lots of other Scotts out there. But doesn't it feel like it's kind of chipping away at your individuality? I'm sure we're very different people. It just doesn't sit well with me."

Scott, the front-desk guy, sucked in his lips and nodded.

"Okay, Mr. Ferdowsi. If it helps, my name is Scott *Hanover*. Now, if you'd like to book another night, that'll be thirty-five dollars."

"Hanover . . . like the hostel?"

"It's my father's," he explained. "We own sixteen of them around the country. The DC location hardly gets any business, so he's letting me run it for the summer."

I noticed Scott Hanover was wearing another inspired shirt today; this one simply read PHONY in bold white letters.

"Do you want to know the truth?" I asked.

Then I spilled. I told him about my parents and Professor Mallard, the bike chase and Fiora and Trent. I walked him through every detail of my roller-coaster runaway, and Scott Hanover's jaw dropped like you wouldn't believe it. At first he thought I was lying. He'd just finished his freshman year at Yale; he was a smart, discerning guy with every reason to be skeptical. But the longer I went on, the more he saw my genuine desperation. And for whatever reason, he stood behind my motives.

Scott Hanover wasn't going to let me stay at his hostel for free—that would be bad business. I paid for two more nights, whittling my cash stash to a painful low. However, he let me off with an IOU for the rest of the nights. As long as I found a way to pay him something every few days, and as long as the hostel didn't fill up, I could stay.

CHAPTER 11

BACK AT TONIC, the scene was airy and infinite. Physically, we were packed by the bar like sardines, but the place felt pregnant with possibilities this time around. Trent was bartending tipsy tonight after coming from a Libertarian networking event. Fiora had gotten into a fight with her boyfriend, so she was late again.

I told them about my success with Professor Mallard. "I knew it," Fiora said smugly. Trent fixed me up a celebratory old-fashioned, which tasted way too strong, so I took small sips.

Now it was Fiora's turn to honor her end of our deal. She grabbed a napkin from behind the bar and pulled a pen out of her bra. Trent and I watched closely as she drew a fifteen-by-fifteen grid in a matter of seconds.

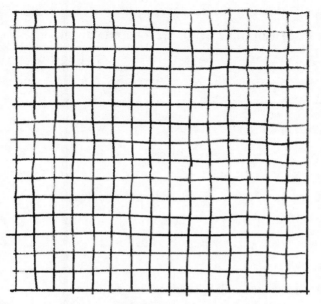

"This is a classic crossword grid," Fiora said. She crumpled the napkin into a ball and chucked it at the trash can, missing by at least half a foot. "Most people think you start a crossword with this. Nope. You start with a theme. All good crosswords have a handful of theme answers that serve as the building blocks for the rest of your grid. Usually they're the longest answers, and since they're *theme* answers . . ."

"They should be related," I finished. I picked up my glass. "So could a theme be, like, types of drinks? Old-fashioned, gin and tonic, dirty martini?"

"Sure, but that's a really simple one." Fiora stole my old-fashioned and took a long sip. "A better one would be . . . hmm." She fished out an ice cube with her fingers and plopped it on her tongue. Her eyes were focused on Trent, who was fixing up a drink for a couple at the other end of the bar. She smiled. "I got it. Trent's Republican views don't *hold water*. His opinions are incredibly *dense*. See what I did there, with the liquidy words? That's a better theme."

Once again, I was astonished by the wheels, assembly line, alphabet soup . . . whatever function controlled Fiora's brain, and how it functioned so differently from mine. Before I had a chance to chime in, Trent leaned in between us.

"I'll have you know," he said, half smiling and squinting his eyes, "that I'm no Republican. I'm a *Libertarian*. Like Renault Cohen."

Fiora nudged me. "Trent's idol. You may think Senator Cohen is a regular Republican scumbag, but *oh, no*. He believes in laissez-faire values! You know, hugs *and* drugs. Legalize cannabis, right, Mr. Future Senator?"

Trent leaned over the bar and smiled dreamily. "I accept the office and its responsibilities," he buzzed. For a moment, Trent disappeared into a world I knew well: the World of What Ifs. His eyes embraced the fantasy of possibility. He held on to that fantasy for just a second longer before reality shoved it into a closet. Trent snapped back into bar mode and poured Fiora a drink of her own. She took a sip.

"He's drunker than I thought," Fiora said.

"Yeah, he's acting pretty funny."

"No, no, Trent always acts like that. I can tell because he made my gin and tonic with, like, ninety percent gin."

Fiora assured me that most beginner cruciverbalists don't come up with swanky themes on their first try. She suggested we try an activity called "theme-storming." To start, I had to come up with a ridiculous word, so I scanned the bar for a cue. Then I took my cue one step further.

"Sexting."

Fiora's eyes shot open. "Whoa!" she howled. She honestly looked proud of me. "That's perfect. Very hip. Modern crosswords are totally moving in that direction." She bobbed her head excitedly. "Where'd you pull *sexting* from?"

"Well, Trent's drunk at work," I said. "It feels out of place, like sexting in a church."

"Eh, I've done it," Fiora said. "When I was fourteen, Trent dragged me to Easter Mass back in Charleston, and it was *so* boring, right, Trent?" Trent nodded, even though he was busy taking orders and cleaning up a spilled cocktail. "Yeah, super boring. Anyway, the Wi-Fi was especially shitty inside the church, so with God as my witness, I resurrected an old text thread with my crush from summer camp and, well . . . Let's just say Jesus wasn't the *only* thing to rise that Easter."

"Oh my God . . . Fiora, that's dis—I'm about to—*Can we just get back to the puzzle?*" I curled up on my bar stool and shuddered.

"All right, all right. Chill out," Fiora said, holding back giggles.

"Sexting," I said very seriously.

"Sexting," she repeated. "What else?"

"Church," I said.

"Good," she said. "What else?"

I kept rattling off random words and phrases, and she'd rattle some off, too, and eventually we had theme-stormed quite the list of answers:

SEXTING

CHURCH

JESUS

MUHAMMAD

MUHAMMAD ALI

ALLEY

ALLY

NEMESIS

OPRAH

ELLEN

PORTIA

PORSCHE

BMW

VOLKSWAGEN

ANGELA MERKEL

SNL

SATURDAY

DRUNK

AA

BINGE

TWINKIE

HOSTESS

CLEOPATRA

PYRAMID

SPHINX

PERSEPOLIS

REVOLUTION

BEATLES

HIPPIE

HIPPO

HUNGRY HUNGRY HIPPOS

APPLES TO APPLES

CARDS AGAINST HUMANITY

UN

EMMA WATSON

HERMIONE

RON WEASLEY

GINGER

PAPRIKA

TEQUILA

PATRON

MEXICO

COLOMBIA

COLUMBIA

DC

NYC

PA

RUNAWAY

PROFESSOR

DUCK

GOOSE

GEESE

GOOSES

POND

WATER

LIQUID

CUP

CONTAINER

POT

"Hm," Fiora said, biting her bottom lip. She scanned the napkin.

"What?"

"We've got at least a few options. What are you thinking?"

I scrabbled through the file cabinet of my mind. There were a million drawers and files to pull from, and they were constantly getting shuffled around. Sexting was now in the same drawer as church and religion. I didn't want any of those files. I wanted something more fun.

"Cards Against Humanity," I said, circling the part of our list that included HUNGRY HUNGRY HIPPOS, APPLES TO APPLES, and CARDS AGAINST HUMANITY.

"Games," Fiora said. "Nice theme. Nothing crazy, but it's broad enough to get interesting with our answers.

Sports and board games and romantic shit."

"Romantic shit?"

"All that 'love is a game' stuff. I try to make my crosswords female friendly," Fiora said proudly, "since it's such a dude-dominated hobby."

"Your personal contribution to feminism."

"Saaket, my *presence* is a contribution to feminism."

I couldn't argue with that.

"So games," I said, fumbling with one of the bar candles.

"Games," Fiora repeated. "Let's theme-storm a list for that."

"What's wrong with the games we already came up with?" I dipped my finger into the candle. It never got old watching hot wax dry so fast.

"They won't fit on our grid," Fiora said. "Hungry Hungry Hippos—eighteen letters. Apples to Apples—fourteen. And Cards Against Humanity? Twenty. Freaking. Letters."

She crossed those words off of our original list. "The max we should do is, like, twelve. Plus, if we come up with more games, then maybe we'll find a subtheme."

TIC–TAC–TOE
TWISTER
MONOPOLY
TRUTH OR DARE
WORLD CUP
SUPER BOWL

WORLD SERIES
TABLE TENNIS
TUG–OF–WAR
MARIO KART
BACKGAMMON

"In Farsi," I said, "backgammon is called *takhteh*."

RISK
JENGA
CANDY LAND
MANCALA

"I forgot about Mancala!" Fiora exclaimed. "I used to live for that game. One time, in second or third grade, I told this kid Joey that if he stuck all the stones up his nose, they would go to his arms and give him more muscle."

"I thought the point was to get the stones on your side of the board . . ."

"Obviously, but Joey was an idiot. He was, like, the class bully. Anyway, he listened to me and ended up in the nurse's office." Fiora raised her chin proudly. "All the dorks worshipped me after that."

BLACKJACK
POKER
GO FISH

CRAZY EIGHTS
BEER PONG
HUNGER GAMES

Fiora shook her head. "I'm judging you so hard right now," she said.

TRIWIZARD TOURNAMENT

"*Saaket*. Would you like to show me your fan-fiction account?" I couldn't tell if Fiora was genuinely embarrassed or entertained, and I kind of liked it.

ETCH A SKETCH
CONNECT FOUR
THE PRICE IS RIGHT
FAMILY FEUD
CASH CAB
DEAL OR NO DEAL
AMAZING RACE
SURVIVOR
AMERICAN IDOL
HELLS KITCHEN
THE X FACTOR

"Anything else?" I asked.

"Really?"

"Hey, it's an accurate depiction of modern romance. Passion and fizzle. Even the most independent lady needs her fix of trashy TV," Fiora said. "In between MSNBC and the History Channel, of course."

Fiora said the words "in between" exactly when I looked down at the first entry on our list. Something clicked.

"Hold on," I said, grabbing the pen out of her hand a little too forcefully. I brought the napkin closer and circled:

TIC-TAC-TOE

Fiora grinned like I had guessed her favorite song or *Bachelor* contestant. She snatched the pen from me:

SUPER BOWL

And together we continued:

MARIO KART
ETCH A SKETCH
DEAL OR NO DEAL
AMAZING RACE
HELL'S KITCHEN
THE X FACTOR

"This is incredible," I said. "There are words in between our words. This is really good, right? It's like a theme and a subtheme."

Fiora didn't say anything. Her eyes stayed fixed on the list.

"Fiora?"

She kept scanning the napkin while I waited for her to respond. Then she scrunched up her face and went, "Yeah. No. It's not going to work."

"What? Why?"

"It's a cool idea," Fiora admitted. "But based on what we have, there's no theme connecting all these bridge words. Theoretically we could *force* a subtheme, like just half-ass something, but then we'd have no freedom with our grid. Filling in the rest of your squares would suck immensely. Especially when you're new to this, you always want to leave a little bit of wiggle room with your theme."

I let out a loud grunt. "Well, that's just—" and then I smiled and thought for a few moments. "That's so 'cool American' of you."

"What?"

I spelled it out for her: "C-O-O . . . L-A-M-E . . . R-I-C-A-N," I said, pausing strategically around the bridge word. "Cool American."

Fiora looked like she was going to punch me. I braced myself. Yep—she was going to—wait. No. All of a sudden she started laughing. Hysterically!

"Wha . . . I . . . Who even *are* you, Saaket Ferdowsi?"

"You know what, Fiora?" I grabbed another napkin and drew a giant question mark. "That's what I'm figuring out."

□□□□

Fiora announced that we were done for the night and would finish later.

"Come on," I begged.

"My therapist says you have to divide big projects into manageable pieces," Fiora said. "Building a crossword puzzle isn't easy. You have to take it step-by-step."

This was the second time Fiora had mentioned her therapist around me. I was surprised by how openly she talked about therapy, like it was a weekly piano lesson and not an expensive appointment for your mental health.

I'd seen a therapist exactly once in my life. Throughout sophomore year, I tried convincing my parents to get me evaluated for ADHD. I begged and begged. *If I were the conductor of the train of thought, I'd steer it right into the Bermuda Triangle*, I told them. They never budged. My parents didn't "believe" in therapy. They were convinced all shrinks were con artists, no different from palm readers or Nigerian prince spammers.

This time, I didn't make a PowerPoint presentation. I took matters into my own hands.

It was a chilly November morning. Every corner of our cul-de-sac was covered in a thin coat of frost: car windshields, stray soccer balls, even the littlest blades of grass. It was so cold, you could see your own breath. My mom shrieked something about hypothermia and offered to drive me to the bus stop for school, but I insisted on walking like I always did. Truth was, I had plans to take a different bus—into Philly, to see Lydia Sparrow, a shrink who administered ADHD tests for $150 a pop.

"It's nice to meet you, Scott," Dr. Sparrow said. Her voice was tough—not Mafia tough, but like a piece of well-done steak. Inelastic and consonant-heavy.

"So why are you here today?"

"I'm having trouble following through," I said. I realized I was sitting uncharacteristically still. I started tapping my foot, little taps—fast—and cracking my knuckles.

"My thoughts are scattered, doctor, and it's been like that for a while. I'm starting to worry that I'll never be able to focus on . . . you know, things that are important. College classes. My job. Life."

Dr. Sparrow took some notes and nodded. I caught her eyelids drooping for a split second; she tried covering it up with a cough.

"So you have attention issues?"

"Yeah," I sighed, "I guess you could call it that. My grades aren't awesome, and I have a hard time focusing at school or doing homework without my mind wandering off."

"Yes, yes. This appears to be a theme . . . a theme song! Ha."

"Ha-ha, sure."

For the rest of our meeting, Dr. Sparrow asked about my childhood, how my parents treated me, relationships with friends, siblings, bullies, and sex, with a lot of questions about violence, to which I repeatedly answered "No." At one point I asked when we would begin the actual ADHD test, and apparently, this was it.

"Scott, evaluating someone your age for ADHD is a relatively complicated process. Usually the disorder is diagnosed when a person is much younger—"

"My parents never took me to a psychologist when I was younger. They don't believe in psychology."

Dr. Sparrow cleared her throat. "And so it's going to take more sessions to determine what's going on. It might be ADHD, it might not, but whatever it is, I'm sure we can help you overcome the symptoms and perform at a suitable level."

"Can't you just write me a prescription?" I asked, cracking my knuckles.

Dr. Sparrow smiled sweetly. "That's not how it works."

"I've read online that Adderall would help. Vyvanse is also the new—"

"We can explore treatment options after a few more sessions." More sessions? I wasn't expecting a marathon. "I enjoyed meeting you, Scott, and I look forward to seeing you again."

Clearly, I had misdiagnosed how therapy worked. I never went back.

□□□□

"Oh, wait! I almost forgot to ask."

I waved my hand in front of Trent to get his attention. He was pouring a beer that resembled liquid dark chocolate. He raised a finger from the glass—*hold on, one second*—and eventually he came over. I cleared my throat.

"I'm, uh, running low on funds."

Fiora raised an eyebrow, and Trent looked at me skeptically.

"I'm not asking for money," I blurted out, lifting my elbow from the sticky bar top. "Well, I'm not *not* asking. I need it. But I'd like to earn it. Is there any way I could wash dishes or wipe tables here part-time? I'll do anything, really."

Trent thought for a moment. A group of cute girls tried to make eye contact with him at the end of the bar; he completely ignored them.

"Tell you what," he said, raising a patient finger at the girls. "I'll ask my manager later tonight or tomorrow. I'll you let you know as soon as I can."

I smiled. "Thanks, Trent."

Trent rushed over to tend to his customers, leaving me alone with Fiora.

"You'll do anything, eh?"

Fiora was half smiling, gently stroking her chin. I could see fire in her eyes. The wheels in her head were spinning, and it wasn't about puzzles.

"If I eat cheap, I can make what I have last through the

weekend. Maybe even Monday. But after that . . . I don't know."

"I'll give you fifty bucks for a dare," she said.

I remembered what Trent had told me about Fiora after the biking accident. *Fiora's life these days is about as messed up as a bunch of lawmakers trying to do their damn jobs.*

"What kind of dare?"

"I haven't figured out the details yet. Hmm. What could you, Saaket Ferdowsi, possibly do that would give me unadulterated pleasure?"

Lord knows she's not the kind of girl to let the world get away with giving her a kick.

"I've got it!" she burst out. "I dare you to pick someone up."

"Pick . . . who up?" I asked hesitantly.

"A *girl*," she cried. "Or a guy. Whatever floats your boat."

My eyes and eyebrows and lips all shifted in different directions. "And where am I supposed to pick up this girl?"

"That's where the dare gets fun," Fiora said. "I want it to be somewhere interesting. Somewhere challenging. Like a sexual health clinic, but less risky. Or a cancer support group, but less immoral."

Sometimes, she'll kick back.

I shook my head. "This is wrong on so many levels."

"Come on! I'm serious!" Fiora flailed her arms like a sports fan reacting to a bad call. "How about . . . Oh God, not . . . Oh!"

"Oh no," I muttered.

"The zoo. The *National Zoo*. Oh, it'll be perfect," Fiora said, clapping her hands.

"The zoo isn't even open this late!"

"Not tonight," Fiora said, like I was the crazy-sounding one. "Tomorrow—no, that won't work. Tomorrow's Friday. I've got my crossword group in the morning and class during the day. We'll go Saturday. Yes! There's bound to be so many people on Saturday."

"People?" I squeaked.

"Girls! Cute, single DC interns wandering around, *ooh*ing and *aww*ing at the animals."

Fiora practically galloped in her seat, flailing her hands in mock excitement. "Saaket, they'll be *so* vulnerable. That's why they're at the zoo, to feel loved vicariously through the giant pandas and koala bears and other cuddly animals."

"Honestly, Fiora . . ." I bit my lip and cracked my neck.

"You don't know how to pick up a girl? It's easy. You walk up and make a smooth comment about how cute and cuddly the pandas look. She'll glance in your direction and check you out, and you'll be making these cute-and-cuddly-but-sexy eyes at her, and BAM." Fiora smacked her hand on the bar top. "You seal the deal."

These things give her a necessary thrill.

"What exactly do you mean by, um, 'sealing the deal'?" I couldn't believe I was playing along with Fiora. It was like Stockholm syndrome.

"A phone number. Proof that you scored digits."

"Don't you have something better to do with your Saturday? Instead of paying to watch me embarrass myself, you could donate to the Ferdowsi Fund and visit the zoo with your boyfriend . . ."

"He's been in a shitty mood since that bike chase," Fiora said sharply. An icy rage crept up my spine, since technically that bike chase was her fault. But also . . . relationship problems? I was listening. "And on the contrary, I've got too *much* going on. Believe me, after last weekend, I could use the distraction. You're helping me here, too, you know."

My palms were sweatier than my entire body after the bike chase.

"I don't know, Fiora. I'm not comf—"

I stopped myself. Comfort was not a luxury I could afford right now. That wasn't the point of my journey. Sure, I recognized the absurdity of Fiora's dare, but the money would let me stay in DC and work with Professor Mallard, and my earning it would do something for Fiora. We had a chance to provide each other with a stipend of sorts. A bridge that would carry us over for a little longer.

I cocked my head back and smiled. All along I had seen Fiora as this lovely interruption, as her own complicated entity, but the intersection of our grids made for a stronger puzzle. Finally, I was getting somewhere with grit. I was clearing my head. You don't clear a table and wipe it with a grimy old rag.

"Scratch that," I told her. "I'll do it."

CHAPTER 12

THE AMAZING RACE is a game-slash-show (not to be confused with game shows, like *Jeopardy!*) where teams of two race around the world competing with each other. The teams could be married acupuncturists, pro wrestlers, Roller Derby moms, and other absurd types of people. My parents used to watch it all the time, and from the way they raved, it sounded like a dramatic, daredevil-ish, entertaining-enough smorgasbord of television.

Today it sounded graceful.

> *A-M-A-Z-I-N . . . G-R-A-C-E.* Grace.
> *T-I-C . . . T-A-C-T . . . O-E.* Tact.

I spent all of Friday morning trying to make our theme work. To win any game, you needed grace and tact. It was the best pattern I could come up with. The answers would be games where the "bridge" word was an ingredient for success. It was genius, I thought. I just couldn't come up with more than those two.

❑❑❑❑

By day five, I was finally getting the hang of this running-away thing. I'd made remarkable new friends like Fiora and Trent. I'd worked hard to win Professor Mallard's attention. Heck, I had even started making a crossword puzzle. I came to DC to get gritty, to discover myself, and I was reaping the rewards on this whirlwind adventure.

Then my parents called again, and this time I knew I had to pick up. Three weeks. Three calls. More lies than I could count. I could do this.

"Allo?"

"*Salaaaaaaaam, Saaket jaan!*" my dad practically sang into the phone, the bad reception giving his voice some extra vibrato.

"*Saaket joonam,*" my mom crooned. "We miss you so dearly. Are you eating enough? Are you healthy?"

Dad added: "What time is it there?"

"Uh, around three," I said.

"So early!" Mom said. "It's midnight here. Are you still at your internship?"

"They let us out early today. It's Friday," I said. It was so easy to make stuff up on the phone with your parents.

"That's wonderful," Dad said. "Isn't research wonderful? Your mother and I are so proud that you are applying yourself to this internship. One day, it could even look good on your medical school application, or for your PhD—"

"Dad."

There was a palpable moment of silence. I clenched my teeth. I wanted to remind my dad that *he* applied to this internship for me. I wanted both my parents to know that I was here in DC, happy with the trajectory of my future—even if I didn't quite know what it looked like. I was learning that I could focus, that I could be gritty.

My mom cleared her throat. "Saaket, I have to say, I wish so badly that you were here with us. It's a shame you haven't seen Iran yet. The royal palaces, the bazaars, the bridges . . . And it's been wonderful to be with our family and friends. You know, your dad and I haven't been back since before you were born. Everyone asks about you, of course. We tell them you're busy doing important things!"

I appreciated my mom changing the subject, but I was still stuck on my dad, who clearly had no real interest in my happiness. I couldn't get over his one-track mind, his obsession with my life, my future, even from ten thousand miles away. I knew for a fact his own father never put half as much pressure on him as he put on me. Baba Bozorg let Dad come to America at sixteen and live an independent life.

"How's Baba Bozorg?" I asked.

Another fat, pulpy silence.

"He's fine," Dad said.

My grandpa's health went to shit last winter. I don't know the details because my parents never talked to me about it. I just overheard them arguing a few months ago about whether or not we should all fly to Iran to see him. Dad won that argument. He didn't want me to miss my precious internship because it would be "crucial" for college admissions. I wasn't overly upset—I'd only met my grandfather twice, when I was much younger, and have always felt a hazy, distant connection to Iran—but I wondered: What if that's me in thirty years, choosing between my father's deathbed and an opportunity to get ahead? What would he want me to do?

"It's getting late," Mom said softly.

"Yes, yes. It is. Your mother and I have to go," Dad said.

"Okay."

"*Saaket joon*, is everything all right at home? Don't forget to lock the door and set the alarm at night," Mom reminded.

"Yes, everything is fine," I said. I couldn't remember if I had set the alarm before leaving home on Monday. I hoped so.

"Have you been getting my emails?" Dad asked. "There was an article . . ." The reception got shoddy for a moment, and I didn't catch the tail end of Dad's sentence.

"Yeah, yeah, I saw that."

"Okay, *joonam*. Let us know if you need anything," Mom said tenderly. *"Delemun barat kheili tang shodeh."* There was no familial way of saying "I love you" in Farsi, so my parents got around it with other statements of affection like "You are my world" and "I would sacrifice my life for you." Or in this case: "Our heart misses you deeply."

"*Khodafez*," they said. *Goodbye.*

"*Khodafez*," I said, hanging up the phone.

❏❏❏❏

I stepped outside for some fresh air. An ambulance blazed down New Hampshire, wailing like a petulant child. I sat down on the stoop of the hostel and logged in to my Gmail account, cupping my hand over my phone to prevent glare from the sun. I hadn't checked my emails since before I left home.

FROM: Dr. Bhupendra Mehta
SUBJECT: Re. Internship Absence

> Dear Scott,
> I am very sorry to hear about your predicament
> with lice . . .

Success. I knew it would be a solid excuse.

FROM: Dad
SUBJECT: Fwd. Early decision affords major edge to engineering applicants

FROM: Dad
SUBJECT: Fwd. College Admissions **SHOCKER**

FROM: Dad
SUBJECT: Fwd. 5 Top Premed Programs for the Uncertain Doctor

FROM: Dad
SUBJECT: Fwd. A professor discovered the secret to happiness. You won't believe what it is.

Delete, delete, delete . . . Tempting, but delete.

FROM: Kevin Ho
SUBJECT: GREETINGS FROM WIFI-WONDERFUL WUHAN

Dude!
We miss you!!!!!!
So it turns out we're not totally disconnected from the Western world. Jack and I got lucky with our student host here in Wuhan. We got this chill dude named Xu who's letting us use his computer for TWENTY MINUTES. Can you believe we're in China?!? Anyway, we have generously decided to spend five of our precious WiFi minutes emailing you. (The other fifteen were for Facebook. We got past the Great Firewall!!! Priorities, man.)

How's the internship going? You sounded pretty excited about it before we left. Still bummed you couldn't be here with us, man. We give the SAYLT people shit all the time for not accepting our best buddy Scotty.

China is crazy. Check out the photo we just posted on Facebook. We'll tell you more stories when the gang's back together at the end of the summer.

Kevin & Jack

The email was time-stamped 2:35 a.m. on Tuesday, so they must have already moved on to the next Southeast Asian city. The next adventure. It sounded like Kevin and Jack were having exactly the kind of worldly, eye-opening trip that we'd imagined.

All three of us applied to the Southeast Asia Youth Leaders Tour. We loved saying the acronym out loud. "I submitted my SAY-LIT application last night!" "I got in touch with my SAY-LIT interviewer." The program was supposed to be highly selective—they only accepted 4 percent of the nearly one thousand high school juniors who applied. Kevin, Jack, and I never discussed that part. We were hoping for a miracle. No, we *expected* a miracle. For a month after submitting our applications, we spent every lunch fantasizing about our all-expenses-paid trip together. "What happens at SAY-LIT . . ." became a running joke.

It was an awkward day when I didn't get in. We had plans to meet at Kevin's locker at exactly 2:58 p.m. on the day results were coming out. Kevin and Jack could hardly contain their excitement; they'd crushed their interviews the week before. I felt less certain. "Earth Club, Model UN, Iranian instruments . . . You're all over the place, Mr. Ferdowsi," I remember my interviewer saying over Skype. "Where do you see yourself in ten years?" Needless to say, I was stumped.

At 3 p.m., we refreshed our phones one more time. Kevin and Jack jumped in the air almost simultaneously, high-fiving and pounding their fists. I looked up from my phone screen and forced a smile. Their expressions dropped.

"Admissions processes aren't perfect," Jack said, patting my shoulder. He was always more sympathetic to my shortcomings than Kevin.

Jack the aspiring diplomat. Kevin the aspiring economist. I knew exactly why I wasn't selected. My friends were more qualified than I was, plain and simple.

❑❑❑❑

Later that day, after the sun had fallen and a soft gust of wind replaced the stuffy air, I went out again for a walk around the neighborhood. I needed to clear my mind. Being so close to GW and Georgetown, Dupont Circle was one of those places where the average age plummets on weekends. Flocks of college-looking people had swarmed to the local restaurants and bars on this Friday night. All the groups looked the same: mostly white, attractive, and an even guy-to-girl ratio. The guys looked nothing like my friends from home. They were dressed in pastel-colored shorts and oxford shirts, downing beer and bellowing phrases like "What's up, player!" and "No way, bro!"

The girls were another story. There was one in particular who spoke exclusively through her nose. She stood outside a Spanish restaurant, stick thin and brunette, suffocating in her little black dress. One by one, her girlfriends arrived, and she greeted them the same way:

"Ohhh mey gawwwd. How are yaaaewwww?" High-pitched. Expressionless. It was like a bad horror movie.

Later I noticed an elderly Muslim woman sitting alone outside a coffee shop, her hair covered in a flowery hijab. She started talking to this African American man who was wearing horn-rimmed glasses and a tweed jacket. The two clearly didn't know each other, but their conversation was filled with gestures and smiles nonetheless. A few doors down, a father and son stood before a tiny patch of purple flowers. The son, who was maybe five years old, turned to his dad and gave a high-pitched assertion: "Blue!" The dad retorted: "Purple!" They went off on a list of colors—pink! lavender!—talking over each other like snappy firecrackers.

This Friday-night crowd felt all too familiar. Everyone was a friend, a father, someone's something. Short bursts of memories went off in my head—the same ones that had been haunting me since I came to DC. Perhaps I couldn't shake off my past. It wasn't something you could leave behind or bury in the ground.

I found myself back outside Tom's Foolery. I was tempted to go inside for some Etch A Sketch or Mario Kart—a fitting "blast from the past"—but they were checking IDs.

The bouncer turned me away, and within seconds, I heard a crack of thunder. The sound punched at my bones, and it started to drizzle. I ran back to the hostel, but not before getting soaked by the torrential downpour that ensued.

CHAPTER 13

THE SUN SHONE relentlessly on Saturday morning. I trekked more than two miles up Connecticut Ave to the National Zoo, the back of my neck burning, and by the end of it I was sweating through every fiber of my T-shirt. I hated sweat. I realized no one was going around saying they loved sweat, but I hated it for so much more than the physical discomfort. It reminded me of all the other things in the world that made me uncomfortable. It reminded me of my lanky body, which people were always commenting on. "Eat something, why don't you!" "You look like you could disappear into thin air." Because how could I be self-conscious about my body image if I wasn't fat, right? It reminded me of salt water, which was half the reason I couldn't stand the beach. Being shirtless was the other half. And it reminded me of sex, because I hadn't done it yet, which was fine a few years ago but was becoming less fine—or at least, it felt that way.

When I reached the zoo, I noticed that the space inside the gates resembled my quiet cul-de-sac back in Pennsylvania, with a granite ledge where the houses would be. I sat on the part of the ledge that would have been my house, not for any sentimental reason, but because it was the only dry space. Most of the ledge was still soaking wet from the night before. I figured the sun needed more time.

A few minutes later, Fiora biked through the gates and braked abruptly in front of my house on the cul-de-sac. She skidded just past the doormat.

"Where'd you get that bike?" I asked suspiciously.

"It's mine," Fiora said, ruffling her hair. She wasn't wearing a helmet.

"You own a bike?"

"Of course I own a bike," she said, locking it in the rack near the entrance. "I wouldn't have given you the other one if I didn't."

I looked stumped. "The *other* one? You mean—" The *stolen* one. Which didn't come with a helmet, either. Now that I thought about it, I was really quite lucky to have survived that accident with just a few scratches. If my mother knew . . .

"I mean what?" Fiora raised one eyebrow.

"Never mind."

She perked her ears. "You know what I hear?"

I listened for a second. "The soft mating call of a tufted sparrow?"

"No, you goddamn sap. I hear the lions all the way in the back of the zoo, roaring at us to get a fuckin' move on!"

Without so much as a nod, Fiora led me into the zoo. I trailed behind like an obedient puppy on a leash; I was following through with her dare. We walked down a stone path with benches and concession stands—no animals in sight. I couldn't even hear any birds. I wondered whether Fiora had taken me to an imaginary zoo, or a sexual health clinic or a cancer support group like she had joked. Maybe Fiora really didn't have any boundaries.

We crossed a small bridge to enter the Asia Trail, the first section of the zoo, where we were surrounded by gentle streams and gangly bamboo. Unruffled silence. A shadow fell upon us and cooled the back of my neck. The entire world shrank into that twenty-foot radius, and for a few seconds, time swelled into an eternity. It was the kind of stuff you'd expect Fiora to scoff at, but instead, she took it all in, literally. She paused over the stream with her hands on her hips, puffing her chest to fill it with 1,256 square feet of oxygen.

Before I knew it, we stood face-to-face with an animal exhibit:

A Case of Mistaken Identity
Sloth bears are not sloths?

Early biologists mistakenly thought sloth bears were very large sloths. Both have shaggy fur and long, curved claws, but sloth bears are not related to slow-moving sloths.

The actual sloth bear was nowhere to be seen. I didn't blame it. I wouldn't have wanted to live in an "exhibit," either. The word sounds so impersonal, like it needs a letter or numerical label—Exhibit A or Exhibit 3.1.5.

"The sloth's not home," I told Fiora.

"Patience, dude. Just look around."

"Maybe he's still hungover from his Friday night," I joked.

"Maybe he ran away," Fiora said.

Pretty soon we dismissed the Case of the Missing Sloth Bear, and we went looking instead for clouded leopards. We followed a curvy path that was concealed by trees and hedges. It felt strangely private.

"Can I ask you a question?"

Fiora gave me a look.

I gave her a look back that said: Okay, yes, *technically* that was a question.

"I didn't even have to use any words," she remarked. "But yes, you may ask me *another* question."

"The other day you said there was too much going on in your life . . . that you weren't doing this out of boredom or because you feel bad for me—this pickup challenge—but because it takes your mind off the other stuff."

"First of all, I don't feel bad for you. You're refreshingly genuine. And flawed, but not in a fucked-up way. I like that. Second, what's your question?"

I held back a smile at Fiora's comment. *I like that.*

"Aren't you flawed, too?"

"Excuse me?"

I'd been curious about the details of Fiora's discombobulated situation, and I was feeling ballsy enough behind these green walls to bring it up.

"Sorry, that wasn't my question," I said. "I'm just saying, I know all these half facts about you, but I feel like I don't have the full picture."

Fiora laughed shyly, like she was aiming for confidence but fell just short.

"What do you want to know?"

Lucky for me, I had an arsenal of questions ready to fire. I started with her dad.

"He's a workaholic," she began. Her tone was raw and exposed. "I didn't see much of him growing up, especially after the divorce."

"Why'd your parents split up?"

"Because they're terrible adults. One shut down after a tragic life event and the other had a drug problem. Not exactly a compatible pairing."

"Your mom's got to be doing better if you visited her last weekend, right?"

"She, um—jeez, do we really have to talk about this?"

Clearly I'd struck a chord with Fiora's mom. Had she relapsed? Or was there something about her new life in Philly that rubbed Fiora the wrong way? I stopped thinking these questions when I realized I might actually say one of them out loud.

"Sorry," I said, kicking at the dirt trail.

"No worries." From the corner of my eye, I saw Fiora turning her face and smiling. She knew I felt embarrassed. This almost evened out the playing field, the fact that I had suffered at the hands of Fiora's predicament for just one second. Her pain had to be orders of magnitude worse, but still.

We turned around after realizing we had missed the clouded leopard. Halfway up the curved path, a yellow squirrel leapt out and scurried in front of us.

"What's her name?" Fiora asked.

"Mustard," I replied.

All of a sudden the squirrel sprinted out again. Fiora almost tripped, because this time Mustard stopped mid-sprint and glared at us—the pesky humans who were arrogant enough to assign them a gender and name.

"Silly Mustard," Fiora said. "You know what's an even weirder name?"

I knew where she was going with this. "Definitely Fiora."

"*Saaket,*" she said, eyeing me intensely. "Where'd your parents come up with a name like that, anyway?"

"In Farsi it means 'quiet.' It's not really a common name. My mom and dad wanted something unique, and they were hoping I'd be a quiet baby, so boom, Saaket."

"I bet you were the whiniest baby," she said. "I bet you cried ironically all the time."

"Still do," I said proudly.

"Really?"

Shit. I thought I was making a smooth comment, when in fact, I'd just admitted to being a teenage crybaby.

"Um. I guess sometimes. Just with my dad, really. He puts a lot of pressure on me to figure out my career. You know, apply myself and get my life together."

"You're lucky he cares," Fiora said.

"Are you freaking kidding me?" I burst out. "It's the worst. I'm not even a senior in high school and he expects me to know exactly what I'm doing for the next four hundred years of my life. *Focus, focus,* fucking *focus.* Like, I need to discover the one thing I'm passionate about tomorrow? Or in five years? And it has to be something practical, too, because, well, 'Your mom and I immigrated to America and worked hard so that you can have a better life.' What if I decide that the one thing I want to do for the rest of my life isn't law or medicine or engineering? That I'm not going to make buckets of money? He would explode. I can't just wake up and say I'm going to write crossword puzzles for the rest of my days. I don't have that stupid luxury."

"Okay, okay," Fiora said, looking down and tensing up her jaw.

"I think we passed the clouded leopard again," I said softly.

The clouded leopard was hidden behind a tall, perfectly trimmed hedge at the center of the loopy path. It was the first zoo animal I'd seen all day, perched atop the highest branch in its zoo habitat. My eyes traced the soft, splashy black spots on the leopard's fur. The kids around us giggled and yelped, and I became giddy, too. My fingers tingled, knees fidgeted, all that. But then I noticed something: the clouded leopard did not actually look happy. It upset me that no one else was the least bit concerned for its happiness.

"What a nice place to take a nap!" one boy shouted, tugging his mom's arm.

"Make it do something," whined another.

I look over at Fiora. She had this hollow expression on her face, a mirror image of the clouded leopard's. It was as if they were saying to each other: *All right, yeah. They'll see whatever they want to see.*

"Hey," I said, tapping her shoulder. "Look, I'm sorry for my soliloquy of sucky parenting over there. I didn't mean to get fired up like that."

Then, almost in sync, Fiora and the leopard shook themselves back into motion.

CHAPTER 14

WE FINALLY REACHED the panda exhibit, and Fiora smiled wickedly.

"This is where you're going to pick her up."

I grimaced. I could feel my body turning inside out, like the prank my swim teammates used to pull on my duffel bag. They would dump all my stuff out, turn it inside out, throw everything back in, and zip it shut so that it looked like a chicken nugget. The prank was called "nuggeting." Real clever.

At swim meets, I would get butterflies in my stomach right before diving into the pool. Fiora didn't even give me a diving board. She pushed me into the deep end, retreated to the benches, and crossed her legs. She might as well have brought popcorn and a jumbo soda—she was ready for a show.

I took a deep breath. All I had to do was find a girl, get her number, and maintain some amount of dignity. Boom. Fifty bucks. Easy enough when there's a cute panda exhibit, right? Except the panda, like its sloth brethren, was noticeably missing.

"Look!" shouted a heavy man with an even heavier Southern accent, pointing his finger below the guardrail. "There it is!"

Everyone looked down. These two twins even turned their faces toward each other and whacked noses. The man let out a roaring laugh; he was pointing at a squirrel. The rest of us were less amused.

"He's in the tree!" exclaimed a girl with turquoise highlights in her blonde hair. She was wearing a yellow-striped halter top and looked about my age. *This feels creepy*, I thought, rocking back and forth on my heels and toes. I took a deep breath and stepped forward to say . . .

Swoop. An older man came out of nowhere and curled her into his arms. He planted a big, wet kiss on her now-undesirably thin lips. Pickup Fail #1. I looked back at Fiora with the most desperate puppy-dog face, wide eyes and all. She pretended not to notice.

The panda was, in fact, hiding high up in the tree. It was hardly noticeable except for a patch of fur where the black turned to white. I didn't even know pandas could climb trees. Everyone around me was twisting and bending to get the best glimpse of this high-up, distant sonuvva-panda. One girl didn't seem to care, instead doling out pieces of bread crust to a flock of pigeons.

"I'm pretty sure there's an underground bird operation going on here," I said, just loud enough to feel like I tried, hoping she wouldn't actually hear me.

"Do I know you?"

"Sorry, sorry. I wasn't talking to—"

She got up and smiled sweetly. "Me. You were talking to me. Don't worry, I'm curious. What's this underground bird operation you speak of?" The girl was curvy and cute, wearing jeans and a hot-pink V-neck with sneakers. Her hair was tied back in a tight ponytail. I looked behind me to make sure Fiora was paying attention.

"Uh, well, obviously the birds were planted around the zoo to . . ." I needed to come up with something clever. "To eat all the . . . From the other animals, you know." Shit. I was initially thinking shit, literal shit, because that was my expletive reaction, but because I wasn't a complete freak, I stopped myself. Birds eat bread, not shit. Or feces. Wait, saying *feces* could make me sound intelligent. Or better yet, "Bowel movements," I said proudly.

The girl's face turned inexplicably sour. "Ew, what's wrong with you?"

She harrumphed as if I had actually splattered feces all over her cheap pink blouse and stormed off. The birds stuck around. Now I was the crazy bird person.

Clearly Fiora had set me up to fail. She had picked up on my impressive ability to crash and burn, from the bike accident to my attempts at getting Professor Mallard's attention, all the way to this pickup dare. She'd figured me out in just a few days. *Here's a guy who always takes the first step, and he always trips. And it is kind of funny when he trips. Like a kitten trying to climb out of a fishbowl.* I took some artistic license with the last bit.

"I hope the panda comes down," a girl said. I kept staring ahead, thinking of the kitten, pretending not to hear an opportunity for Pickup Fail #3.

"That might have been a more effective pickup line," she added. "Instead of that silly bird comment. Everyone knows people who talk about birds are crazy."

I looked quickly over my shoulder to glance at this mystery girl. She seemed to be about my age, wearing a gray T-shirt tucked into a pencil skirt that stopped just above the knees. She was pretty. Not edgy or drop-dead gorgeous, but pretty.

"Wouldn't that make her crazy, too?" I asked.

"All girls are crazy," she said. "Except me. I'm Jeanette."

Jeanette shot her hand out. I stared for a second, like a prisoner of war meeting his rescuer for the first time. Then I shook her hand. It was a firm handshake, and my expression must have revealed my surprise, because she reacted immediately.

"Firm handshake. Part two of an effective pickup."

"Are you picking me up?"

"No," she answered, as if my question were a totally reasonable one. "I'm just helping you get better at it. I don't appreciate ineffectiveness in any form." She paused and bit her lip. "Also, if you don't mind me making a few more observations . . . Your eye contact wasn't exactly direct, and your tone was hesitant at best."

Jeanette spoke—no, *lectured*—with the authority of a professor. Every word that came out of her mouth had staccato, like logs crackling in a fireplace.

"How magnanimous of you," I said. Big words felt right for our conversation.

"You're welcome."

I looked around, unnerved, and Jeanette raised a dubious eyebrow. She was about as interested as the clouded leopard. Fiora, on the other hand, was struggling to contain her laughter back on the bench.

"Your choice of a pickup venue is also quite baffling," Jeanette continued. We were only half facing each other, like stage actors reading scripted dialogue.

"I didn't pick the venue. A friend picked it."

"You're with a friend?"

"No, no," I said quickly. "It was more of a friendship . . . contract."

Out of nowhere, someone handed me a small digital camera, and before I knew it, a family of Asian tourists stood posing in front of me.

"If I were your lawyer, I would deem that contract null and void," Jeanette said as I took two pictures—horizontal and vertical—making sure to get the panda in the shot.

"Are you . . . a lawyer?" I gave the camera back.

"Someday. I just finished my freshman year at Liberty University. Pre-law. I'm interning at a think tank this summer. You?"

I'd never heard of Jeanette's college, but the bigger issue was that I didn't attend any college at all. There was no way Jeanette would keep talking to me if she found out I was still in high school. So I lied.

"I'm interning for Professor Cecily Mallard at Georgetown." I gulped and smiled from the side of my mouth, like a cartoon character. "I'm a research assistant."

"What kind of research?"

"Grit. It's the psychology of success and perseverance. I'm studying important historical figures who accomplished amazing feats by, um—persisting."

"That sounds like a fascinating subfield! I—" Jeanette stopped midsentence. If a face could kick itself, that was exactly what Jeanette did with hers. "Hold on. I'm sorry. This is wrong. I'm doing precisely what you did with that poor girl. I didn't mean it. I was simply calling attention to your subpar pickup line, and in doing so, I'm now somehow picking *you* up. My magnanimous individual agency became a pickup line of its own. This is wrong."

"No, no," I blurted, worried I was losing my one shot at winning this dare. "This is totally the universe speaking. It's for sure, like, an act of God."

Jeanette's face instantly un-kicked itself. She was beaming. "I like the way you think. Did I mention my name? I'm sorry. I'm Jeanette."

"Scott," I said.

I had the feeling that even though Jeanette had commented on my poor pickup skills, she didn't do this very often. That put me at ease.

"Care to check out the elephant?" I asked.

Jeanette shrugged her shoulders. *Sure*, I interpreted. I looked smugly back at the bench where Fiora had been sitting. She wasn't there.

I didn't actually care to see the elephant, but I thought it would be tactical to see one more animal exhibit before asking Jeanette for her number. Jeanette was generally an interested person. She wasn't interes*ting*, per se, but she was interested.

The elephant was living large. It had a freaking amusement park all to itself. There were giant tire swings on metal chains, patches of trees surrounding small ponds—the space could've fit another zoo. The panda might have been the star of the National Zoo, but the elephant was king.

"Wild elephants move ten to thirty kilometers a day," Jeanette commented. "It sounds silly, but they don't mobilize themselves purely for food and water. They have to fight boredom."

"Fight boredom?" I scoffed. "I fight boredom every day."

I thought about how Fiora would have responded to my joke. She would have scoffed right back and called me a boredom-fighting superhero. *Pow! Whack! Kaboom!*

Jeanette wasn't much of a joker. "Confining elephants to a small space with minimal autonomy can lead to serious behavioral problems. Increased aggression, chewing their own body parts, unnatural lethargy. These are all problems that would inevitably shave time off the elephant's life span. All of this space is an investment in the elephant's longevity."

"Can't have elephant suicide," I joked.

"That would be tragic," Jeanette said. "Though I can't imagine how it would manage."

I could tell Jeanette was smart. Insanely smart. The kind of smart that demanded to be noticed and brought to mind words like *brainy* and *sharp as a tack*. She was the girl whose hand shot up each time a teacher asked a question—the girl who forced that teacher to go, "Does anyone *besides* Jeanette know the answer?" She'd sit there in her seat and squirm anxiously while no one else answered. But more than that, Jeanette's world was black and white. No gray. Because if there was one thing I'd figured out about this girl, it was this: her brain was confident. It might look squishy like other brains, but it was made of sharp-as-anything tacks.

Jeanette insisted on seeing more of the Asia Trail. I noticed a pattern at each exhibit: I would make a stupid comment to loosen her up, and Jeanette would follow up with an intelligent observation. We were never quite in sync.

Take the pink flamingos. I'd never seen so many flamingos in one place. They sounded like clown cars in a traffic jam, honking over each other! It was a beautiful cacophony of noise, but Jeanette focused on their feathers. She hypothesized that the zoo was putting artificial pigment in the flamingos' food to keep their feathers pink. I was skeptical, but Jeanette didn't *do* skepticism. She marched right up to the nearest zoo employee and demanded an answer. Everything had to be black or white, or pink . . . Anyway, the guy looked at her funny. He said he was on his way to feed the panda, but Jeanette wouldn't let him leave, so he reluctantly corroborated her hypothesis. I patted her on the back, because that was the closest thing to an A+ I could give her.

Inside the Bird Center, we found a pond of whistling ducks. Apparently they didn't actually whistle very much, so I blew my own tunes. Jeanette groaned.

"I don't understand why Americans idolize birds," she complained. "We name our sports teams after them: Ravens, Cardinals, Seahawks. We have state birds. We've even made a hobby out of bird-watching!"

"Maybe it comes from an inner human desire to fly," I said.

"That would be silly. We have airplanes for that."

⊔⊓⊔⊓

Jeanette had moved to DC two weeks ago and was intent on making this "the most adventurous summer of her life." She'd already visited *five* Smithsonian museums and now she could check off the National Zoo. I suppose we had different definitions of adventure. Unbeknownst to Jeanette, mine involved asking for her number, which I checked off promptly after the Bird Center. It wasn't an intense or exciting ask, because it felt like another scene from the script we were reading. We played our parts well. This predictability put me at ease, and the end result was weirdly satisfying. Not electrifying, not frustrating—just satisfying.

Saying goodbye to Jeanette felt like leaving school on a regular day. It marked the completion of a task that I had to do. I walked over to the zoo's entrance, where I found Fiora. That felt like running into a bulldozer. Literally. She shoved me in the chest.

"Did you get it?"

I played dumb. "Get what?"

"Herpes," Fiora said. "Pencil Skirt is a *total* slut. I could tell."

"Ha!" I laughed just a single laugh, like a snooty 1920s aristocrat. Or Sherlock Holmes. *Ha! Elementary, my dear Fiora.* "Pencil Skirt was actually super nervous. She introduced herself twice. But yes, to answer your question. I got it."

"Show me."

I took out my phone and scrolled down to Jeanette's name. "Jeanette Dumont."

"Jeanette Dumont," Fiora read. "540-555-8309. Got it."

"Got it? Huh?"

She ignored me, tapping at her phone screen. "Have you texted her yet?"

"No? I literally just left her."

"And . . . Sent."

"What in the—what?! What did you send?"

Fiora showed me her phone. It was a text message:

> Hey! Scott here. It was great to meet you and hang out just now. Thanks for showing me around the animals. I'm actually going out with some GW friends tonight around U Street, care to join?

"*Fiora.*" My jaw dropped. "When— How— When did you even write that?"

"While I was waiting for the two of you to finish your lovely stroll." She smiled so wide that her eyes became tiny slits, slicing into what little dignity I had left.

"You're insane," I said. "Certifiably insane. There's no way she'll actually—"

Buzz buzz.

Fiora read the message to herself. She smiled.

"What?" I said, leaning in to see it. Fiora turned her phone away. The phone with a text for *me*. "What did she say?"

"You really must have made an impression on her, Saaket."

"I did?"

She read the message out loud in a squeaky, mouse-like voice: "Hi! Yes! I would love to!" Fiora paused. "But didn't you say you're doing research at Georgetown? *Winky face.* I don't understand why you're hanging out with GW kids. *Dot dot dot . . .*"

Fiora snapped out of her Jeanette impression. "This girl doesn't understand why you're hanging out with GW kids? Who the fuck does she think she is?"

"She's actually really smart."

Fiora rolled her eyes. "Whatever," she said. Then she smirked. "Wait. You told her you work at Georgetown?"

"I may have taken a lesson or two from your playbook."

"Oh man," Fiora said, chuckling to herself. "What have I done to you, Saaket?"

"Well, first, you dared me to pick up a girl. And I did. So you owe me fifty bucks."

"Fair," she said, reaching into her back pocket. She handed me a crumpled fifty.

"More recently," I continued, "you told Jeanette we're all hanging out tonight. Mind explaining that?"

"We're going to a bar called Saint-Ex."

"All right, well, thanks for the heads-up. How am I supposed to get in?"

"I already texted Trent," Fiora said, unlocking her bike from the rack. "He's going to get you that guy's ID . . . Carlos, or whatever."

"Okay," I said, feeling a little nervous. "I should probably get your number so we can be in touch and coordinate plans, right?"

Fiora gave me her number and took off while I was saving it to my contacts. I ran and caught up to her, and she rode slowly as we made our way down Connecticut Avenue. I sweated even more than in the morning, but I didn't feel embarrassed around Fiora. Because walking back with her felt like the last day of school, and parting ways outside the hostel felt like the last bell. I knew I'd see her soon, but still. Something about Fiora made each goodbye pinch like it could be the last.

CHAPTER 15

I ARRIVED AT Café Saint-Ex a few minutes early. I power walked the whole way over, because fast walking is the moving equivalent of nervous fidgeting. I didn't want to wait outside the bar by myself, so I did a loop around the block. The second time I arrived at Café Saint-Ex, Fiora was there.

"So where's Pencil Skirt?" she said. "I thought of all of us, she'd be the most punctual."

"No clue. Maybe she panicked and changed her mind," I said.

Fiora shrugged. She was wearing a black tank top and baggy parachute pants, an outfit that reassured me Saint-Ex was not a fancy-pants establishment. I wore the same polo and corduroys I'd been wearing all week. Turns out there were washing machines in my hostel, so instead of spending money on new clothes, I spent some quarters washing the ones I had.

A few minutes passed.

"Are any of your other friends showing up?" I asked.

"Don't worry about it," Fiora muttered.

She bit her lower lip, and I stared at the ground. It was going to be uncomfortable for both of us if Jeanette flaked. But she didn't.

"Hey, Scott!" Jeanette said, coming in for a firm hug. Her boobs pressed into my chest forcefully, which made me flinch. Then she turned to Fiora. "Hi. I don't believe we've met. I'm Jeanette." She extended her arm. "Scott and I met today at, well—"

"Yeah, yeah, I know the story." Fiora shook Jeanette's hand skeptically, fishlike. "Pleasure to meet you."

You know that expression . . . *two worlds collide*? That. Handshake. By normal standards, I shouldn't have been invested in either of their worlds. I'd only known Fiora for a few days and Jeanette for a few hours. But here I was, orbiting aimlessly within a universe of girls.

"Shall we go inside?" Jeanette proposed.

"We have to wait for Trent," I said.

"Trent's going to be late," Fiora said. "He can meet us inside."

"Yeah, but remember Trent has that thing that I need . . . ?" I was trying to be discreet.

"Riiiight," Fiora said. "Your fake ID. I forgot you're, like, a baby."

I gave Fiora the quickest death glare. Jeanette giggled.

"Freshman problems," she said sympathetically, fumbling through her wallet to show off her own fake ID. "It's my older sister Frankie's license. She's the wild one in the family—left Virginia, lives in Brooklyn now . . . Frankie says I should have fun this summer."

Technically we were all underage, but Jeanette had no idea just how "under" my age was. She didn't need to know.

Trent arrived what felt like an hour later with a lost expression on his face. He seemed focused on something else, muttering an excuse about how he'd gotten held up with his coworker Carlos. He hugged Fiora absently, and then he snapped on, introducing himself like a gentleman to Jeanette, who practically gawked in his presence. (She must have been thinking, *Am I really with Scott when I just met this hunk?!*)

Trent handed me Carlos's ID. "Memorize everything," he said. "In case the bouncer gives you shit 'cuz you don't have a five o'clock shadow like Carlos."

"Or because I'm not Hispanic . . ."

I quickly memorized Carlos Barroso-Valderrama Zambrano's insane name, height, address, birthday, and organ donor status (yes, he'll give you his kidneys). The bouncer didn't even ask for any of it. He just took a long look at the ID, then my face, then the ID again, and when I itched my nose, he took one last suspicious look at me. I held my breath. The others were already inside, waiting for me, watching nervously by the door.

"Go ahead," the bouncer mumbled.

I shot past him and—WOW, MY EARS FELT LIKE THEY WERE GOING TO EXPLODE. I didn't think it was possible to scream my own thoughts, but I also didn't realize that Café Saint-Ex was actually the inside of a giant boom box. Top 40 beats blasted like hammers hacking away at my eardrums. We all followed Fiora, who led the way toward either "the back" or "a rack."

Did I mention it was loud?

Saint-Ex was also packed. Everyone stood around in awkward circles, each group sardined against another. Sleazeball bros bumped into girls from adjacent circles and offered to buy them tequila shots. They drank. They spilled. They grazed hands, hips, legs, any body part available. I didn't know where to look. My senses were going berserk.

Fiora led us to the *back* of Saint-Ex, where we spiraled down a nondescript staircase into a basement of sweaty chaos.

"I'm gonna get drinks," Trent yelled. The music in the basement was even louder than upstairs. "Scott, come with me."

We squeezed through the crowd to the bar, where three layers of drunk customers separated Trent and me from our drink orders. I thought maybe Trent would use his bartending expertise to con our way to the front, but alas, we waited with the masses.

"So what's with this new lady?" Trent asked.

"It was a dare," I said. "Fiora offered me fifty bucks to pick someone up at the zoo."

"Classic Fiora."

"Sure, but now she's acting weird around Jeanette. I don't get it. She's the one who invited Jeanette out tonight, and she's practically ignoring her."

Trent kept his eyes straight ahead, focused on getting us closer to the bar. "Fiora might play dumb, but she knows exactly what she wants, man. She's lookin' for a show."

I wasn't convinced it was that simple. Fiora had already gotten the show she wanted at the National Zoo; why take it this far? I wanted to believe Trent, but he had a tendency to simplify Fiora's motives and misdoings. He'd assert himself on all matters Fiora like he knew the girl better than she knew herself. Sure, they had been friends for a long time and Trent was older and theoretically wiser, but Fiora didn't come across as the kind of girl you could just put in a box.

There was nothing glamorous about the basement of Café Saint-Ex. To an outside observer, it might have looked like the sort of college party you fetishized growing up. But if you truly looked at the basement crowd—girls swinging their hips and guys bopping their heads to the beat, void of real energy—well, it was a sad scene. Saint-Ex felt like a sweaty sex pool without the sexiness. No one was really committed to their moves. Instead, they were hungry for action. Eyes wandered the dance floor, ricocheting off each other. *Move a little to feign amusement, but don't forget to scan the room for a* really *good time.* A new dance partner. A hookup. A fuckbuddy. The love of your night, at best.

You can't spell "Saint-Ex" without sex. But if you try, you

get "aint." And from early on I knew: ain't nothing good comin' out of this night.

Fiora, Trent, Jeanette, and I huddled around each other in the middle of the dance floor, bouncing awkwardly to the music. Around eleven, Fiora checked her phone and left abruptly, pushing through the crowd and running upstairs. She showed up five minutes later with two tall, older-looking guys.

"Everyone," she screamed over the music. "This is Benji and his friend Quentin."

I ducked my eyes immediately. I recognized Benji: bald, bearded, bike-less. He was Fiora's boyfriend—her TA. I was his accidental bike thief. Holy shit.

The DJ played a remix of "Everytime We Touch," and the beat rang through my body.

It felt like someone had punched me in the stomach—which was a real possibility given the situation. Was Fiora trying to get me killed? That would explain everything: the stolen bike and the pickup challenge and the fake texts with Jeanette, all the way to her mood tonight. All those punches led to this one final knockout. Fiora was going to spill the beans to Benji and Jeanette, and they would rip me apart, right here, in the middle of the dance floor. This was the show she'd been rehearsing for all along.

Sweat dripped down the back of my neck. Hell hath no fury like the basement of Saint-Ex, and it hath no devil like Fiora Buchanan.

To my relief, Benji cared very little about meeting us. He gave a quick nod of acknowledgment, ignoring Trent's excitement ("Finally, I get to meet Fiora's man!") and Jeanette's extended hand. Instead he wrapped his arms around Fiora's tiny waist and pulled her to a roomier, isolated corner of the basement. Quentin followed along.

Trent turned to me and tilted his head. He must have just made the connection.

"Isn't that—"

I nodded slowly, closing my eyes to reset my nerves.

"Classic Fiora," Trent said.

□⊓⊔⊓

The volume dropped from earsplitting to a more bearable loud when the DJ played a sultry, slower song. Some R & B mix I'd never heard before. Trent, in his infinite politeness, struck up a conversation with Jeanette. I zoned out quickly, peeking through the crowd for Fiora. I caught a flash of her dancing in between Benji and Quentin, swinging her hips to the music, creating ripples in her parachute pants until Benji grabbed on to her hips. I jerked my head back to Trent and Jeanette.

". . . we need to get our country back on the right track," Jeanette said, poking into Trent's chest. "We need to make America great again. Our Founding Fathers weren't crazy. They had values. We are a great nation *because* of those values, not in *spite*—"

"Scotty!" Trent slapped me on the back. "Another drink?"

Jeanette announced she was going to the bathroom. Trent and I pushed to the bar.

"Holy. Cow." Trent's eyes bulged. "Man, where did you find Jeanette? She's . . ."

I didn't hear the last part of his sentence. I asked him to repeat it.

"INSANE," he shouted. He threw his arms to his side. "Gosh, I don't know how we got down that slippery slope with the Founding Fathers and our nation's values. Oh *wait*. I know how. Because she's interning at the freaking Foundation for American Traditionalism. FAT. That organization's got its head so far up its own ass that they never thought to come up with a better acronym. She's a religious nut, Scott. A crazy, conservative, homophobic, xenophobic nutcase. I tried to be polite with her—you know, I'm a Christian and all for less government, so we're not worlds apart—but good Lord. Jeanette is on another level."

"But how is she xenophobic if—"

"I just know it. She's gotta think you're, like, Greek or Italian or something. That has to be it. You never mentioned the Iranian part to her, right?"

I realized he was right, that it never came up. Most of my conversations with Jeanette until this point had been about zoo animals.

"Good," Trent said. "Don't. Better yet, we could ghost on her right now."

For some reason, instead of worrying about my standing with Jeanette, I thought about Fiora, dancing at the center of Benji and Quentin's universe. I was curious what her goal was for orchestrating this night. This puzzling plot. How the themes intersected and conflicted but didn't actually make much sense together.

"Nah," I said. "Let's get our drinks."

On the way to the bar, I noticed these two guys standing on the sidelines of the basement. They weren't your usual wallflowers. Call them Backward Yankees Hat Guy and Washington Wizards Jersey Bro. They were clearly buddies, built and dressed like athletes, towering over a sea of girls. BYHG and WWJB stood shoulder-to-shoulder, their arms crossed like bodyguards. Every now and then, BYHG played ball. He'd scout out a girl he was interested in, eye his sidekick for approval, and then approach the girl and grind up on her. He was swiftly rejected three times in the short period of time that I watched.

I couldn't blame BYHG; I couldn't even blame the male species. Everyone, and I mean *everyone*, in that basement was hungry for action. Especially Jeanette. Soon she started dancing with Trent, face-to-face. This was incredibly awkward to watch, because Jeanette was so into Trent's face, and Trent's face was less interested in hers . . . and neither of their bodies appeared to be into the dancing. So I swooped in and started dancing with Jeanette, which turned out to be a good call because our faces quickly got closer and closer with each swing until we were almost kissing. Kissing with our cheeks. Sexual tension escalating.

Suddenly Fiora appeared out of the side of my eye. "Cigarette?" she said to us, motioning a puff with her two fingers and wrist.

"Oh God yes!" Jeanette cried.

What? I looked at her like she'd admitted to being a Russian sex worker named Anastasia. Could Jeanette honestly have been so relieved to get out of dancing with me? Had I imagined our synchronized motion? Her hands on my hips? Her eyes and my eyes meeting until they couldn't meet anymore because our cheeks were almost touching? All chemistry aside, I wouldn't have pegged Jeanette as a smoker. Fiora, sure—but Jeanette was too practical, too smart, and according to Trent, too rooted in her values.

Trent was down for a breath of fresh air, so we stepped outside, and Fiora offered the three of us cigarettes. I politely declined.

Fiora smiled when she got to Jeanette. "I didn't think you smoked," she said.

"Intermittently," Jeanette replied. She couldn't have sounded less cool with her word choice. "I've made the decision to rebel a bit this summer. We aren't allowed to drink at Liberty, for example." She smirked boozily.

"Tsk, tsk. Liberty University," Fiora said. "So you're . . . Christian."

"Yes," Jeanette said matter-of-factly.

"You know he's Muslim?" Fiora said, pointing at me. Killed. She was for sure trying to get me killed.

Jeanette gawked. "No, I did not." She paused, and slowly another smile crept up on her face. Jeanette rubbed my arm robotically. "I suppose I'm rebelling again."

I couldn't help but puff my chest proudly. Trent was wrong about Jeanette. She might have been a conservative white Christian girl, sure, but she wasn't xenophobic. She was an intelligent, reasonable human being. And she was into me. I glanced over at Fiora to make sure she noticed Jeanette's hand on my arm.

We stood outside Saint-Ex a little while longer, Fiora and Jeanette taking casual puffs of their cigarettes, until Benji popped outside. He scolded Fiora for "treating herself to a fine serving of lung cancer" and ushered her back into the bar. Jeanette blushed at the mention of lung cancer and threw out her cigarette.

Honestly, that was how I saw it, too. These two girls bonding over a shared disregard for their health. "You want lung cancer, too? Same! Twins!" But the way Benji came right out with verbal punches . . . It was like he accepted Fiora and belittled her at the same time.

Conflicting, crisscrossing, confused. The plot thickened.

❑❑❑❑

The bar was even more jam-packed when we reentered five

minutes later, which meant only one thing: Café Saint-Ex was *for sure* made of some fourth state of matter. A special blend of solids (people), liquids (alcohol), and gas (body odor) came together in this hellhole to form a state where you could pack infinite twentysomething-year-olds into a confined space as long as they were drunk enough. And boy, were they drunk enough. On our way back down to the basement, I had beer spilled on me twice. Even the most revolutionary states of matter don't protect against party fouls.

Trent announced he was going to the bathroom, which I took as a cue to get back to dancing with Jeanette. It was all right, and this time we made out. I'd made out with exactly two girls before—my eighth-grade ex-girlfriend, and a few times with Annie Choi at some parties last year—and they both complimented me on my soft lips. The problem was Jeanette. She kept suction-cupping my mouth with her thin, fishy lips. She played tonsil hockey. She did not know how to kiss.

Every now and then I'd stop kissing Jeanette and just nuzzle my face against hers. Not only was this a break from our exhausting make-out session, but it gave me a chance to peek across the room at Fiora. She kept alternating between dancing with Benji and Quentin; they were passing her around like a basketball. At one point she was sandwiched in the middle of them, their hands clasped together over her head. (I later learned this move was a variation of the "Eiffel Tower.") Fiora didn't look thrilled or sad or exhausted or any emotion in particular—she looked empty, as if dancing in between ghosts. To be clear, it wasn't just me eye-stalking Fiora; our eyes met exactly twice. Both times I apologized profusely with my expression, and both times hers just stared right through me. We'd deflect eyes quickly, like two magnets of the same polarity.

Then I lost her. I looked into the crowd, and Fiora was nowhere to be found. I told Jeanette I was going to the bathroom, and I went looking for her. I searched every corner of the basement, the area by the DJ booth, the upstairs bar— nothing. I knew I had no right to be annoyed that Fiora left without me. The past hour should have been forewarning enough.

I just hoped she was okay.

I came back to find Jeanette somehow drunker than when I'd left. The guys she was waving goodbye to had probably bought her shots while I was gone, because the ever-articulate Jeanette was now slurring her words. "*Skuuhhh*-hot," she said. That was a new one. Admittedly, I was a little turned on. "Let's get . . . outeff . . . here," she said slowly, suggestively, but with full conviction. Drunk-conviction. That had to be a thing.

Things were winding down at Café Saint-Ex anyway, so we pushed through the crowd and left. On our way out, I caught sight of BYHG and WWJB. I was happy to see that one of these players ultimately found success on the court. WWJB, the sidekick, scored big-time. He ended up dancing with a tall, beautiful Indian goddess while BYHG stood against the wall checking his phone. Alone. I chuckled. Only in the most special of sweaty basements can Robin prosper over Batman in a blaze of carnal glory.

Outside, Jeanette asked in more or less words, "What's your plan now . . . because you should come back to my place." An ask-turned-suggestion. I politely declined, making up some excuse that involved my nonexistent roommate. Well, technically I had a few roommates, Swedish this time, but none of them were "sick and in need of my immediate attention." Whether she believed me or not, Jeanette nodded, and we agreed to hang out again soon. I put her in a cab and made sure the driver knew exactly where to take her before I hailed one for myself.

The cab cost me a lofty twelve bucks: eight for the fare and four for tip. I probably didn't need to tip that much, but I did it for good karma.

I fell asleep hoping Fiora was okay.

CHAPTER 16

THE MORNING AFTER Saint-Ex, I woke up feeling surprisingly alive. My head felt a little heavy and my breath could have used a toothbrush, but it was nothing like my first hangover, when my body ached like I'd rolled out of a drying machine. Maybe I was getting the hang of drinking.

Trent had texted me to make sure I got home safe. He also had good news: he'd talked to his boss and gotten me a part-time job at Tonic. Success! I could help out behind the bar a few days a week, starting today.

I didn't hear from Fiora or Jeanette that morning. Not like Jeanette had my real number. But with Fiora, half of me just expected her to be there. You know—sitting on the other top bunk, waiting for my "hungover ass" to wake up and freak out about her intrusion. I smiled until I remembered the last time I had seen her, in the basement of Saint-

Ex, trapped in the Eiffel Tower of Benji and Quentin.

What did Fiora see in Benji? From what I could tell, he was more of a soul-sucking parasite than a boyfriend. I wondered if Fiora was curled up in bed now with Benji or if she'd decided to mess with him again. I thought about BYHG and WWJB, and I pictured Fiora wearing the backward hat, the basketball jersey, the backward hat *with* the basketball jersey. These images all flooded my mind—

I stopped myself. Switch gears. I picked up my phone, scrolled past Fiora's number to find Jeanette's, and texted her:

Hey it's Scott, different number

If Fiora was going to shove Benji in my face, I decided I might as well pursue Jeanette. After all, *she* was interested in *me*. How often did that happen? I added:

Had fun last night! Let's hang out again.

A minute later, I went back and texted Fiora the same thing.

❏❐❏❐

I rolled into Tonic later that morning. The atmosphere inside was eerily calm. There was a family sitting in the back of the restaurant and a couple at the bar, picking apathetically at their omelets and roasted potatoes. It was a sleepy Sunday brunch scene. I couldn't imagine why anyone would choose to have their first meal of the day—of the week!—at a place that's usually packed with drunk, sweaty college students. I would rather eat at McDonald's.

Trent was cleaning up behind the bar. I walked up and slapped my hands on the bar top. *"Ready for duty!"* I shouted. The bar top was wet—the kind of wet that forms rivers between your fingers. I tried shaking the wetness off.

"Hah, sorry, bud." Trent chuckled. "Just cleaned the bar. Kind of a dirty rag, so you might want to wash your hands."

"It's okay," I said. "I came here to get my hands dirty."

"All right, my man, but you should still wash your hands." He pointed at the sink behind him. "Here."

I slid under the bar's lift-top entrance to join Trent on the other side. I felt powerful behind that bar, like when I used to be a patrol officer for my elementary school bus. All the patrols at Deer Valley Elementary wore neon belts with shiny gold badges, giving us full authority over nose-picking bullies and cliques of popular girls. I didn't truly appreciate this power at the time. I mostly did it for the pizza parties.

Bartending was hard work. Trent put me on dish duty, so I spent most of the afternoon picking up dirty glasses and washing and drying them. My palms were prunes by the end of it. Later Trent showed me how to serve a couple of drinks—simple ones, like beer on tap and the gin and tonics Fiora loved so much. We gave away my practice drinks, and I got solid reviews from my customers. Probably because they were drinking for free, but whatever.

Just after closing, Trent and I started cleaning up. He took dishes, and I wiped down the bar top with the same brownish rag as before.

"You know," I said, "I always thought there was something sexy about working in the service industry. Don't get me wrong, I worked hard today. But I feel good. My parents never let me get a job like this—they always wanted me to focus on school."

"Sound like terrific parents."

"Eh." I shrugged. "I never really bought their 'We worked hard so you wouldn't have to wait tables' excuse. They were overprotective."

Trent shook his head. "Man, shut up. It sounds like your parents wanted the best for you. Plain and simple."

The rag was getting too filthy to effectively clean anymore, so Trent went back to get another one. Except he didn't give me the rag; he finished wiping down the bar himself.

"Hey," I said. "Why do you have to work anyway? I thought you said your dad did business with Fiora's . . ." I assumed Trent came from a wealthy family.

"My parents cut me off," Trent said. He dug harder into the bar's cherrywood surface.

"I'm sorry."

"Eh." He shrugged. "Their loss."

"Why'd they cut you off?"

"I'm gay," Trent said. He said the words without wavering, as if he were just stating another fact, like the color of his eyes or what he had for dinner. From what I could tell, he was completely and proudly unashamed. "I came out to them after graduation last month. Haven't spoken to 'em since."

"Oh," I said.

I never would have guessed that Trent was gay, but to be fair, I didn't know a lot of gay people back home. It wasn't within my realm of possibilities. Of course I didn't mind. Who was I to mind? Who was anyone? I was Iranian, and Jeanette was Christian, and Trent was gay. These were facts, and the world kept spinning.

I leaned back against the sink, staring out the window into the dark night. Suddenly I felt a gust of homesickness. I pictured my bedroom window, overlooking the usual suburban yard fare: two-car garage, weedy lawn, our Leaning Mailbox of Pisa. I used to stare past the cul-de-sac, which connected to the rest of our quaint neighborhood, which connected to a small street that intersected our town's main street. There was an ice-cream parlor at that intersection called Scoops, where I sometimes went with my mom.

"What if I was gay?" I asked her once over a salted caramel cone. I was confident enough in my straightness as a twelve-year-old to test my mom by joking about it.

"Astağfurullah." Mom sighed. Don't say such things.

"No, really! What if?"

I was always thinking too much, but it felt okay to over-think when I stared out my bedroom window, or other windows—like the ones in classrooms, buses, or bars.

I poked my mom. "Would you still looooove me?"

"*Saaket bash*," she snapped. *Stop talking.*

What if I only thought that way—through the literal medium of windows—because that was how society molded me to think? What if thousands of years ago, one man looked out a window and thought, so he wrote about his thoughts, and someone later thought to paint the thinking scene, and someone else thought to depict a dramatic window-gazing thinking scene in a movie, and it proliferated decades of movie scenes, sometimes serving as a pivotal plot moment, sometimes just filling time, and eventually this scene made its mark on me, and that was why I'd think the way I thought, or thunk. Fuck.

"Maman," I said softly.

She shut her eyes painfully, holding her breath for two seconds before releasing the pain. "Yes," she said, utterly exasperated. "Of course. Yes, I would still love you."

I snapped out of my daydream when I realized that Trent had finished wiping down the bar. He was standing by the front door.

I walked up to him. "I don't care that you're gay."

Trent half smiled. "I don't care, either," he said. "And I don't care if you care."

□□□□

I stumbled home around midnight and fell into bed. My feet were sore, like I'd run the New York City Marathon and mixed drinks for all the spectators along the way. Equally dead was my phone. I plugged it into the wall charger and saw I had two missed texts:

> I had fun, too! Wish we were able to spend more time together outside the bar, but it was an enjoyable night nonetheless. Although my lips are kind of chapped now, ha!

Jeanette. She was either making a kissing joke or a hangover joke, or her lips were actually chapped. I cringed at all these possibilities. The second text was from her, too:

> Want to do something today?

It was time stamped 4:30—almost eight hours ago. In my defense, I was busy working when her text fluttered into my very dead phone. Working my *shift* at my *job* where I got *paid in cash*. I felt pretty legit.

Instead of responding to Jeanette, I couldn't help wondering why Fiora hadn't texted me back yet. I dialed Fiora's number—no pickup. Maybe my phone was broken, so I found a pay phone a few blocks from the hostel and dialed it there. She still wouldn't pick up. I became suspicious of the fact that pay phones still existed in the twenty-first century.

Shouldn't they be extinct? Clearly, I was too tired to think straight, so I went back to the hostel.

I assumed Fiora had likely spent the entire day with Benji, having brunch and picking flowers and such, so I decided to text Jeanette back:

> Hey, sry was working all day today. How about tomorrow?

She replied almost immediately:

> Georgetown makes you work on Sunday? How un-Catholic of them.

Oh, shit. I forgot that Jeanette thought I was interning for Professor Mallard, which was only partially true. I replied:

> Lol no I was working from home

And she said:

> Of course. Sounds like you're a hard worker ;) I get off work at 5:50 tomorrow. There is a 6:35 movie at the Georgetown AMC, which is approximately in between the two of us. Interested?

I groaned, shoving my head into my pillow. Did I really

want to see Jeanette again? Monday was going to be my first day doing research for Professor Mallard.

Fiora may have had a Benji, but did I really *need* a Jeanette?

That's when I realized something: Jeanette was gritty. Not closed-minded like Trent had cautioned, but confident. The girl knew what she wanted: She wanted a summer of new experiences away from her Christian college. I could benefit from being around someone like that, with clearly defined goals. Also, I couldn't deny that I was a little attracted to Jeanette in, like, a rebellious Catholic school girl way. So I replied:

Sure :)

WEEK TWO

CHAPTER 17

WHEN I ENTERED Professor Mallard's office on Monday, I felt a crisp sensation of freshness, like I had stepped out of the shower and put on a brand-new T-shirt.

I felt clean.

DC had given me a fresh start. It threw me into a cold washing machine, where I tumbled around a ruthless cylinder of rejection, but now I could feel the positive effects. All that insecurity and doubt were purged from the fabric of my future. Sure, I had no passion, but that didn't mean I had to settle on a career I didn't care for. I needed more time. I needed to keep experiencing life through new paths like crossword construction, pickup dares, nightlife, drinking, even identity theft. (Carlos Zambrano's five o'clock shadow was literally starting to grow on me.) None of those paths qualified as a future career, and yet they helped me feel closer to the life I wanted.

Something inside me was convinced I had the potential to change. I'd figure out my passion one day, but for now, I was living. And that was important.

I couldn't tell you how my work with Professor Mallard would translate into my future, but I knew this: grit was just one small piece. I was solving a much larger puzzle than I had originally anticipated.

⊔⊓⊔⊓

Professor Mallard led me into the office next to hers. It was a cramped and messy space . . . nay, it was a disaster zone. I figured the last occupant must have gotten swept up by the micro-tornado that had clearly passed through. I took a seat in the swivel chair as Professor Mallard logged me in to the computer. She noted that while I wasn't technically a paid research assistant, I should aim to research one new historical figure each day and summarize those findings in an email to her.

Before I knew it, it was just me and a blank Microsoft Word document. I stared at the glaring white screen for a full minute before realizing that my first historical figure was obvious: the poet Ferdowsi. I already knew the gist of his story; I just had to fill in the gaps.

I'd been surfing Wikipedia for an hour and was ready to dive into the twenty-seven tabs I had opened from the citation links, when I heard a harsh sob from the other side of the wall. My ears perked up. Professor Mallard?

I knew it was wrong of me, but I pressed my ear against the wall. I was never very good at resisting curiosity.

"God, Bridgette, you wouldn't believe how difficult these last few months have been. One day I'm fine and the next day I'm falling apart . . .

"Is he? Is he really in a better place? He was one of the happiest men I knew. He existed in a state of pure happiness. Now he—he doesn't exist . . .

"No . . . Yes, Bridgette, I would say that . . . Yes, that is what I mean . . .

"He was my rock, you know, Bridge? . . . God, I'm such a mess. I'm always wired tight, one way or another. Tight as a bowstring, he always said. But he never accepted that as a permanent state. He made me more adventurous, spontaneous . . . I'm a fucking mess now.

I ripped my ear away from the wall. I couldn't believe it. Professor Cecily Mallard, the world's leading adolescent psychologist, was having an emotional breakdown. And rightfully so. From what I could tell, her husband was dead. Gone.

I took a deep breath, exhaling slowly, and refocused my eyes on the computer screen. Under my breath, I whispered a small prayer for Professor Mallard. One more breath, I thought to myself, and back to work.

Dear Professor Mallard,

Thank you again for letting me work on

this project under your guidance. I want to emphasize that you are making a difference in my life.

Today, I researched the renowned Persian poet Ferdowsi. His masterpiece, *Shahnameh*, is the national epic of Iran and took thirty years to write. He wrote tens of thousands of lines of poetry about kings and queens and the hardships they endured in the name of Iran. Ferdowsi was a brilliant, gritty man who created gritty characters for a country of gritty people. Technically his stories are myths, but when you're caught up in fiction for that long, it becomes someone's reality, right?

My findings are attached.

I have to admit, I was distracted by another important and gritty person today: you. I am not going to spend my time here researching you, of course, because that would feel creepy from five feet away, and I presume you already know everything about yourself. But I want to point out that you are one of the grittiest people I have ever met. You earned three degrees from Harvard and have dedicated your life to a noble field. I hope that in five hundred years, another runaway is writing his research-summary email about your poetry of grit.

Sincerely,
Scott Ferdowsi

❑❐❑❐

Jeanette and I met up after work to watch a movie. I got to the theater early, and she arrived exactly on time. It was a romantic comedy where the girl conspires to win over the hot guy's attention, and the girl fails over and over until the very end, when the hot guy professes his love for her—but she picks her best friend instead.

The entire time, Jeanette couldn't keep her hands off me. She alternated between holding my hand tight and stroking my inner thigh, slowly and rhythmically. After the movie we went out for overpriced cupcakes. I paid for both of us, which took a hit on my wallet, but what was I going to say? "Can we split the check? I'm trying to budget better so I can make my runaway money last." Then we went back to Jeanette's place and made out tamely on her bed. Well, I kept it tame. I was thrown off guard by how far she wanted to go. Jeanette tried getting other body parts involved at least three times, but I respectfully declined.

CHAPTER 18

TUESDAY I WAS bogged down by a case of the Tuesdays.

Texted with Jeanette in the morning. Told her I was researching Martin Luther that day. Won some major Christian Girl Points.

Learned Martin Luther had dropped out of law school when he was twenty-one, against his parents' wishes. His father hoped he would become a lawyer.

Said hello to Professor Mallard. Asked how she was doing.

"Excuse me?" Her eyes shot up.

"I was wondering if everything was, um, all right in your life."

"As a matter of fact, Scott, I've been dealing with a major loss lately."

"Oh." Pause. "I'm sorry."

"Don't be sorry." Smile. "It's why I took you on for this

project. After he died, I lost my focus. Your enthusiasm for my work . . . It revived me, unexpectedly."

Got shifty and changed subjects.

Finished up my work a little early that afternoon. Found a bench at Georgetown; attempted to solve the *Washington Post* crossword puzzle. Kept getting stuck. Called Fiora each time I got stuck. No pickup again and again and again. Attempted to pick up where we left off on the puzzle we started constructing together. No luck there, either.

Another date with Jeanette in the evening. Free show at the Kennedy Center's Millennium Stage. Beautiful venue— adorned with the richest red curtains I'd ever seen—but subpar folk music performance. Bleh.

Told Jeanette I had a headache, which was actually kind of true. Rushed back to the hostel. Called Fiora one more time. No pickup. Left a voice mail. "Hey . . ." My voice trailed off. "It's Scott. Surprise me sometime." Hung up. Thought about calling again, but maybe Fiora was sending me a message. I hoped she was okay.

I hoped she was okay with me.

CHAPTER 19

WEDNESDAY MORNING, I heard my phone vibrating from my bed when I got out of the shower. I groaned—it had to be Jeanette, following up on my pretend headache. I took my time drying off and putting clothes on before I climbed up my bunk for my phone.

Two missed calls: Fiora.

I dialed back immediately. She picked up on the third ring.

"Hello?" she croaked. Fiora sounded surprised that I had called her back. Almost frightened. There was something feeble about her voice.

"Hey," I replied quickly. I heard heavy breathing from the other end.

"Hey," she said, warming up.

"Is everything okay?"

"Not really," Fiora said. "I had an accident. I'm . . . at GW Hospital."

I jumped out of my bunk bed, grabbed my wallet and keys, and stormed out the door. "I'm on my way," I said before hanging up. I didn't miss a beat. I just missed Fiora.

A stranger at the corner gave me directions to GW Hospital. I sprinted toward Washington Circle, which was on the other end of New Hampshire Ave.—a straight shot from Dupont Circle. Fiora always made me run in DC.

A million possible scenarios played out in my mind. I wondered if Benji had abused her. He was being an asshole Saturday night, and I hadn't heard from Fiora since then. It seemed unlikely, though, if she had just made it to the hospital. Did Fiora do drugs? Perhaps she'd overdosed. Or maybe it was a regular old accident, like a broken arm or fractured wrist. Maybe she was crosswording too hard. No, stop. How could I be so flippant about this emergency? Fiora was in a real-life hospital. I was lucky she was alive.

Holy fuck, I finally thought. What could she have done?

I stumbled through the hospital doors and slipped on the floor. A nurse came over to help me up, and I immediately told her I was there to see Fiora.

"Let me check with the front desk," the nurse said calmly.

I followed her to the receptionist, emphasizing that I needed to see Fiora *right away*. They looked up Fiora's file and said she was okay. I processed those words. "Okay." So it wasn't a freak accident. "Okay" was better than "She's not okay" or "We think she's going to make it." They asked me to take a seat for a few minutes. Okay, I replied.

There wasn't a single comfortable couch in the waiting area. I tried all of them. Every couch was too firm. I adjusted my butt, tried sitting crisscross, wedged my hands under my quads—nothing worked. I didn't know whether to attribute it to the couches or nerves. Instead, I stood up and tapped my foot incessantly to unwind the tenseness. Maybe I was building it up. Or both. It was like a yo-yo: Wind, unwind. Wind, unwind.

I wondered briefly if Dad was doing the same thing in Iran. Squirming in an unforgiving hospital chair. Waiting for news on Baba Bozorg's health.

Breathe in, breathe out.

Pretty soon they let me into Fiora's hospital room.

I never would have described Fiora as pristine and angelic. Fiora herself would scoff at those adjectives. Sure, she had cheeks like a cherub, but the second she opened her mouth it was all edge. In the hospital bed, though, lying there . . . she looked nothing but innocent. Any impulse I had to scream "What happened?" or "What the fuck?" or "Are you all right?!" vanished, and for a long moment, all we did was rest in each other's silence. In each other's confused, exhausted, what-are-we-doing-in-this-room eyes. It was my first time making eye contact with Fiora since she disappeared from Saint-Ex, and I had nothing to say.

She spoke first.

"Don't flatter yourself," Fiora muttered, her eyes dropping.

"What?"

"I know how you're looking at me. Like it's your fault I'm here." She breathed heavily. Carefully. "It's not."

I inhaled, then exhaled with my words: "I tried calling the past few days . . ."

"I know."

"And if—"

"I know."

I couldn't reason with Fiora. That wasn't what she needed right now, anyway. She was putting up a guard, and I could tell it wasn't a stable one. Fiora needed me as a friend. She needed some of my momentary stability to rub off on her. So instead of asking questions—like why Fiora didn't pick up my calls, or how she wound up at a hospital, or what inspired her to call me instead of someone she knew better—instead of saying anything, I sat gently by Fiora's side and held her hand.

❏❐❏❐

With crossword puzzles, I always saw Fiora's brain as this badass, indestructible assembly line of downs and acrosses. But sometimes, assembly lines break. That's why we were at the hospital. Fiora didn't get into a car accident or anything physical; the wheels were in her head. She had a mental breakdown.

"Fucking Benji," Fiora said. She buried her face in her exceptionally pale hands, whimpering softly. Then she finally opened up.

Fiora met Benji four months ago in Intro to Sociology. She was the student; he was the teaching assistant. Benji was older than Fiora by about a decade, which I thought was funny, because Benji is the kind of name you hear on the playground. He's the twerp who pushes kids down the slide before they're ready. That's Benji.

Fiora's Benji was the son of a Belgian diplomat and was getting his PhD in sociology and marijuana, she told me. He made the first move. Fiora was never much of a class-goer, so Benji asked her to come in for office hours after the third week of classes. He demanded an explanation for her absences, and Fiora, desperate for an excuse and someone to talk to, told him about her mom's letters—how they'd caused her so much stress. Benji looked at her with a combination of pity and intrigue. Without batting an eyelid, he urged Fiora to reconnect with her mother. "He was so confident with his prescription that I made up my mind. I booked a trip to Philly," she said wistfully.

The next week, Benji invited Fiora over to his apartment for a glass of wine. One thing led to another led to his bedroom. It was 100 percent consensual, she assured me.

Two weekends later, Fiora saw her mom and her new family for the first time. It went better than she could have expected: Her mom hugged her tight, stroked her hair, and apologized in all the right ways. She was clean and even volunteered at a rehabilitation center for drug addicts. Her husband managed a chain of grocery stores, and they had the sweetest two-year-old. But still, when Fiora came back to DC, something didn't feel right. Her heart thrashed against her chest and her vision turned splotchy.

Fiora hadn't had panic attacks since she was fifteen, so she checked herself into the hospital. She didn't want to call her dad; she'd never told him that she was visiting her mom in the first place. So she called Benji.

After he came to her side, their relationship changed. At least, it had from Fiora's perspective. Benji became a constant presence in her college life, one that hadn't included many friends up until that point. Benji was different from the premeds and sorority suckers. He had edge; he was an *adult*. They kept hooking up, and Fiora kept seeing her mom in Philly, and for the rest of the semester, life was peachy.

"This summer, though, we've been fighting. That's why I stole his bike in the first place—after he'd made a couple of douchey comments in a row," Fiora said. "The morning after Saint-Ex, he broke up with me. I was half-awake, and he just started yelling at me about how I acted around Quentin the night before. Telling me I was immature, just looking for attention, that I would never amount to more than an atom in the universe."

Fiora's voice was so faint, I could barely understand what she was saying.

"Why would he say something like that?" I asked.

An atom. In the *universe*. Just one atom.

"Because he believes things, Saaket. For a while, I liked that about him. He had firm opinions. His confidence . . . It was dickish and arrogant, but I told myself it would always soften for me. I thought I was his exception.

"Of course, now I see that I was being delusional." Fiora rose slightly in the hospital bed, narrowing her eyes at nothing in particular. "I don't need a fucking trust-fund baby telling me I'm worthless. No one deserves that. I spent a lot of time thinking about myself these last couple days, my sense of self-worth. And then Benji called this morning, all 'What's up, babe?' as if nothing had happened. I told him he owed me an apology, and the balding bastard had the gall to demand one from *me*, so I hung up."

I bit the inside of my lips, afraid of saying the wrong words.

"I should have felt like a champion, right?" Fiora said, her eyes reaching. "I felt like shit. Then I went to check my email, and . . . Do you remember the puzzle I wrote last summer, the one the *New York Times* accepted?"

I nodded hesitantly.

"Well, they take forever to actually publish them. Sometimes years. After I got off the phone with Benji, I found out they're running my puzzle in the paper next week."

"Fiora!" I burst out. "That's incredible news."

She looked at me with ferocious gratitude and a dollop of pride.

"Thank you."

"I don't understand, though. How did you get from there to here?"

"Saaket . . . I couldn't even muster a smile. That's what did it. I knew I should have felt happy for myself; I just couldn't. I thought about taking another dose of my antidepressants and anxiety meds, but I stopped myself and came here instead."

Empathy stirred inside of me. I wanted to tell Fiora she was a warrior. I wanted her to know I was proud of her for telling off Benji. For the puzzle that would be printed a million times over. For taking care of herself. But I didn't want to overstep.

"Why did you call me?" I asked gently. My voice was hardly audible over the ambient noise of the hospital. Heart rate machines beeped in the background. It struck me that each rhythm was unfazed by the others, like blinking car turn signals. That every one of these sharp beeps belonged to a person who, like Fiora, had endured. This seemed like a profound realization at the time.

Fiora looked off to the side.

"I would have tried calling Trent, but he has an important networking event today at the Cato Institute. So I called you."

"And your dad?"

She rolled her eyes. "He's useless. My dad was never very 'hands-on' with his parenting."

"But shouldn't you let him know—"

"That I'm in a hospital bed? I'll tell him later. Maybe tomorrow. He'll pretend to be concerned, ask if I need to switch therapists, switch my medication or something. He'll pay the hospital bill and send more money. He's too busy with the paper business and his rotating cast of big-boobed bimbos to actually care, Saaket."

Once again, I was at a loss for words. I didn't know how to react to the reality that there were parents out there who didn't prioritize their kids over all else. I couldn't believe that wasn't a guarantee—a constant in Fiora's life.

"Your dad . . ." I said, searching for the right words. "I guess he just . . ."

"I promise you he doesn't care. When Grams died and my mom left, my dad shut down and never rebooted. I told him I was seeing Mom again—he knew about the letters—and all he had to say was 'Make sure to let Dr. Daniels know.' That was always his style. He'd send me to shrinks, and of course shrinks don't know how to parent, so they did what they do best."

"Bullshit?" I said.

"Prescriptions," Fiora said. "The most fucked-up cocktails of medication. More pills than anyone should see in their life-time."

I thought back to my session with Dr. Sparrow. How I expected her to take one look at me and cry, *Adderall! Two a day! All your problems will be solved!* Because what I wanted was a quick fix. An easy way out. What's easier than popping a pill?

I straightened my back a little bit. Fiora continued: "Between therapy and crosswords, I've stayed pretty sane. But Benji broke me."

"God damn it, Fiora," I whispered under my breath. She nodded.

I felt a rush of blood to my head. I also felt relief. Half my relief was for the wrong reason—for my own mental health, a privilege I had always taken for granted—but the other half was for Fiora.

"I don't understand how a girl like you could let anyone affect you like that."

She pressed her eyes shut, bobbing her head back and forth slowly. "Well," she said, opening her eyes. "It happened."

I squeezed Fiora's hand, because the tighter I held her, the more confidently I could guarantee she was alive. That she would be okay. Fiora spread her fingers free.

"I guess the cat's out of the bag, then, isn't it?" She laughed softly. "I'm not such a free spirit. Life gets to me. Sometimes . . . I take my downs and acrosses seriously."

"Guess so."

"Guess so," she echoed.

Almost simultaneously, we both let out a deep breath. She looked down at her fingernails; I cracked my knuckles, two by two.

"Hey," I said, poking at her with hopeful optimism. "Now that you're going to be a published cruciverbalist, I think we need to celebrate properly."

"Oh yeah?" Fiora smiled.

And so began the rest of our day. The nurse walked into the room, and Fiora asked her for paper and a pen. She winced a little when Fiora said the word *pen*, because pen equaled potential harm, but she brought us one anyway. Fiora flattened the sheet of paper on a book and drew a large, gridded square. I'd learned a lot since our last crossword session, and Fiora had been through a lot. So we started over.

Every now and then as we constructed this new puzzle, our hands and arms brushed. When this happened, I didn't pull back. Neither did Fiora. Instead we would both freeze, on purpose. It was like each time our bodies touched someone whispered into our ears, *Let the moment happen*. And then Fiora would tilt her head, and I'd wonder again: Should I pull back? But I didn't. So Fiora kept smiling, and we kept freezing together, and we melted into puddle after puddle of puzzle ink.

CHAPTER 20

"GOODNESS, THAT'S . . . that's right out of a movie."

I was back at Professor Mallard's office Thursday morning, filling her in on Fiora's incident and the whirlwind day that followed. I felt guilty for skipping a day of research, but Professor Mallard didn't seem to care; she was fascinated by my story.

"So you're telling me," she continued skeptically, "Fiora—this girl you befriended by chance on the bus to DC—she had an anxiety attack yesterday morning, and *you* were the first person she thought to call?"

"She doesn't have the best relationship with her dad," I said.

Professor Mallard's eyes wandered off to the side. "That's a shame."

"Fiora doesn't really have a lot of friends," I explained.

"At least, from what I can tell. Just this one guy Trent who she grew up with—he moved here from Charleston—and I think she has some crossword puzzle friends. I mean, I don't think she wants more friends. She's incredibly spontaneous. One of those really independent, confident girls. I've only known her one week and . . . well, I can't help but feel lucky. She's definitely pushed me out of my comfort zone in some ways," I said. I chuckled to myself. There was no way I could tell Professor Mallard about Jeanette and the pickup challenge and the night at Saint-Ex. "Anyway, I can't help but worry about her after yesterday."

Professor Mallard was still staring off to the side of her desk. "Where did the crossword puzzles come from?" she asked absently.

"Oh man. Fiora is obsessed. She's been solving crossword puzzles since she was a little girl, and now she writes them. She's a really good constructor," I said.

Professor Mallard looked back at me and forced a smile. "The psychology of puzzles is interesting. Many studies link puzzle solving with exceptional cognitive skills. Memory search. Problem solving. Facial recognition. Intuitiveness."

"What does that say about Fiora?" I asked impatiently.

"What do you think?"

I gave Professor Mallard a funny look. "You're the brain expert . . ."

"I wouldn't worry about Fiora, Scott. Of course it's within reason, as a friend, to be worried after her breakdown yesterday. But the way you describe her, with this penchant for crossword puzzles . . . Her brain is wired a certain way. She likely moves fast, yes? She likely makes quick, intuitive decisions."

Professor Mallard hadn't even met Fiora yet, and she understood her better than I did. "So, you're saying she's 'likely' impulsive?" I asked. It made sense. All signs up until now pointed to Fiora being 100 percent, no-telling-what-she'll-do-next impulsive.

"I'm saying the same way she jumps from box to box, puzzle to puzzle . . . It's likely she's already moved on from yesterday's incident. She has a bigger issue than this ex-boyfriend, yes, but she'll deal with it. The irony is that you're still worried about her."

I bit my lip. "I worry a lot," I said. We were thinking the same thing. *That's why I'm here in DC, in your office—because I couldn't stop worrying about my future. Because I was desperate to get gritty.*

Professor Mallard smiled in a familiar way. Her smile had arms, and they wrapped around me and squeezed tight. It was my mom's smile—the way she smiled on my first days of school and my birthdays. Growing-Up Smiles. That thin and sympathetic curvature of the lips always said the same thing: *You'll be fine.*

"Growth mindset, Scott," Professor Mallard said.

"Everyone worries and everyone fails. I get it."

Professor Mallard pressed down on a stapler. She tilted it over to reveal a single staple, which she swept into the waste bin.

"Failure isn't permanent," she said. "Grit is the ability to learn and fail and learn some more. That ability is fluid, not fixed. You have the power to change."

Dear Professor Mallard,

Last week, Fiora mentioned a gritty artist named Marina Abramović. I'd never heard of this woman, so I decided to focus my research today on her life and art.

I was astonished with what I learned. Marina Abramović is a world-famous performance artist who, time and time again, has pushed herself to the limit (and past it!) for her work. She is very avant-garde. In her first performance over forty years ago, Abramović cut herself twenty times with twenty different knives. She recorded the sounds and tried replicating each cut, not because it looked gory or cool, but to explore her body's limits and her state of consciousness. It's meta, isn't it? The performer is the performance, and as a viewer, you're supposed to get inside her head. What is she thinking? How does she go on? How is she making herself go on? Is she even thinking?

Abramović has put on hundreds of other

thought-provoking, inflammatory (sometimes literally) performances over the decades. She has disciplined her mind in the most unique way to let her audiences' minds run wild.

My findings are attached.

Sincerely,
Scott Ferdowsi

As I was closing out my tabs, Professor Mallard poked her head in the door.

"Marina Abramović," she said, giving the cluttered office floor a look of disapproval. "Interesting choice."

I shrugged. She looked up, just barely missing my eyes.

"You know, Scott, my dad was a big fan of hers. I haven't jumped into your research yet, but did you happen to come across her bow-and-arrow piece?"

"Of course. *Rest Energy.*"

"Yes!" Professor Mallard's face leapt, and our eyes finally met. "My dad was simply obsessed with her Ulay collaborations. He believed they were too good for this world, Marina and Ulay, as artists and as a couple."

"They sure were something," I said, remembering how they had walked the length of the Great Wall to end their twelve-year relationship.

"They were absolutely nuts, but so were my parents. When I was seven, they recreated *Rest Energy* for Halloween.

My mom carried the bow and Dad carried the arrow, and every house we stopped at, he would load the bow and pull it back and aim it at her, and they'd laugh like maniacs. 'Trick or treat!' Can you imagine? I was mortified."

By this point, Professor Mallard had fully entered the office and was actively recreating the scene, pulling back an imaginary bow and bending over to laugh herself.

"They were intellectual goofballs," she said, bent over her knees and shaking her head. "As grown up as you could be in Oakland back then."

"What did you dress up as?" I asked.

"I think I was a surgeon that Halloween," Professor Mallard said, moseying back toward the door. "I believe that's what I wanted to be at the time."

Her expression turned sober. Finished with the story, but still longing.

"Thanks for your help today, Scott."

❑❒❑❒

I headed straight to Tonic after a full day at Georgetown. I had a six-hour shift ahead of me with Trent. I was working hard these days, but I liked my work.

Fiora had already called Trent and told him about everything that had happened the day before.

"What do you think is next?" Trent asked, stacking clean

glasses behind the bar like a house of cards. I thought he'd stop at the second or third level, but he moved on to the fourth. Very precarious.

"She keeps on keeping on," I said, quoting a cheesy Tumblr post I saw once.

"No, I mean with, like . . . you. You and DC, you and *Fiora*. She's officially single now, you know."

I sighed and pressed the glass I'd just dried against my forehead.

"I don't know. I'm pretty happy these days doing research with Professor Mallard and working with you. And with Fiora, I don't even— I mean, even if I did . . . Like—"

"Like what?"

"Like, look at me," I blurted. "She wouldn't go for me. If I did."

Trent stopped wiping the bar and tossed his dirty rag at me.

"Hey. Buddy. Scott." He put his arm around my shoulder the way a coach does right before giving a pep talk, which was exactly what I was getting. "I don't know if you realize this, Scotty Too Hotty, but you're a fucking catch. A jawline like that? Man, you could cut a marble statue with it. Your olive skin? Damn. Share a little with pasty ol' Trent. And those green eyes? Boy, oh boy, I feel sorry for all the girls who got lost in those eyes. May they rest in peace."

I closed my eyes, laughed, and shook my head, but Trent kept going.

"Plus, you've got an actual personality, which beats most other guys. All you need is some confidence."

"Where do I get that?" I asked. As if confidence were something you could buy off Amazon. Free two-day shipping!

"You'll find it when you need it," he said, slapping me on the back so hard, I bumped into the bar—which sent his tower of glasses tumbling down. Fortunately, none of them actually fell to the ground or broke.

We laughed tremendously.

❑◻❑◻

At the end of my shift, Trent pulled out a small wad of cash. "Here," he said, counting five crisp twenties. "A hundred bucks. Good work today."

"I'm confused. That's double what you paid me Sunday, but I only worked half the hours," I said.

"You earned it," Trent said.

I never had a job growing up, so earning money was a new concept for me. My parents were by no means rich, but they had a strict internships-only rule, because anything else would distract from my studies. Salaries meant nothing to me; I'd never seen ten bucks an hour or $60,000 a year in material form.

"I don't deserve this," I told Trent. "Definitely not this much."

"Come on, man, you're doing a good job," he said.

"But—"

"Scott! Here we go again. *Confidence.* Con-fi-dence," Trent repeated. "You need to stop seeing yourself as a pansy and start seeing yourself as the badass, runaway *rock* star that you've become."

"That's very nice of you," I said.

He shoved the money back in my hands. "Here. Take it."

I counted the money in disbelief. Twenty, forty, sixty, eighty . . . one hundred.

All of a sudden I experienced a feeling that could only be described as ecstasy. Like the drug. I'd never tried ecstasy, but Kevin's cousin did it in Europe, and he told us it felt like the most attractive girl in the world had just given him a compliment. That's how I always pictured confidence, and a hundred bucks and a pep talk later, that's how I felt. Confident. I even quashed my What If doubts. I considered them, sure, but I squashed them with a series of So Whats. So what if my confidence was shallow? So what if it was a placebo? So what if it wouldn't last forever?

I knew I hadn't quite swallowed confidence yet; I was just getting a taste. But I nonetheless savored the moment with a grin.

Trent noticed. "There we go," he said, smiling. "Right on, buddy."

"But—"

"Oh, Lord."

"What about taxes?"

"Ha! Fuck Uncle Sam. You're dealing with a Libertarian, remember?"

I chuckled. "A Libertarian who wants to run for office. I could blackmail your future campaign."

"And you're a runaway who won't admit he likes my best friend," Trent shot back. "I could blackmail your operation, too."

We entered an intense staring contest—which I of course lost after, like, four seconds.

"Fine," I said, giggling helplessly like a toddler. "I won't tell the government."

"And I won't tell Jeanette," Trent said. "Or Fiora." He stepped out from behind the bar, untucking his shirt along the way. "Our stupid little secret."

❑❑❑❑

At the end of the night, I dragged myself back to the hostel. My body ached with exhaustion. The last two days had been such a whirlwind that I'd forgotten about my phone, which died God-knows-when. I plugged it into the wall outlet and crawled into bed.

I was dozing off when I heard my phone fire off. *Buzz, buzz, buzz-buzz-buzz-buzzzzzzzzz.* I must have missed a lot of calls or texts. From who? My parents?

Reluctantly I climbed down from my bunk bed to check.

I had an onslaught of text messages from Jeanette. Eleven. *Eleven* individual messages.

Wed. 6/30, 3:01 p.m.: Had a wonderful time yesterday! Hope you are relieved of your headache.

Wed. 6/30, 3:04 p.m.: Lmk if you have any free time after work today.

Wed. 6/30, 6:01 p.m.: I'm sure you are swamped at work, but I sincerely hope to hear back tonight! :P

Wed. 6/30, 8:05 p.m.: Scott, is everything OK? Did the headache manifest into something more serious? I have an hour for lunch tomorrow so if you are not feeling well I can bring you soup or Advil. Let me know.

Wed. 6/30, 8:11 p.m.: Just let me know you're alright.

Wed. 6/30, 8:50 p.m.: Scott?

Wed. 6/30, 10:00 p.m.: Perhaps you had a grueling

day of research! Sorry for the incessant texts, I'm just a bit . . . puzzled.

Thurs. 7/1, 7:01 a.m.: Strange that I haven't heard back from you.

Thurs. 7/1, 7:02 a.m.: Happy July.

Thurs. 7/1, 12:02 p.m.: Scott, please let me know you're alright. Or if you would rather not see me again. I can't say I am not a little bit worried.

Thurs. 7/1, 9 p.m.: OMG! I'm so sorry. I had dinner at Tonic tonight and I saw you working behind the bar. You looked so busy. I didn't know you worked two jobs! I'm so, so sorry for bugging you. I can only imagine how busy you must be. Reply when you have a free minute, dear Scott!

"Did someone die?"

The guy in the bunk below mine, a long-haired hippie who was in town for a protest, looked on with concern as I read Jeanette's texts.

"No, no," I said, wiping the horrified expression off my face.

By this point, I should have ignored Jeanette or just cut things off. I should have replied saying: *Hey, you're great, but I'm not interested.* All signs pointed to Jeanette being crazy, anyway—crazy obsessed with me. But I didn't want to shoot down her persistence. I had to admire it, right? She was being gritty, and grit should pay off. So I texted her back:

> Hey. Yeah, been swamped with my two jobs.
> Shoulda mentioned that earlier. Coffee this
> weekend?

CHAPTER 21

HOLY SHIT—who was calling me at six in the morning?

I climbed down from my bunk to unplug my phone from the charger. It was Fiora.

"Hello? Is everything okay?"

"Saaket!" she cheered. I cringed at her enthusiasm. "Good morning! How's my favorite DC runaway doing?"

"Kicking myself for picking up the phone . . ." I said as I climbed back up the ladder.

"Are you still in bed?"

"Um. It depends," I said. I lay on my back, staring at the ceiling. I followed the white wire around the edge of the room all the way to the corner where Fiora was sitting a week ago. "Do you need me to get out of bed?"

"*Saaket*. I don't feel comfortable dictating your bed activi-ties," Fiora said. I was speechless. Literally—my jaw dropped for about three seconds. "However, if you are so willing, my crossword buddies and I are puzzling in Dupont at seven a.m. if you'd like to join."

"That sounds fun. But, um. Why?"

"Because." She paused. "The last time I called you this early, it was for something depressing. I wanted to fix that."

"How are you feeling, by the way?" I closed my eyes, picturing the white hospital sheets, white walls, white gown . . . and our black-and-white grid. "Better?"

"I'll feel better if you join me at seven."

I bit my lip, containing a smile that surged throughout my body. I could feel Fiora smiling through the phone, too. I had to go.

"Okay. Sure," I said coolly. Inside I was leaping for joy.

I heard an extended *beep*. Fiora had hung up.

I would see her before work.

◻◻◻◻

There was something invigorating about DC so early in the morning. You could hear chirping sparrows just as plainly as roaring Ford Escalades carrying bureaucrats. It was a short walk to Dupont Circle, but I made the most of it, taking long strides up New Hampshire and thinking, for the first time, that maybe I was better off here in DC than in Southeast Asia with Jack and Kevin.

If my friends believed they were experiencing foreign cultures abroad . . . they clearly hadn't met Fiora's "crossword buddies." I had figured out early that Fiora marched to her own drumbeat and didn't get along with her classmates. She made those points very clear. But I still expected her to have cool friends. Other people who hated other people and marched to their own percussion instrument. I figured that among the 1 percent of her classmates who didn't suck, there might have even been a few who also liked crossword puzzles. Maybe those friends did exist, but they weren't who I'd meet today. That became clear as soon as I saw Fiora in Dupont Circle.

"Saaket!" She perked up in an uncharacteristically friendly way, like she was actually happy to see me—like she had dropped her poker face at the crossword table. Fiora pulled out a chair for me. "Guys, this is Saaket."

The guys appeared less enthusiastic. There were three of them seated at the table, all middle-aged, balding, cookie-cutter dorks.

"Hello," I said, and I repeated it after a few seconds of awkward silence. I sat down in the plastic lawn chair Fiora had pulled out for me.

One of the men greeted me with an inaudible mumble. He was busy organizing a thin stack of papers. The other two kept their heads down, fiddling with their fingers. One played with his thumbs in a masturbatory thumb war, and the other was cracking his knuckles two at a time. Obviously I could relate to their fidgeting, but still. Social awareness is a thing.

The guy with the papers suddenly jerked his head left and right, like a paranoid alien, before standing up. He cleared his throat: "Ahem. Welcome. Let us begin today's fun with some anagrams."

Fiora leaned over and whispered into my ear, "That's Eugene. He's the leader of this whole mafia. We all pitch in puzzles and take turns printing, but he runs the show."

Eugene looked exactly like you'd expect a Eugene to look—bald, pasty, and white, with a turtley head and gentle blue eyes. His demeanor was almost as square and straight-edge as his checkered shirt, which was buttoned all the way to the top. "I prepared a roundup of some of this year's most noteworthy pop culture icons. May we begin?"

"Awww, come on, Eugene," Fiora said, leaning back in her seat. "Don't you want to tell us how your week was? Anything exciting?"

Eugene shriveled his nose. "It was fine," he said dryly. For the group leader, he wasn't much of a talker.

The guys, Fiora told me, called themselves the Crossword Crusaders. Something to do with the *sword* part of *crossword*. I imagined they had secret handshakes and gang symbols and such, but I didn't get a chance to ask. They jumped right into their anagram activity, which, contrary to my first impression of the group, was actually a lot of fun. Eugene would say an anagram, like "So Long, Lane Skew" and give a description like, "She's a popular R & B singer whose sister is married to Shawn Carter." (Answer: Solange Knowles.) I got one or two of them, which was one or two more than I was expecting to get. We blew through about a dozen anagrams before Eugene revealed the answers and declared Stu the winner.

Stu was a funny dude. He wore a short-sleeve Hawaiian button-up shirt with a rubber ducky–themed tie. He also had these humongous, thick-rimmed glasses that kept sliding down the bridge of his nose, and every few seconds he would push them back up. "But he's a crossword BAMF," Fiora whispered in my ear. "He can solve anything you give him in ten minutes or less."

The time came to put that claim to the test. After the anagrams, Eugene pulled out a paper-clipped stack of papers from his heap and passed one sheet to each person, facedown. I could see through Fiora's that it was a crossword puzzle. I used to do this with quizzes and exams all the time. I'd lean in a little closer to the exam and try to decipher a few of the questions before we were allowed to flip it over. Who was I kidding? I still did this. No one's perfect, but so many people pretend to be. That was why I liked Fiora. She lied, stole, manipulated, teased, and broke down just like everyone else. But she was an honest liar, self-admitted thief, straightforward tease, and transparent manipulator. And like the rest of us, she had bad days.

"What about the third guy?" I whispered to Fiora, pointing at the Humpty Dumpty–looking man on her other side.

"That's just Charles," Fiora said, not really whispering. "He's a total loser, as you can probably tell. But what you *can't* tell is, he writes these trippy puzzles that are surprisingly fun . . . if you're high enough."

Charles leaned over. "I heard that, Fiora."

"Love you, too, Charles," Fiora joked. "You're my favorite weirdo constructor."

Charles winked back at Fiora.

Eugene shot a harsh look to our side of the table. "Ready? Begin."

Charles, Stu, and Fiora immediately flipped their sheets over and attacked the puzzle. (Eugene didn't get one because he constructed the puzzle, and I didn't get one because I wanted to watch the first time around.)

"There are an awful lot of threes," Stu mumbled under his breath.

"Shit. There are a shit ton of threes," Fiora said, tapping her pen furiously. "Way too many threes." She bounced her pencil from box to box; each time she'd draw tiny, vigorous circles in the air before filling in the boxes with invisible letters. Sometimes she wrote the letter down, but more often than not, Fiora just shook her head and hopped over to the next clue.

I took a peek at her grid and imagined the thought process behind each hop.

The third letter in 43-Across has to be a T, *I thought. But 27-Down is* TR_M_ _. *And the last letter in 43-Across intersects the third letter from 27-Down, so first I should figure out the remaining two letters of 27-Down. Then I'll figure out all the other words that intersect 27-Down, and I'll have more context for 43-Across.*

My head was already hurting from the crossword logic, which seemed more complex than an Ikea instruction manual. I looked over at the group of men playing chess about thirty feet away. Those guys had nicer chairs than we did, not to mention proper stone tables with superimposed chessboards. Our table was one of those cheap plastic ones you'd buy and keep in your storage shed for when you're *really* desperate.

"Cocky chess freaks," Fiora muttered. She must have caught me staring.

Whoa. I looked down at Fiora's grid, and somehow, in the time that I got distracted by the Cocky Chess Freaks, she'd gone from an empty grid to halfway done. Fiora was hopping and nodding and filling in squares with real, not-invisible words. Something was definitely going right, or at least in the right direction. I started nodding in support, chock-full of secondhand adrenaline, knowing that even though it wasn't exactly a competition, Fiora could actually win—

Flip. Showing no reaction whatsoever, Stu flipped his puzzle over. He was finished. He checked his watch and marked the time: six minutes and forty-three seconds. Fiora wasn't kidding; this guy was fast. No one looked up to congratulate him, no one was jealous, nothing—and Stu didn't seem to care. He simply took a sip of his iced tea. And you know what? *That* was what got him. As soon as he gulped the tea, Stu's eyebrows shot up, as if the bittersweet drink caught him more off guard than a HUNDRED RANDOM CLUES.

Crossword puzzles were supposed to be Fiora's way of taking the world less seriously, yet here she was, stressing out over the one in front of her. Her pencil hovered over the grid as if casting a spell—expecting the words to magically appear in their boxes. All of a sudden she stopped hovering and pounced at the grid, but a minute later, she retreated, rubbing her temples in defeat. Meanwhile Charles bounced his eraser and nodded in unison, all the while twirling his pencil intermittently and filling in some squares. Even Eugene picked up his pencil and tapped it against his head every now and then. These guys were all fidgety with their hands. Maybe it was a cruciverbalist thing.

Then it hit me: *these* were Fiora's friends. Not the future dickheads or the imbeciles or the fraternity bros and sorority girls, but three middle-aged crossword dudes at a picnic table in Dupont Circle, sitting in the shadows of the "cool kids," aka a slightly less scrappy league of Bobby Fischer wannabes. At least those guys had proper chess tables. But despite their shortcomings, the Crossword Crusaders' spirit never waned—and Fiora was never nicer to me. She never appeared more comfortable or at ease, it seemed, than she was around puzzles. Crossword Fiora was a gentler Fiora.

Twenty minutes later she turned her puzzle over, and shortly after, Charles either admitted defeat or finished up, too.

"It appears all pens and pencils are down," Eugene announced. "Shall I read out the answers now?"

I half expected Fiora to fire back with something sarcastic like: *No, Eugene, get them tattooed on your back and then we'll talk.* Instead, she nodded along with the other Crusaders. Eugene revealed that the theme of this particular crossword was quite the mindfuck. Literally, the theme was "mindfuck." With each theme answer, you had to change the first letter—the "head"—so that it worked with the intersecting word. So if the clue was "Dragon-related circus performer," then the answer would be FIREEATER, *except* you'd have to change it to TIREEATER for the word intersecting the "head" to work. (Because the only thing weirder than a guy who downs fire is the woman from *My Strange Addiction* who ate rubber wheels . . .) Mindfuck.

"So pretty much every theme answer was a lie?" I asked.

"Precisely," Eugene said.

Charles banged his head against the table in slow motion. Fiora and Stu exchanged spirited high fives. Eugene collected everyone's puzzle to determine the winner—obviously Stu. And me? I just grinned from ear to ear, thankful to this quirky squad for letting me in on their unadulterated fun.

❏❏❏❏

"So Fiora . . ." Stu began. His voice had a shaky lilt to it. Not from nerves or anything—Stu was still soaring from his hotshot victory. He just sounded dorkily pubescent. "Who is this friend of yours?"

"Ah. Gentlemen, this is Saaket," Fiora said. "He's in town this summer doing research for a professor at Georgetown. I brought him along because he's curious about our art."

Stu's eyes narrowed, and Charles stared at me like I had something on my face. I broke the silence: "I'm not a pro like you guys, but Fiora's been showing me the ropes. It was incredible watching you solve just now. What exactly is your— well—your method for solving crossword puzzles?"

"Eh," Fiora said.

"Eh," Stu said.

"Method my ass," Charles chimed in.

"Well," Eugene said, "you generally begin with a toehold."

"What's that?" I asked.

"Just a fancy word for the first answer you fill in," Fiora said. "It's pretty important, actually. It anchors the rest of the puzzle."

"The tricky part," Eugene said, "is that often you will feel compelled to begin with a certain toehold because you believe it will reveal more answers. But it's more complicated than that. The surrounding clues may cause you to get stuck."

Charles burst into laughter.

"What's with the chuckles, Chuck?" Fiora seemed irritated.

"Hey, you can solve however you want," Charles said. "I just find all this strategy talk to be a bunch of bull. I start where I feel like starting. If I get stuck? Whatever—I'll save myself. Makes the process more exciting anyway."

Charles and Stu broke into a side argument about toeholds, which for some reason involved Charles making fart noises. I whispered into Fiora's ear, "This guy reminds me of you."

"Do *not* compare me to Charles," Fiora asserted. She pointed at him below the table. "Adult," she said. Then she pointed at herself. "Kid." She took a deep breath. "I know what I am. People like Charles are delusional. That's the difference."

Eugene stood up and clasped his hands together. "All right, friends. *Friends*. Let us continue with our puzzle play. I'm sure Saaket would like to continue observing."

I agreed to participate in the next round, since it was supposed to be collaborative. Every group project has that guy who gets away without doing any work, right?

It turned out that wouldn't be possible here. We were solving a "meta puzzle"—four mini-puzzles that come together to solve an overarching puzzle. Only one was a crossword, and the other three were logic puzzles. Since there were four of us working on it (Charles constructed the meta puzzle, so he sat out) we each took one of the smaller puzzles. I picked the one with pictures because it looked easiest, but of course everyone still finished their part before me. That was when it really got collaborative.

Fiora, Stu, and Eugene huddled over my shoulders.

"What if we . . ." one of them said.

"No wait! Try this!" someone else cried.

We got through seven of the eight pictures. It was the picture-perfect model of teamwork. We were just stuck on the eighth picture. For a suspenseful minute, we all stared at it with intense focus. Eight brows furrowed, four brains working furiously, one mind-boggling image. Anyone who didn't believe puzzles made you smarter would have to be as delusional as Charles, who kept hollering random words like *penis* and *appendicitis* to throw us off.

"Got it," Fiora declared, taking the pen out of my hand just like she did when we were constructing our puzzle at Tonic. "There."

We laid out the four puzzles next to one another, and together, they spelled the solution to the meta puzzle:

HEY FIORA LETS ELOPE

"God damn it, Charles," Fiora said, shoving his arm.

"I'll always be here for you, babe," Charles proclaimed, making kissy faces.

"It is a running joke among our group," Eugene clarified. "That Charles is, quote unquote, 'in love' with Fiora."

"Not a funny joke," Fiora groaned. "Can we just move on?"

Maybe Fiora meant we should move on from the *idea* of the joke, but Eugene took it literally and fumbled with his paper stack. He pulled out another paper-clipped set of crosswords and passed a sheet to each person, facedown. He stood up to speak.

"This next puzzle is particularly special," Eugene said. "Will made it for NPL and has given us an exclusive first look."

"National Puzzlers' League," Fiora clarified. "It's a big convention in July. Will Shortz is the crossword editor for the *New York Times*. He's like the Beyoncé of our world."

The Crusaders all looked at each other eagerly, and without another word, they flipped the puzzle over and dove right in. Fiora immediately stuck her pen down on a box near the heart of the grid. She held it there for a few seconds. Would that word be her toehold? Yes. Yes, it would.

□□□□

"So what did you think?" Fiora asked as we left Dupont Circle.

After the last puzzle, Charles pulled out a bottle of what could only be cheap liquor, concealed in a brown paper bag, and offered plastic cups to the group. Fiora scrunched up her nose and made up an excuse for us to leave.

"Who are those guys exactly?" I asked.

"Day-drinking geniuses," Fiora said. "They're cooler than you think, I swear. We meet up a few times a month to do puzzles together."

"That's so cool. You guys were all so into it. I couldn't believe how detached you got from the world and everything."

"Deep," Fiora teased.

"Now, when are we going to finish *our* puzzle?" I asked.

"Ah, yes. Our little boxy bitch." Fiora tapped her fingers against her chin, like she was playing trills on piano. "Hmmm. This weekend's no good, since I'm going to Philly again to see my mom. She wanted me to visit for the fireworks."

I couldn't believe the Fourth of July was already upon us. My parents would be back in less than two weeks.

"Philly is great for the fireworks," I said absentmindedly.

"You sound like my mother. *Anyway.* Let's jump back into our puzzle when I get back next week. In return, you can listen to me recap an entire weekend of passive-aggressive niceties with my new family. Do we have a deal?"

I tried my hardest to resist smiling; it was like a balloon had swelled inside my chest, with little balloon animals pushing their way into my limbs. I wasn't just a distraction to Fiora anymore, but a real friend worthy of the details of her life. If she was a jigsaw puzzle, the image was finally beginning to come together. I was getting a semblance of the full picture.

I checked my phone—it was almost nine. I had to run to Professor Mallard's.

"Deal," I said.

The faintest smile slipped out the edge of my lips.

CHAPTER 22

WHEN ONE DOOR closes, another opens. Apparently this rule applies to girls, too. Fiora may have left town, but Jeanette was still around, and I had almost forgotten about our coffee date. Not that I was really feeling it. After early-morning crosswords with the Crusaders, a full day of research on Mandela, and two nights in a row working at Tonic, I'd had enough of this truly long weekend. But America's birthday was upon us, and Jeanette—patriotic as a tacky American flag pin—would not be spending the day alone. I agreed to meet her for coffee on Sunday before the fireworks.

We picked a spot called Bourbon Coffee. Well, Jeanette picked it; I replied with a quick smiley to end our conversation. (Does it still count as a conversation when the ratio of texts received to texts sent is eleven to one?) Bourbon Coffee was located just south of Dupont Circle. On my way over, I passed an abandoned, fenced-off yard with a dilapidated red sign hanging off the side: CAUTION WATCH DOGS. It reminded me of the CAUTION AGGRESSIVE CRANES sign back at the zoo.

"Scott!"

I heard Jeanette's shrill exclamation as soon as I stepped into the coffee shop. She was sitting at the table closest to the door. Naturally. Jeanette wore a white polo, navy Bermuda shorts, red flip-flops, and a starry ribbon in her hair. She looked like a limited-edition American Girl doll. She also looked nervous.

"Hey, Jeanette," I said. "How've you been?"

"Wonderful!" she said. We both kind of widened our eyes. Eleven unanswered texts did not translate into *wonderful*.

"So . . ." she began. "It sounds like you had a busy week?"

"Oh man, you wouldn't believe it. I—"

"Do you want coffee?" she interrupted. We got in line and ordered. I paid for Jeanette's coffee, because I felt bad about the unanswered texts.

Jeanette sat down and took a big gulp of her extra-hot cappuccino. She puckered her lips and raised her brows; I wasn't sure if she was reacting to her drink or nudging me to fill the conversational void.

"How was your Sunday?" I asked, changing subjects.

"Good!" she said cheerfully. "I went to church this morning, and the pastor gave a really lovely sermon on reconciling technology with our faith."

Church. Technology. Sexting. Without realizing it, I snorted.

Jeanette shot me a look that I hadn't seen on her before. It wasn't admonishment or shame like I'd expected.

"I suppose it *is* funny," she said.

I searched Jeanette's face for a clue to this apparent humor.

"This is our fifth date"—of course Jeanette was keeping track— "and we still haven't talked about religion!"

"Do we . . . need to talk about it at all?" I said carefully, doing my best to tiptoe around what was evidently an important subject for Jeanette.

"My mother and father firmly believe it should be the first conversation on any date," Jeanette said. "But my sister Frankie says I shouldn't bring it up, ever. I told you about Frankie, right?"

I crossed my feet under the table. My eyes got shifty, and I pressed my thumb deep into the center of my left palm. Until this point, I'd been a pro at limiting my interactions with Jeanette to mutually agreeable subjects like zoo animals, Smithsonian museums, and making out. I took a big gulp of my iced coffee, and in a surprising turn of events, Jeanette perked up and shed all her nerves.

"I grew up with five sisters. I can't believe I never told you that! I'm the youngest, and Frankie is the second youngest. Frankie dropped out of Liberty after a year and moved to Brooklyn, where she plays in a folk band. They're actually quite good!"

"Are you and Frankie close?" I asked, genuinely curious

about this seemingly cool person and how she could be related to Jeanette.

"Best friends. Always." Jeanette's words were clipped with assurance. "Although it doesn't mean I'd drop my faith like Frankie did. Two summers ago she read Dawkins, and just like that, she decided Christianity wasn't for her anymore."

Jeanette paused and took a deep, deliberate breath.

"Are you religious, Scott?"

"Well . . . Technically speaking . . ." Jeanette already knew I was Muslim, thanks to Fiora. No need to bring that up again. "No, I'm not very religious."

"But Fiora says you're Muslim."

"Ish," I said. "A long time ago I asked my parents what religion I was, and I accepted what they told me. Haven't gotten around to reevaluating it or whatever."

"Would you ever consider converting?"

"To what?"

"Christianity."

I gave Jeanette a look that said, *Are you serious?* She let out a defeated sigh.

"What is it with our generation's fear of religion?" Jeanette spoke intensely but quietly, like she was reasoning with herself. "I saw it with Frankie when she converted to atheism, I see it in my research reports at FAT. . . ."

(It's worth noting that Jeanette said the individual letters, not the word.)

"Fundamentally," she continued, "you have nothing to

lose with religion. You've taken economics, right?"

I quasi-nodded, bobbling my head in a circle. It was a tactic I'd developed every time Jeanette asked about my "classes" at GW.

"So you know all about opportunity cost," Jeanette said, jutting her shoulders and straightening her already-straight back. "It's the idea that when you're faced with a choice, there will always be a cost associated with not choosing the other choices."

Why are we talking about this? I thought, and the words almost slipped out.

"Logically, I'm better off in the long run with my Christian faith."

"I'm sure you are," I said quickly.

"It minimizes my opportunity cost!" she exclaimed with delight. "I keep my parents happy, who believe for their own reasons. I keep God happy. I keep my community, my morals, my values. There is absolutely nothing to lose."

Jeanette's eyes had grown to the size of golf balls. As she gesticulated her hands with acute awareness, I remembered that this girl aspired to be a lawyer one day.

She kept going: "And in the unlikely event that God doesn't exist—"

I felt my phone vibrating in my pocket. Jeanette was wrong: There *was* a God. He had blessed me with an escape. I answered without looking at the caller ID.

"Hello?"

"*Saaket joonam!*"

My heart sank. Call #2.

"Hi, Maman," I said.

Who is it? Jeanette mouthed.

"*Saaket jaan, salaam!*"

"Hi, Dad," I said, looking directly at Jeanette. She nodded and mouthed: *Oh.* For such an intelligent girl, you'd think she would have picked up on the Farsi word for "mother."

"Saaket, what is this 'hi' and 'dad' business? *Farsi harf be-zan!* You're speaking too much English lately."

"Okay, Maman."

"*Azar joon*, let the boy speak whatever language he wants to speak!"

"But if he doesn't speak Farsi, he's going to forget—"

"Maman and Baba, I'm out with a friend," I interrupted.

"Oh, how nice," Mom said. "Is everything at home all right, *pesaram?* Do you have enough money? If you need more, we can have Majid drop some off."

"Yep, everything's fine!"

"Scott, uh, about your internship . . ." Dad began.

This was it. He knew. I didn't think it was possible, but Dr. Mehta must have told Dr. Sen, who told his wife, who told my dad. How could I have been so stupid? Of course they would figure it out. My parents had warmed me up to take me down, an over-the-phone execution, in front of Jeanette . . .

"Are you enjoying it?"

Those were not the words I was expecting to come out of his mouth. Those were not words I had ever expected to come out of his mouth.

"I . . . I think so? Actually, I don't know. It's early to tell. But . . . I'm trying to be gritty about it. I'm trying to be gritty about my internship. I think you'll be impressed."

"That's good," Dad said, as if he were still pondering this new concept of enjoyment. "The rest will figure itself out."

I looked up at Jeanette. She'd finished her cappuccino and was tapping the weightless cup against the table.

"I need to go," I told my parents. "My friend is waiting."

"Okay, *Saaket jaan*," Mom said.

Dad cleared his throat.

Mom spoke: "Ah, yes. One more thing, Saaket. I don't want to worry you, but . . . Baba Bozorg had another heart attack this week."

"He's better now," Dad said quickly.

"The doctors say he's recovering very well. They'll run some tests—after all, it's the second one this year—and continue with his cardiac rehab, and . . ."

"He'll be fine." Dad had had enough.

"I'm . . . sorry to hear that," I said. I wanted to press further, even if I wasn't very close with my grandfather, but I knew better. For Iranians, sensitive matters are like Terms of Service: check the box to acknowledge what's necessary and move on. You never read the fine print.

"*Insha-Allah* he stays healthy," Mom added.

"*Insha-Allah*," I said.

I couldn't say for sure, but I was fairly certain I caught Jeanette wincing out of the corner of my eye. I said good-bye to my parents and turned back to her.

"It means hopefully," I clarified. "*Insha-Allah.* 'God willing' is the direct translation."

"Fantastic," Jeanette said. "Now, as I was saying . . . So what?"

"Excuse me?"

"I was saying that in the unlikely chance that God doesn't exist, so what? I'll have lost nothing. There is no opportunity cost. *Insha* . . . you know." She smiled.

I sighed.

"That's great, Jeanette."

❑❐❑❐

The National Mall was predictably packed for the fireworks, but as a party of two, Jeanette and I were able to claim a small patch of grass without much problem.

As soon as we sat down, the fireworks inside my head went off like the bursting reds, blues, and oranges over the Washington Monument.

I wondered about Jeanette, who was so assured in her beliefs that she knew exactly how to shoot down the skeptics. Wouldn't that be nice? Not to question your identity every second of every day, but to simply know.

I wondered about Fiora, who, in that moment, had to be questioning every piece of her identity: her parents, her relationships, her mental health. Yet, despite these variables, something about Fiora felt steadier than Jeanette.

The fireworks suddenly became more intricate. Greens! Indigos! Pinks! Pink hearts! Multicolored starbursts! My favorite was the fizzling gold streamers in the foreground during the grand finale.

The sky had filled with smoke by the time the show ended.

Families picked up their picnic blankets and left. Jeanette and I both had work the next morning, so we kissed goodbye on the steps of the Lincoln Memorial.

On my way back to the hostel, I thought of my parents, and finally, I wondered about my own situation. What was left of my time in DC? The string of lies I had woven only kept getting longer and longer, and the odds that my parents would actually be impressed with this new internship felt slim. I had betrayed their trust; that probably tipped the scale. In fact, it struck me that they wouldn't just be angry— they would explode. It would be unlike any punishment I'd ever seen. But even if they dragged me home from DC and grounded me for life, I could keep up my grit research. I'd still have these experiences.

WEEK THREE

CHAPTER 23

"HE PLAYS THE kazoo, Saaket. How am I supposed to come to terms with that?"

I was laughing so hard my sides were beginning to cramp. It was Monday evening, and Fiora and I had reconvened on a bench in Dupont Circle. I sat upright, and Fiora lay perpendicular to me, her legs propped up on my lap.

"Aside from that minor flaw, it sounds like he's not such a bad stepdad?"

Fiora drew her lips in and nodded.

"Mom found a good one," she admitted. "He's not even, like, too nice, you know? Sometimes stepparents are dicks, but it's almost worse when they make it obvious that they're trying to impress you. Franklin is just the right amount of cool."

"And your half sister?"

"She's two. She was literally clapping and dancing to the

fireworks all of last night. Don't worry, though, she's got plenty of time to piss me off."

"Sounds like the perfect weekend."

"It wasn't so bad, yeah."

Fiora stretched her arms out, reaching for the sky. She wiggled her fingers at the ostentatious sunset—a flashy spectacle of grapefruit pink and sweet-nectar orange that dyed the entire skyline, one-upping the previous night's color show. There were hardly any clouds in sight. We studied the sky carefully for a few moments, until Fiora dropped her legs to the ground abruptly and sat up.

"I brought you something from Philly," Fiora said. "Picked it up from the station this morning."

"I hope it's not a miniature Liberty Bell. I have so many of those that I've thought about turning them into teacups or shot glasses."

Fiora handed me a folded piece of newspaper.

"I paid for it in Philly, but you could say it's from New York . . ."

It was a crossword puzzle, ripped out of the *New York Times*. And in tiny, bold letters at the top-right corner of the grid: BY FIORA BUCHANAN.

I stared at the flimsy gray paper for what had to be a full minute.

I could have said: I'm so, so proud of you.

I could have said: This is an incredible accomplishment.

I could have said: Congratulations!

"You are a freaking beast."

Fiora bent over and buried her face in the palms of her hands, laughing.

"You know, that's *exactly* the sort of review I was going for," she said, coming down from her giggles.

Unfortunately, neither of us had a pen on hand, so I promised Fiora I'd work on her puzzle later and finish before the next time we hung out.

"I can't believe I know someone with a crossword puzzle published in the *New York Times*. Now, if you could work on publishing an article . . ."

Fiora punched me in the rib cage. I fell over on my side, pretending to be hurt; Fiora pulled me back up, and we sat straight for a moment.

"My dad texted me this morning," she said gently, almost surprised—like a carrier pigeon had delivered the message and not her biological father. "He still does the *Times* puzzles, you know. Anyway . . . he said he was proud of me. That Grams would have been proud."

My body warmed up with happiness for Fiora. A gust of wind passed, though it did nothing to ebb the tingly sense of delight I was feeling.

I realized it was getting dark. I placed my hand on the small of her back.

"That's great, Fiora."

❑❑❑❑

During the rest of the week, I found confidence in familiar places.

I found confidence in solving Fiora's *New York Times* puzzle, even if it took three hours and twenty-six minutes.

I found confidence in paying back the hostel for a few more nights.

I found confidence in my steps on M Street each morning. The route to Georgetown had become second nature to me, like a house I knew well. My eyes grazed over the same candy-colored town houses, and I cut across the same campus lawns, and I opened the same wooden doors at White-Gravenor Hall. All things considered, I felt more grown-up than ever with my daily routine.

I found confidence in the lives of Marie Curie, Steven Spielberg, and Thomas Edison, who overcame sexism, rejection, and ten thousand failed attempts to invent a lightbulb. They all made it in the end.

I found confidence in working with Trent behind the bar. Weeknights were slower at Tonic, so we passed the time by telling stories about our lives before DC. Trent got a kick out of my escapades with Jack and Kevin, like the time I tricked them into showing up at a real party, complete with loud music and alcohol, by pretending it was a *Star Trek* viewing. Trent told me about life growing up in Charleston—how for him, it revolved around the Church. Trent may have been gay, but he was still Christian. He couldn't shake off his faith. We agreed that religion, like friends, can take on many forms.

Thursday night, I presented my finished puzzle to Fiora at Tonic. I pointed out the corner where I'd gotten stuck, and she was proud that I pushed through. We got right back to constructing our puzzle, and here, my confidence skyrocketed. Fiora and I filled about 80 percent of the grid before calling it a night. We would fill in the rest over the weekend.

I decided that I wouldn't worry about my parents anymore, who would be back in America the following week. Even if grit didn't save me from their wrath—even if I was sentenced to spend the rest of my days counting staples in my bedroom—it would all have been worth it.

Dear Professor Mallard,

Happy Friday!

Today my research focused on Khaled Hosseini, one of my favorite authors. He wrote *The Kite Runner* and is Afghan American, making him one of the few popular writers who actually looks like me. I was surprised to learn that Hosseini wasn't always an author; he went to medical school and was a doctor for more than ten years. When he was writing *The Kite Runner*, he would wake up at 4 a.m. every morning to crank out new pages before work.

Khaled Hosseini's family moved to the United States when he was eleven. They sought political asylum after the Soviets invaded Afghanistan. His father went from being a diplomat to a driving instructor, and his mother took a job working the night shift at Denny's. They lived off food stamps. Hosseini says he became a doctor to ensure his own financial security—because his family, despite their struggles, sacrificed everything for him.

His story bothered me at first, but then it gave me hope. It's never too late to take over the steering wheel of your life. Everything works out in the long run.

My findings are attached.

Sincerely,
Scott Ferdowsi

CHAPTER 24

I ALWAYS HAD a feeling that I wouldn't be very good at break-ups. My eighth-grade girlfriend was the one to break up with me (we'd "lost our spark," she explained over IM), and the jury was still out on my on-again-off-again fling with Annie Choi. It wasn't my style to reject the people I let into my life, whether they were telemarketers or girls I'd picked up at the National Zoo. But this week, I decided enough was enough with Jeanette. Our last date had been a disaster. The texting was getting out of hand.

I asked her to meet me at Bourbon Coffee on Friday.

"Scott!"

Again with the shrill exclamation. Jeanette was sitting at the same table as last time, dressed professionally in a purple frilly blouse and a black pencil skirt that sufficiently covered her knees.

"Hey there," I said, my eyes flickering like broken taillights between the table and Jeanette's face. "How was work?"

Jeanette lit up.

"It's been so rewarding, Scott," she gushed. "I've been working on a pamphlet all week about the urgent need for more stay-at-home mothers."

I knew I couldn't jump into it right away. (Not that I was capable of a quick and clean breakup, anyway.) I'd have to entertain Jeanette's right-wing chatter until I could segue into those callous words: *We need to talk.*

"Our generation's obsession with equal rights, equal pay . . . It's nice, but don't you think we're taking it too far?" Jeanette asked.

"Oh. Sure, I guess you could say that."

"Exactly!" Jeanette shouted. "We need to talk"—I flinched—"about *families*! Everything shouldn't be about what women need, but what their families need. Kids need their mothers. Husbands need their wives. They need their full attention."

"But don't you want a career?" I asked, remembering the girl who said she planned to attend law school one day. "Isn't that why you're in college?"

Jeanette looked at me sweetly. "Well, of course I want to work. Where else will I meet my future husband?" She may have been joking, but I didn't laugh. Her face turned straight. "Look, I understand my views are more traditional than most people our age. But I've thought it all through, really. I want to experience things while I'm young, just like you and Frankie—

that's what this summer is for! It's just . . . At the end of the day, I know what I want as an adult. A family. I value that more than anything else. I want a happy, traditional family."

On one hand, I was astounded by Jeanette's total rejection of all things modern and feminist. On the other hand, though, I couldn't help but respect her. She had her life mapped out. I envied that.

"What do you want, Scott?" Jeanette asked, her expression filled with genuine interest. "Do you want to keep studying psychology—get your PhD and teach?"

I laughed. "I have no clue. I mean . . . maybe? I'm doing grit research, I'm bartending at Tonic, I'm here with you. I even got into crossword puzzles lately."

"That's so interesting!" Jeanette exclaimed.

I came up with an idea.

"In fact," I said, "I have one on me."

"Oh, can I see?"

I pulled the puzzle out of my back pocket and slapped it on the table. I grinned with a cocky sense of pride.

"There's this metaphor about crosswords—"

Jeanette interrupted: "I used to love doing crossword puzzles with my mother when I was—*oh*. You're constructing a crossword! That's so neat, Scott." She looked at me with eyes that made me regret this idea immediately—eager eyes that saw no boundaries. I had let her get too comfortable with me.

"I want to t-talk . . ." I stuttered. "Our grids, the intersection, it's not—"

Jeanette wasn't listening to me; she pulled a pen out of her purse.

"You should insert an interesting first name in here," Jeanette said. "A modernist writer, because that would appear quite crossword-y. Virginia Woolf!" Before I could object, Jeanette scribbled in VIRGINIA.

"Oh, yeah," I said meekly. "That's wonderful."

"And here you need a four-letter word that ends in R. How about REAR? You could come up with a fantastic clue for that. A *blank* admiral, or the trunk of a car, or perhaps even . . ." Jeanette blushed and giggled. Oh God, was she making a sex joke?

I felt paralyzed. Jeanette was molesting my crossword puzzle—the one I'd started with Fiora. My plan to segue into the flaws of our intersecting grids had failed. I lost track of time. Had five minutes passed? Ten? Forty-five? Words kept coming out of her mouth and falling onto the puzzle. I nodded robotically the whole time.

Then I snapped out of it, snatching the puzzle out of her hands.

"Let's go for a walk," I said.

I led Jeanette toward Dupont Circle, hoping that we could find a bench where I could breathe and spit the words out. "I don't want to see you anymore." Seven words. No, even shorter: "It's not you; it's me." Five. Better yet: "We're done." Two.

I should have thought through my plan of action. Instead,

my mind kept wandering to Fiora, and how I would explain to her that Jeanette had violated our crossword.

Sometimes, the universe takes the exact thing that's on your mind and puts it right in front of you. By this logic, I shouldn't have been thinking about any person at all; I should have thought about a million dollars or a mega-mansion. Lo and behold—

"Saaket!"

What had seconds ago been eclipsed by a mammoth tree revealed itself to be none other than the Crusaders, sitting at their flimsy plastic table. They were not solving crosswords. Instead, they wore different-colored party hats: Stu's was green, Eugene's was periwinkle blue, Charles's was pink, and Fiora's had *Happy Birthday* written in cursive.

"Oh, hi, Fiora!" Jeanette squealed. She looked around, and then twisted her face consideringly. "Who's Saaket?"

I noticed Eugene was about to speak.

"It's my nickname," I blurted.

Fiora rolled her eyes but preserved her smile. She seemed to be in a happy mood.

"Hey, is it your birthday?" I asked.

"It is not," Eugene said. "We are celebrating a milestone far more important than birth! Fiora's debut crossword puzzle was published in the *Times* this week."

The Crusaders instantly broke out in syncopated applause. Fiora blushed.

"These guys are too good to me," she said, resting her

hands on Eugene's and Charles's square shoulders.

"Goodness, con-*grat*-ulations, Fiora!" Jeanette clapped, her jaw practically touching the grass. She nudged me. "Scott, perhaps our puzzle will be next?"

"Your puzzle?"

Fiora's smile faded.

"Scott is working on his own crossword puzzle," Jeanette explained. "We were just working on it together. It's almost finished!"

I couldn't place the exact emotion Fiora's happiness was morphing into, but the transformation was palpable. The Crusaders noticed, too, and became fidgety.

"Show her, Scott," Jeanette added.

I looked at Fiora desperately. Apologetically. I was already begging for forgiveness. Eugene shot Stu a questioning glance, who bounced it off to Charles, who looked left and right and then stared at his feet.

I planted my hands into my pockets; I did not take them out.

"Let me see it," Fiora said, forcing a smile. Fiora was not happy that I was making her bring out her poker face, especially in front of the Crusaders.

I handed her the crossword. My shoulders tensed up, sending a chill down the back of my neck as she scanned the sheet of paper.

"So you guys are what, boyfriend-girlfriend now?" Fiora's tone was prickly, almost mad. "Getting married already?"

Jeanette and I answered simultaneously.

"No!"

"Are you crazy?!" Jeanette said, looking truly horrified.

Fiora and I glanced at each other quickly, then turned to Jeanette. *Huh?*

"I mean—" Jeanette grew frazzled. It didn't help that Fiora was staring her down intensely. "Scott and I aren't *serious*, Fiora."

I glared at Jeanette. "What do you mean?"

"I mean—I mean . . . Gosh. Don't you remember what we talked about last Sunday, Scott? You're a Muslim. I'm Christian. My parents wouldn't approve, and they would cut me off like they did to Frankie, and—"

Jeanette spoke these words matter-of-factly, as if it was common knowledge that Muslims were a special, wholly un-datable breed.

"Don't get me wrong," she said. "I like you as a person. But you must be able to acknowledge that we're worlds apart. We could never be more than a summer fling."

Fuck you, Jeanette, I thought.

The Crusaders had gotten up during Jeanette's hyper-rationalized bigotry and moseyed over to a distant bench. The bench where I should have broken up with her.

"Well, that's delightfully open-minded," Fiora finally said, the fakest smile slithering across her face. "Who could you get serious with, Jeanette? Trent?"

Jeanette giggled. "That's not such a crazy idea," she said.

"Trent is a handsome, conservative Southerner. I'm sure my parents would approve."

"Trent is gay," Fiora said, totally deadpan. Jeanette's eyes shot wide open. She might have even gasped.

"That's . . . I'm very sorry for him."

"Seriously?" I packed so much judgment into that one word.

"Scott, surely as a Muslim you don't approve of that lifest—"

"Fuck you." Fiora spat the words at Jeanette and stormed off.

I stared at Jeanette.

"Did you know about Trent, Scott?"

I took two deep breaths and looked down at my hands. They were clenched tight, the skin bunching up around my knuckles.

"We're done, Jeanette," I said, shaking myself into motion. "I need to go."

❑❑❑❑

Trent was right about Jeanette—she was crazy. She was racist. Most of all, she was a bigot. You couldn't help people like that.

I sprinted back to the Hanover Hostel. I had no plans to go chasing after Fiora. *If it weren't for Fiora, I never would have met Jeanette in the first place.* I bit down hard on the inside of my lip; I failed to draw blood, but nerves flew through the roof of my head. As much as I wanted to blame Fiora, I blamed myself more. I wasn't going after Fiora because I couldn't look her in the eye without feeling like I had messed everything up. I should have seen through Jeanette.

I bit down harder, setting off fireworks inside my head.

Stop thinking. Start doing.

I paced around my hostel room. My vision was blurry. At some point, the Colombian girls I had shared the room with that week tiptoed around me and left. I felt lonely and vulnerable, like when I boarded that Greyhound bus nearly three weeks ago.

Stop thinking. Start doing. Just when I was figuring out my puzzle, I had to jump and throw all the pieces in the air. Start over, or start another puzzle. That was always my theme.

Stop thinking. Start doing. But what?

❑◻❑◻

I remembered the Metrobus stop down the block—the one where I hopped on for an impromptu tour of DC. I knew what I wanted to do. I wanted to run away again.

I let my quarters clink into the fare machine and took a seat. We passed the same landmarks as last time: the pay phone I had crashed my bike into, Ford's Theatre, the Spy Museum, Union Station, hair salons, and chicken joints. Then we reached a run-down neighborhood. Stadium-Armory. No stadium in sight, though. I tightrope-walked along the edges of sidewalks and wandered into convenience stores, wasting away my Friday night. I passed gangs and drug-dealer types, mostly minding their own business. I might have caught a few drug deals in action. Shady handshakes. Men drinking mystery liquid out of brown paper bags.

Midnight came and went. I found myself outside a bar called Trusty's, where drunk men and women trickled out in pairs—slamming the broken door open, laughing carelessly, and hailing cabs to go home and partake in acts I didn't care to think about. Eventually I snapped out of my own daze and checked my phone for directions back to the hostel.

In a perfect world, I would have hailed a cab. But for some sad, consequential reason having to do with the day's events, I wasn't convinced I had earned that luxury. In a perfect world, I wouldn't have been alone on a Friday night. And certainly in a perfect world, I would not have dropped my phone after being pushed into from behind.

"Hey!" I yelled. "What the hell?"

Stumbling past me was a freakishly tall man with green, frosted hair. He stopped in his place and turned around in slow motion. He looked me up and down.

"Fuck you," he slurred.

I picked up my phone and noticed the screen had shattered into a web of cracks.

"Seriously? You broke my phone."

This man stared at me, dumbfounded. His eyes demanded

that I cower in the presence of his massive frame. There was a long scar above his right eye that trailed down the side of his face. Despite my fear, I stood tall.

He huffed. "Fuck you," he said again, shoving me this time. "You fookin' terrorist."

I froze up.

"He-ey!" he said, slurring the nonexistent syllables. Drunk. This man was absolutely drunk, and he was not pleased with my nonresponse. He pushed me harder. "I'm speaking to you, fookin' terrorrrrrist."

I started pulling away when the man whipped his arms back and snapped forward, clinging around my small frame like a crane.

"Let me go!" I screamed. A group of three teenage-looking girls were standing outside the bar, and I turned to them and pleaded, "Excuse me! Help!" They watched uncomfortably for a few seconds before scurrying away. Assholes.

The man dragged me down the block. "Fuck your phone. I'm going to beat the livin' shit outtaya," he said. "I will fookin' kill ya."

I tugged and jabbed, trying my very hardest to escape. He was too strong. I didn't want it to end like this, in a sketchy neighborhood with a green-haired Aussie. Alone. Friend count: zero. The man dragged me halfway down the block, gripping my T-shirt. I could smell the liquor on his breath. I prayed for him to pass out in his own vomit, or for someone to see us and call 911. But the street was empty.

Just before turning the corner, he stopped to cough, and I seized the opportunity to slip out of my T-shirt and break free, shirtless. The whole maneuver confused us both.

It was drizzling. The rain trickled down my trembling body; I was so grateful to be alive. I sprinted for blocks to prove it, and then I hailed a cab.

CHAPTER 25

SATURDAY MORNING, I made up my mind that I would not go home. Not yet. I had every reason to call it quits and run away from DC. I was almost killed, I'd pissed off Fiora, and my parents would be back from Iran in four days. But I wasn't ready to give up. I throttled the idea before it even had a chance.

Somehow I had lost my phone. I must have dropped it while the drunk Irish or Australian man was dragging me down the block.

No device, no friends, nothing to do.

I lay in bed the rest of the day—on my back, on my side, on my face—staring at walls and the ceiling and nothing at all.

CHAPTER 26

DRIP. DROP. DRIP, DRIP. I peeked out my window to confirm the sound of raindrops. It was supposed to downpour today.

I felt restless; I hadn't eaten anything for more than twenty-four hours. I didn't have any way of checking online or texting Trent, so I took a chance and walked over to Tonic. I was drenched by the time I arrived.

"Welcome to Tonic," said the guy behind the bar. It wasn't Trent.

"He—oh. Hi there," I said.

I recognized the bartender. It was almost like looking into a mirror. I knew his full name, address, zip code, and organ donor status.

"Can I help you? We're opening in a few minutes," Carlos Zambrano said.

I smiled. *You've already helped me a couple times.*

"Is Trent around?" I asked.

Carlos's face lit up. He must have just made the connection between us . . . and something more. There was a twinkle of concern in his eyes.

"Trent's not in today," Carlos said. "Are you Scott?"

"Heh. Yeah, that's me."

Carlos reached into his back pocket. "Here," he said, extending his arm. It was a letter. "This girl came by yesterday morning to see you. I told her you weren't around. She was furious, dude. Crazy. She screamed like an insane person. 'Scott, Trent, they're going straight to hell.' She stormed out of here and came back an hour later with this."

Carlos dangled the letter like it was a flaming piece of shit. I snatched it, my heart racing.

"You want any food or drink, man?" he said.

Could Jeanette have done something to Trent? Was this a breakup note? Could either of them have tried texting me since Friday night? I collapsed onto a bar stool, sliding my elbows down the bar top until my chin was resting on it. My stomach grumbled. I felt wholly inoperable, drained by anxiety and hunger.

"A burger would be great."

Dear Saaket,

I consider myself a decent and open-minded woman who is driven by her values. Godly values like honesty, respect, and appropriate behavior. Recently I've learned that you don't live by any of these values.

I could not believe the text I received from you Friday night. Your confession was nasty and outrageous. I couldn't even look at myself knowing that I had been hanging out with you blindly for over a week. I couldn't forgive myself for being such a fool.

But I wanted to understand your side. My faith has taught me to be forgiving, understanding, and so I wanted to give you the benefit of the doubt. I came into Tonic today to speak with you like an adult, Saaket. I wanted to understand the true nature of your relationship with Trent. A part of me even wanted to help you. When you weren't there, I got very irritated. Then I got smart. I went home and did my research. I Googled. I checked the White Pages. Facebook. I learned who you really are.

You are a liar, Saaket. I know your real name isn't Scott. I know you're in high school. Do you know how embarrassing that is for me? Thank the Lord I didn't stray so far as to break the law. (I never would.) I also know that you were never really employed at

Tonic. I called the restaurant's management office and informed them that an underage person was working behind the bar. They didn't even have your name on record. Isn't that funny? I informed them that you were a friend of Trent's, and they assured me that they would take care of the two of you. It would be a shame for the restaurant to get slapped with a lawsuit.

In conclusion, we are done. It's not like we were ever serious, anyway. But I am purging the idea of you and your ungodly friends from my mind. I'm not sure what business you had in DC or why you even approached me at the zoo, but I have no desire to be a part of it. I hope you find a way to live with yourself.

Praying for you,
Jeanette

I sat there speechless for God knows how long. I was waiting for a sign—someone to explain the words I had just read. The Sunday-brunch crowd started to form, ebbing and flowing around the bar, enviably carefree. I hardly took two bites of my burger; I felt sick to my stomach. Half-baked theories rushed through my head. Who had texted Jeanette on Friday night? What did they tell her? What had happened to Trent? Was he okay? Did Fiora have anything to do with this? A part of me believed that she did. The conflict reeked of her touch—a mess not unlike my cycling accident. The whole thing was rooted in Fiora. It had to be her.

Remember how the universe sometimes takes exactly what's on your mind and places it in front of you? I didn't learn my lesson the first time, so instead of a train or a bus to take me back home, I got Fiora rushing through the door.

"Why aren't you picking up my calls?" she said, exasperated. "You weren't at the hostel, and you're not answering or texting me back."

I stared at Fiora, scanning her face in an effort to understand what she was doing at Tonic without asking explicitly.

"Hello?" she said, waving her hand in front of my face. "Trent got fired. Jeanette is furious. She sent you a text saying she 'took care' of you. The girl is crazy, Saaket. Do you know what the hell is going on?"

Hold on, I thought. I jerked my head just slightly.

"Do you have my phone?"

"I don't," Fiora said.

"So . . . How do you know that Jeanette texted me?"

"I— Oh, jeez." Fiora rolled her eyes, but it wasn't in her usual mocking fashion. She had something to hide. "She didn't text *your* phone, Saaket. She texted mine. Thinking it was you."

"Why would she think that?"

"Look, I can explain. Remember at the zoo . . . ?"

My eyes grew astronomically wide. I stared at Fiora with a livid expression—the kind of gaze you fire off at a stranger who spills on your laptop, or a friend who knocks over your house of cards. *What have you done?*

Before Fiora could begin to answer, Carlos approached us.

"Hey," he whispered. "I think you should take this outside."

❏❐❏❐

Fiora marched straight out of Tonic into the summer rain. I tried yelling at her to stay under the awning where it was dry, but Fiora wouldn't stop walking. I ran up and grabbed her by the shoulder.

"Hey!" I shouted. "What the hell is going on, Fiora?"

Fiora turned slowly. Raindrops splashed around her face, bursting at the moment of impact like water balloons. They slipped down her forehead onto her probing eyes, her lush lips, and they soaked her hair into thick strands of rope. I usually despised wetness—be it sweat or salt water or rain—but in that moment, I couldn't stop myself from smiling. Here we were, Fiora and I, afflicted by the same natural form of shittiness. Twenty days ago we didn't know each other. Fiora, Trent, Jeanette: I had never met any of these people. I ran away to DC with the sole goal of meeting Professor Mallard. Here I was, twenty days later, facing a shiny new web of problems.

"Fiora," I repeated, calmly this time. "What happened?"

"Friday night," she said, her chest rising and sinking with each deep breath. Fiora closed her eyes. "I was home alone. I had a couple glasses of wine. Just a couple, okay?"

"Sure."

"I was so angry about earlier in Dupont Circle, the horrible things that Jeanette said about you and Trent. I felt angry with myself for setting you guys up in the first place . . . forcing you to meet her and inviting her out with us that night at Saint-Ex."

I wiped my eyes—rain, not tears—and nodded. "Can't say I disagree."

"And I was pissed about my mom. I'd emailed her my *Times* puzzle, and you know what she wrote back? 'Oh, I didn't know you still did those things.' Maybe she congratulated me somewhere in the email, but the point is she didn't do the goddamn puzzle, and clearly I remind her of my dad now, and—"

Fiora closed her eyes again and shook her head and made a face that admitted she was running her mouth offtrack. So she backtracked:

"I got tipsy, right? And remember how I'd texted Jeanette at the zoo pretending to be you? Remember that? So Friday night, I thought, 'What the hell? Let me mess with this cold-blooded bigot a little.' I texted her . . . I texted her mean things, Saaket. It was supposed to be a joke. I didn't think she'd actually do anything about it."

I wanted to shout at Fiora. Just completely chew her out. I was fuming, but I controlled my anger. I let myself feel the rain dripping down my arms, keeping me calm.

"What . . . *exactly* . . . did you text her?"

Fiora shook her head. "It doesn't matter. It was stupid. I made up stupid things about you and Trent to piss her off."

"Apparently enough to get Trent fired," I shot back. "Do you understand that, Fiora? Jeanette sabotaged him. He lost his fucking job because of her. Because of me." I couldn't stay calm knowing that a good person like Trent had suffered for his kindness. For helping a foolish person like me. "Most of all, because of *you*, Fiora."

"Okay, okay," Fiora said grudgingly. She ran her fingers through her wet, unwieldy locks of blonde hair. "I'm sorry I meddled."

Somehow that wasn't enough.

"That's it, right? You're sorry. You move on." I shook my head. "That's not how it works for the rest of us, Fiora. Trent's going to have to find another job. I'll probably go home. Even Jeanette . . . we really hurt her."

"Oh, fuck Jeanette," Fiora said. "*Jeanette*," she repeated with a thick, mocking French accent. "You didn't even care about Jeanette."

"Who are you to tell me what I do and don't care about?"

Fiora opened her mouth to speak but froze. She turned her back on me.

"This is your fault, Fiora," I said.

She flinched. "You know, Trent never officially got you that job." She looked at me out of the corner of her eye. "He was paying you out of his own pocket."

The pit in my stomach grew heavier. It slipped into the crevasses of guilt.

"Why would he do that for me?" I asked slowly.

Fiora turned back to face me. "Because he's a good person, Saaket. You were desperate."

We locked eyes. Fiora gave me a terrible, hopeless smile.

"I'm the desperate one?" I clenched my fists and tightened up so much, I thought I'd burst like a tea kettle. "I'm not the one who had a mental breakdown because her boyfriend broke up with her. I'm not the one who does crossword puzzles because—"

"Because what?" Fiora said.

"Because you're desperate to escape," I said, forcing the words out. "From your own reality or whatever."

Fiora threw her hands up, laughing like a maniac.

"Here we go," she said. "We have achieved peak irony. The *runaway* is telling me I'm desperate to escape. You want to hear about reality, pal? You came to DC chasing after this thing you really wanted. Grit. But the more I see you, the more I realize you're doing it all wrong. You're obsessed with the future, Saaket. You're obsessed with to-morrow, when the only shit you have control over is today, right now."

"That's hard to believe, Fiora, since your in-the-moment

lifestyle screwed with all the rest of our lives. Maybe if you considered the future—the *consequences* of your texts to Jeanette, we wouldn't be here fighting. No one would have gotten hurt."

"Maybe if you never came to DC, we'd all be fine," Fiora said coldly.

"Easy for you to say. If you had parents like mine—"

"Enough about your stupid fucking parents!" Fiora snapped. "It kills me the way you talk about them. Do you realize how good you have it? Let's talk about that reality. I mean, I get it. They're strict. Maybe too strict. But at the end of the day, it's because you're the one thing they care about more than anything else. I don't have that. My dad's got his own life, other women in his life, and I'm just an af-terthought. Trent has it even worse. We're the real runaways, Trent and me—desperate as hell to get away and get on with our lives. What's your excuse?"

Fiora's tone demanded an answer. She stood there resil-ient to the pouring rain, and I felt myself coming undone in its spitter-spatter.

I wondered what would happen if I just disappeared right there. If I vanished from existence. I didn't want to die, since that would be tragic and painful, but to simply fade out of the world. Would anyone notice? Would my problems carry on or cease to exist? Would there still be thoughts to over-think? Would it all have been worth it?

Fiora's tone demanded an answer, and I wasn't equipped

to give one. I had to believe she saw the helplessness in my expression, because she shook her head and took off.

Maybe she wanted to disappear, too.

I never fully understood Fiora. I never pretended to. But what was wrong with caring about something you don't understand? No one fully understands the universe. It's incomplete. But we care about it anyway. We have to persist.

The universe had rained on me, and now I was soaked.

◻◻◻◻

I allowed myself to imagine a scenario where everything worked out. Fiora apologizes to me, and I apologize to her. We both apologize to Trent. He gets his job back. We become great friends again in no time, except Jeanette, who stays out of our lives. I pictured the three of us inside a coffee shop: Fiora and me solving the *New York Times* crossword puzzle while Trent scans the *Washington Post* headlines. I could reestablish my life in DC. I could thrive in DC. Everything could more than work out; it could be perfect.

If there was one thing I was consistent about, it was being blind to the details of my own reality.

Blind to my own isolation.

◻◻◻◻

The heavy rain pounded the back of my neck as I headed

back to the hostel, simultaneously pushing me forward and weighing me down.

I imagined a puppeteer in the rain clouds, tugging the strings of this sad, dejected person. His body lagged like a wet towel being dragged across the bathroom floor. His steps lacked motivation. His head hung low. The rain no longer fazed him.

I snapped out of my third-person melodrama at the hostel and took a long, warm shower. In a moment of naked clarity, it hit me that I'd missed my last weekly check-in call with my parents. I threw on a dirty T-shirt and ran downstairs. Scott-the-front-desk-guy let me borrow his laptop for a minute, perhaps because he felt bad for me. As I logged out of his Gmail and in to mine, I noticed the date in the top-right corner of the screen. *July 11.* My parents would be back in three days. It was time to let them know that I was working with Professor Mallard, and, in spite of losing my friends and my source of income, that I wanted to stay in DC.

As luck would have it, I wouldn't get the chance.

Saaket jaan,

Where are you? You haven't picked up any of our calls. We have been calling your cell phone nonstop since Friday. And the home phone. The neighbors say they haven't seen you in weeks and Dr. Sen says you left your

internship last month because you had lice?
Is that true? Why didn't you tell us???

Your mother and I are very worried, so we
are flying back immediately. Please, please, if
you see this email let us know that you are all
right. We love you.

Baba and Maman

The email was time-stamped 11:32 a.m. Just hours ago. If I had simply called the day before or earlier that morning, I wouldn't have worried them like this. What made me sick to my stomach were the possibilities that had to be running through their minds—that I might have been abducted, or I might have been murdered, or I might have caught a rare and deadly strain of flesh-eating lice, I might have, might have, might have . . .

I felt like an idiot. Until this trip, my parents had always kept extremely close tabs on me. They made me call every day when I was away at Model UN conferences. They monitored my eating. They stayed awake until I went to sleep, no matter how late. They were strict not because they wanted to torture me, but because they cared. I had taken their inch and blindly assumed they would give me a summerlong marathon. How could I think they wouldn't check with the neighbors or Dr. Sen? How could I even think that if all went according to plan, they would have accepted my actions? "Yes, of *course* we're fine with you staying in DC all summer after you lied to us about your internship and your whereabouts"?

In what universe, Saaket?

I replied to their email immediately.

Maman and Baba,

Please don't worry. I'm fine and I will be home very soon.

Love,
Saaket

WEEK FOUR

CHAPTER 27

MONDAY WAS MY last day working with Professor Mallard. It was hard to focus after deciding so abruptly that I would not be gritty—that I was going home. Not to mention, I was still hung up on the Jeanette disaster. I felt terrible, just terribly guilty about what had happened to Trent. Deep down I knew it was my fault. I was desperate to apologize to him, but I had no way of getting in touch.

The best I could do was to dedicate my last few hours of research to Trent. I researched Harvey Milk, the first openly gay elected official in California. I'd watched a movie about his life a couple of years ago and recalled he was an important figure in the gay rights movement who was assassinated. What I didn't know was that Harvey Milk hadn't always been gritty about activism. After graduating from college, he joined the navy. Harvey Milk was a public school teacher, a stock analyst, even a Broadway producer. It wasn't until his forties that he got involved in politics and advocacy.

After I emailed my findings to Professor Mallard, I walked over to her office to say goodbye. The door was wide open.

"Interesting choice," she said, her face glued to the computer screen. "I'm reading your email right now. Harvey Milk?"

"One of my good friends is gay," I said. "Well, formerly. I mean—formerly good friend. Not formerly gay." I rubbed the side of my face, exhausted. "I kind of screwed him over."

Professor Mallard smiled at me. "Don't worry. People forgive more easily than you would think," she said. I tried my best to smile back.

I told Professor Mallard that I had to go back home today—back to Philly.

"Already?" She sounded more surprised than disappointed.

"Parents," I said.

She didn't pry any further. I promised her I would keep up my research from home, whether it was helpful for her book or not. I thanked her for helping me learn about grit . . . helping me to actually see it. Professor Mallard gave me her business card.

"You're a special kid, Scott. I admire your grit." She walked me to the door, where we first collided three weeks ago. "You're going to be fine."

That night I fell asleep thinking about God. Even when things go wrong, I've always believed in a holy power that controls the world. I wondered about the events that had crisscrossed to bring me to this place. How much of it was fate, and how much of it was my fault? How much control did I really have over my life?

A few days ago, I felt good about this journey I had embarked on. But now that my immaculate house of cards had collapsed, I had to wonder what did it.

Was it Jeanette?

Was it Fiora?

Was it my parents?

Or was it me—from the moment I stepped onto that Greyhound bus, the first time I heard the word *grit*—failing, flailing, gasping for air—me?

CHAPTER 28

STOP THINKING. Start doing. Today, I would go home.

My last round of roommates checked out later than I was expecting, so I hurried to begin my own departure process. I threw a few things in my backpack, paid the rest of my hostel fees at the front desk, and bolted out the door.

I had three crisp twenties left—enough for lunch and a bus ticket home. But by the time I'd picked up a sandwich and made it to the bus stop, I'd barely missed the one o'clock bus to Philly. The next one was at four. *Just my luck.* I plopped down on the concrete sidewalk, crisscross-applesauce, to form a new line. At least I'd be the first to board.

I was sitting there for a while when, out of nowhere, I felt someone's hand on my shoulder. They pressed down and leapfrogged over my head. Guess who.

"Hey-ya."

"Seriously?" I said.

"Front desk guy told me you finally checked out," Fiora said. She took a seat on the sidewalk, facing me. "I thought I might find you here."

I leaned away from Fiora, wondering what she'd done now.

"Well . . . I'm leaving," I said.

For a split second, I thought this might turn into one of those rom-com scenes where Fiora admitted she was in love with me and convinced me to stay in DC. Realistically, I knew that wouldn't happen.

"I'm not here to proclaim 'I love you' or any of that crap," she said.

I looked up to glare at Fiora when I noticed something had changed. Her blonde hair was almost entirely gone—just a short, ruffled pixie cut.

"What happened to your hair?" I said frantically. "Are you all right?"

"Don't flatter yourself. This has nothing to do with Sunday," Fiora said, smirking just enough to imply she was actually fine. "Haven't you ever gotten frustrated with that one piece of hair that keeps falling out of place? Every day, every week, it's always falling out of place. So you finally say to yourself, 'You know what? I'm going to take matters into my own hands and cut it off.'"

"No . . ."

"Well," Fiora continued proudly, "I cut it off. *All* off."

"You're so weird," I said, trying hard to suppress a smile. "Why'd you come here?"

"Look. It's obvious you don't want anything to do with me . . ." Fiora said, her words trailing off. She gazed past me at the side of the bus that had just pulled up.

"Don't flatter yourself," I mimicked.

Fiora turned her attention back, looking me straight in the eye.

"But don't you want to help Trent?"

❏❏❏❏

Fiora admitted that we both still had shit to figure out. In the meantime, our friend Trent was out of a job. She said they had talked over the phone, and Trent wasn't even the least bit angry with me. He wasn't angry with anyone. He was keeping his chin up and looking for other jobs in DC. It's not like he could go back to Charleston or ask his family for money, Fiora said. His options were limited.

"The thing is, we all know Trent's dream is to go into politics," she said, waving her hands like a motivational speaker. "He doesn't want to bartend for the rest of his life. But at this rate, he's never going to get there."

"Unless?"

"Unless *we* get him that dream job."

I rolled my eyes. "We don't even know what that dream job is," I said.

"Of course we do! Remember that senator he's always babbling about? The one who's Republican-but-not-really because he's cool with gay people and pot?"

"Renault Cohen?"

"Exactly."

"How are we supposed to get Trent a job with a US senator?"

I didn't see where Fiora was going with this. Was her plan to pass out Trent's résumé to every person on Capitol Hill? Post it on telephone poles? Scan Craigslist?

"Networking," Fiora said. "I did some research, and apparently Renault Cohen is very involved in the DC French scene. *Reh-nohhhh.* Lucky for us, Bastille Day is this week. There are a million events leading up to it. A big celebration tomorrow night at the French Embassy, champagne happy hour, a picnic during the day—"

"I can't stay that long," I interrupted. I thought about my parents' near-instant reply to my email on Sunday:

> Saaket jaan—Ok. Thank you for letting us know you are safe. We are at the travel agency in Tehran and they say it will be very expensive to move our flights. So we will leave in two days as planned. And we will talk to you on Wednesday.

The last sentence gave me chills. From what I could tell, I was royally screwed.

"You don't need to stay much longer," Fiora said. "There's a super-exclusive soiree tonight at the French ambassador's residence."

"How'd you hear about it if it's so exclusive?"

"Benji tipped me off," Fiora said. "We were supposed to go together before he broke up with me. His family's a big deal in France."

Fiora threw her head back, ruffling her new hair. I scratched mine.

"Why don't you go by yourself?" I asked.

"I don't look like much of a Benjamin, do I?" she said half smiling. "There's no way he'll go. All we have to do is show up, use Benji's name to get in, and find Renault Cohen. If we tell him Trent's story, I'm sure he'll sympathize." Fiora put her hand on my arm. "Come on, Saaket. Let's do it for Trent. What's one more night?"

Fiora knew how to play people. She dangled carrots, she twisted words. But when she truly cared about something, you could tell. First it was crosswords. Now it was her best friend. She didn't always know what she wanted, but when she did, she went after it.

This would be no exception.

My parents weren't due to arrive home until tomorrow morning. It was cutting it close . . . But for one last DC adventure?

"I'm in."

It felt strange to be reunited with Fiora so soon after our fight. Fortunately, there wasn't much time to mull over the strangeness, because I needed a tuxedo for the soiree. She suggested we borrow one from Benji.

"No way," I said.

"Come on—"

"*No*, Fiora! I don't care if you still have his apartment keys. You already stole his bike. If he figures out you took his tux, we're both screwed."

"He has, like, eight of them," Fiora said. "Benji hardly keeps track of his closet. I know it better than he does."

"How in the—"

"Saaket, please. I'll return it tomorrow. He won't even notice it's gone." Fiora's face twisted up like cheap earbuds. She wasn't giving up on me. "Benji hates dressing up. His outfit of choice was always a tank top and cargo shorts, with these stupid Crocs—"

"Okay, okay," I said, smiling inside. I liked it when Fiora made fun of Benji's style. Schadenfreude. I felt like I'd earned it.

Benji was supposed to be teaching a class for the next hour, so we hurried over to his apartment to steal the tux. Fiora moved so buoyantly that you could tell she got a kick out of high-risk escapades like this one. I, on the other hand, followed along like a prisoner marching to his execution. I couldn't have been more terrified.

As promised, Fiora used her copy of Benji's apartment key to get us inside. It reassured me that Benji was careless enough not to take his key back. He definitely wouldn't notice a missing tuxedo . . . right? Right. Riiiight.

The apartment was modest in decor but abundant in mess. Fiora and I waded through a minefield of boxers and dirty shirts to get to his closet. Luckily, the tuxedos (yes, plural) were all the way in the back.

Fiora picked one out and moved to the door.

"Don't I need to put it on?" I asked.

"You can do that at my place," she said.

It occurred to me that Fiora still had to wear something nice, too. It also occurred to me that I'd never seen Fiora's "place"—apartment, dorm, row house, bunker, or whatever form of unique, Fiora-esque living it might be.

◻◻◻◻

Fiora's apartment was less than two blocks away from Benji's. I could see the convenience of their relationship: student/ teacher, neighbors, confident man/neglected daughter. Fiora'd had every reason to keep gravitating back to Benji.

I just wish she had realized sooner that she deserved better.

Fiora threw her clothes off as soon as we entered the apartment. Before I knew it, I was standing in front of a naked and perfect female body covered in nothing but black, lacy underwear. I stared for two seconds before turning away—the first second because I was caught off guard, and the second because my eyes lingered. Fiora's breasts and hips curved beautifully, and her skin was so light it shone even in the darkness. For a girl with such a devilish sense of adventure, she radiated like an angel.

A few minutes later, she was dressed in a long royal-blue dress.

"*On y va,*" Fiora said. *Let's go.*

⌑⌑⌑⌑

We took a cab to the French ambassador's house. For some reason, Fiora sat in the passenger seat, leaving me alone in the back. She kept peculiarly quiet. I pretended to stare out the window at the green landscape along Rock Creek Parkway, but I couldn't help sneaking peeks at her profile. Fiora stared straight ahead, taking small breaths through the tiniest gap in her lips, her chest rising and falling.

I couldn't say for sure, because I only caught a glimpse, but it felt like there was a storm brewing in her eyes. It reminded me of when we first met.

My peeks must have been as subtle as Fiora's haircut—which surprisingly upped her classiness to a level I couldn't compete with—because as soon as I took another one, she piped up.

"Hey, Saaket?" I held my breath. "I've been thinking a lot lately about that trip I took last winter, after I bombed my Spanish final. The one to Madrid."

I grinned shamelessly, because Fiora couldn't see me. She was still staring at the road. "Do I remind you of it?"

"No," Fiora said. She lifted her chin and looked me straight in the eye through the rearview mirror. She wore an icy expression, and I dropped my smile immediately. "It's just . . . Things were so different then. I made my decisions differently. You know?"

I didn't know.

"A lot has changed since Spain, and I don't know how I feel about it."

I sat silently, unsure how to console Fiora about the changes in her life. She didn't need consolation, I decided; she would figure it out on her own.

"So what happens if this *soirée* plan doesn't work?" I asked, placing a hoity-toity French accent on the word.

"*Il faut voir*," she said in real French.

For the rest of the ride, Fiora and I gazed out of our respective cab windows. I would later learn what Fiora's sexy French phrase translated into: *We'll have to wait and see.*

CHAPTER 29

THE FRENCH AMBASSADOR'S residence was the most co-lossal three-story mansion I'd ever seen in my life. It blew my mind. *"Stop staring,"* Fiora whispered to me. She pulled out her phone and began scrolling through her Instagram feed. *"Act cool."* I just couldn't help it. I scanned the lush, green lawn—each blade of grass cut with razor-thin precision—and let my eyes wander up the house's faded brick facade. The French were at it again with their whole *esthétique* thing. Fancy-schmancy. Francy.

Just before we reached the door, Fiora stumbled into a garden of pink petunias. The doorman took note.

"Ahem," he said. *"Bonjour."*

"Ah, one second," Fiora immediately replied with the faintest French accent. Then she nudged me. *"Mon cher,* I be-lieve I dropped an earring on the driveway."

Fiora gently squeezed my nonexistent bicep and guided me—leisurely, then hastily—around the corner of the house.

"What's going on?" I asked.

"He's here."

"Renault Cohen? Good, I would hope so."

"No," Fiora hissed. "Benji. He just posted a picture on Instagram. He's inside."

"Shit. Okay. What's the backup plan?" I asked.

"I don't know. I don't know."

"I thought you had a backup plan?"

"Of course not! It's me!" Fiora sounded agitated.

"Then what are we going to do?"

I was waiting for Fiora to reveal the joke—that there was a hard-but-not-impossible-to-access doggy door in the back-yard, and we were going to crawl through it. That moment never came. She actually, truly looked defeated.

No plan. Nothing to lose. I closed my eyes and channeled my inner Fiora.

Bingo.

"I think I have a plan," I said. "No promises."

We walked back to the front door. Fiora cracked her knuckles as I marched with an involuntary air of self-importance. Inside, my heart was pounding, but I tightened my chest and willed my nerves to stay calm.

"*Bonjour*," the doorman said again. He was a tall, suited Middle Eastern man, in his forties or early fifties, with dark features and bushy brows.

"*Bonjour*," I said, nodding once. I took Fiora's hand, and we swung forward like pendulums, waltzing through the front door.

"Excuse me, sir."

My pulse froze as I turned my head very slowly.

"Yes?"

"Did *mademoiselle* find her earring?"

"Ah, yes. She found exactly what she was looking for."

I gulped dry air, gripped Fiora's hand, and walked inside. Once we were a few steps past the foyer, I turned to her and whispered: "*Holyshitthatworked.*"

"Holy shit is right," she said.

We stood motionless before an extravagant chamber. A crystal chandelier hung from the sky-high ceiling, balancing what seemed like thousands of glowing candles. The room was painted a perfect shade of red that would have rivaled Rudolph's nose, and its edges were lined with intricate crown molding. I gasped, but the sound was swallowed by the hum of high-society chatter. The partygoers were predominantly old, important-looking. White. Waiters floated around the room offering hors d'oeuvres. Fiora picked a crab cake off one of their trays. I went for the mini hot dogs. Our snacks felt out of place at such a lavish event. Like us.

"How did you know he wouldn't check our names?" Fiora asked.

"I didn't," I said. "Blind faith."

"Wow."

"Yeah." I reached for another mini hot dog. "There's no opportunity cost when you're taking a risk like that. We had nothing to lose."

"Sounds like confidence to me."

I smiled. "Not to mention we look dapper as hell."

Fiora raised her eyebrows and laughed. It was a careful laugh, like she was reacting to a joke about François Hollande or the politics of French cheese.

"Okay, okay. Let's not get cocky," she said.

⌁⌁⌁⌁

We stood around idly, scanning the room for signs of Renault Cohen. I was growing uneasy. Not so deep down, I had this feeling that Fiora and I were going to get caught. We were obviously the youngest people in the room. Our hair was the most unkempt, our postures the slouchiest, and my tuxedo by far the worst-fitting. If we intended to track down this senator before our shaky cover was blown, Fiora and I had to strategize. Stat.

I noticed a familiar face across the room. It was a woman's, and when her eyes caught sight of me, her expression changed. She dipped out from her group and hovered toward us, smiling as she turned her full attention to my partner.

"This must be Fiora," she said.

Fiora looked at me suspiciously. She must have thought we were getting busted.

"Professor Mallard," I explained. I wanted to hug her, but I went for a more appropriate hand-hug. Firm grip. "What are you doing here?"

"MacArthur Grant perk," Professor Mallard said. "The award is effectively an all-access pass to DC's most elite soirees. Every intellectual in town invites me out now. I figure I'll play along for a year, enjoy the free crab cake, and fade out of the scene before I resort to stabbing my ears out from all the small talk."

Fiora giggled like a five-year-old girl; I had a feeling they would get along. Professor Mallard shifted to professional mode—not in an intimidating way, but out of genuine concern. "The better question is, what are you doing here? I thought you had left town."

Fiora began: "We have this friend, Trent—"

"And we're trying to get him his dream job," I said, skipping straight to the point.

"With Renault Cohen," Fiora said. "The senator."

Professor Mallard raised an eyebrow.

"Because Trent's a good guy," I added.

Professor Mallard's raised eyebrow rolled right into a smirk.

"A *good* guy in *politics*?" She pitted the words against each other like *church* and *sin*. "Well, if he insists . . . How can I help?"

Fiora and I looked at each other, smiling. I leaned closer to Professor Mallard.

"Who do we need to meet to find Senator Cohen?"

❑❑❑❑

Professor Mallard gave us the lowdown on every dignitary, ambassador, CEO, and deputy secretary of Fine Wine and Cheese in attendance. She pointed out each target to us in the sea of tuxedos and cocktail dresses. Senator Cohen wasn't in the room, but someone who knew him certainly was. Networking 101.

Even before this crash course, I was experiencing massive sensory overload. Too many people, heirlooms, French paintings, silk tablecloths, velvet sofas, and those itty-bitty gold cups holding the candles in the chandelier. It was the kind of party Cinderella would have crashed, except there was no pumpkin carriage awaiting our escape.

We split up for maximum networking. I started with the chief of staff to the deputy ambassador of Monaco. I remembered his description because I found it funny that such a small country needed a *deputy* ambassador with his *own* chief of staff. Plus, he had a big nose—which just seemed kind of un-French.

"Mr. Coruzzi," I said. I caught him as he was bidding *adieu* to a pretty African American woman, or perhaps African French.

"Allo!" he said, joyfully tipsy. "How eez it go-*weeng*?"

"Wonderful," I said nervously. "Um, how are you?"

"Ah, my son. It eez only zee beginning. I must sustain my-self," he said, swaying from side to side and sustaining his boozy smile.

"I know what you mean. Mr. Coruzzi, I was actually look-ing for . . ."

"Oh, Charles!"

Bad things have a tendency to pile up like raindrops in a puddle. And when it rained in DC, it poured.

"Bah, *Benjameen! Comment allez-vous?*" Mr. Coruzzi snapped out of his giddy inebriation into something more serious. Or maybe he was asking, "Are you as sloshed as I am?" in French.

"*Eh, c'était une semaine difficile,*" Benji said. "I'm single again, Charles."

Mr. Coruzzi gasped. "*Comme c'est tragique,*" he said. His reaction was overly dramatic, like a soap opera character. I almost chuckled. Benji turned his attention to me.

"Benjamin. Pleasure to meet you." He sized me up and added: "Sharp tux."

"Scott," I said, shaking his hand with terror. If Fiora had mentioned my name to her ex before, surely it would have been as Saaket.

Coruzzi was obviously clueless, because he kept going with the breakup: "Zees eez zee" (*this is the* . . . moment when his accent peaked) "girlfriend who made zee crossword, no?"

"Indeed," Benji groaned. "The cruciverbalist. Not quite as

productive as our trades—academia, government—but those fields aren't for everyone. Am I not right, my friend?"

"What does she actually do, though?" I interrupted.

"She's a student," Benji said. "If she hasn't dropped out yet . . ."

"So she still has time to figure things out," I said. "You know, there's so much research linking puzzles with other aspects of cognition. Memory search, facial recognition, intuitiveness . . ."

"Anything connecting crosswords and *crazy*? Because that's Fiora," Benji said. He looked noticeably irritated—like he was swatting a bumblebee that wouldn't leave him alone. Professor Mallard passed by us and winked. Coruzzi took note.

"It appears you know *See-see-lee* Mallard," he nudged. "Brilliant lady, no?"

"She's an absolute *genius!*" Benji said, sounding snootier than a Mozart symphony. "Literally. They just awarded her a MacArthur. How are you connected, Scott?"

"Research," I blurted out. "I do research for her at Georgetown."

Benji eyed me hawkishly. "A fellow academic, eh? Well done." He paused. "Actually, you did look somewhat familiar . . ."

Coruzzi smiled. "Zee world eez small!"

"Very. Very small," I said. I needed to get away. "Excuse me, gentlemen. I have to go find the professor now. Nicetomeetyouboth!"

I weaved through clumps of socialites—schmoozing and

boozing—to find Fiora and Professor Mallard standing together, engaged in a heated debate.

"*These* people are the dickheads my GW classmates are being pruned into," Fiora said, her voice growing increasingly tense.

"That's an unfortunately narrow-minded perspective," Professor Mallard said. "The men and women in this room are the movers and shakers—"

I interrupted. "Hey, guys. I just ran into Benji talking to Charles Coruzzi."

Fiora gagged like she'd swallowed escargot.

"You know Benjamin Decot?" Professor Mallard asked.

"*You* know Benji?"

Professor Mallard nodded. "The academic world is regrettably small and connected in this town . . ."

"So is the dating pool," Fiora added.

"Ahem," I said. "How are we doing on Renault Cohen?"

I was itching to finish up and leave. I didn't think Professor Mallard or Fiora felt the same urgency I did. One of them had been legitimately invited to the soiree and the other thrived off these sorts of situations.

Professor Mallard and Fiora exchanged thin, eager smiles.

"Well . . ." Fiora said. "We may have a location."

"The Danish ambassador tipped us off," Professor Mallard said.

Fiora looked left and right. "Balcony," she whispered proudly.

I leaned in and nodded, trying to contain my excitement. We were so close. Not quite finished, but close.

"You guys," I said softly. "It sounds like we're plotting a *murder*."

The three of us burst out laughing. Suddenly I noticed Benji, sitting by himself on the opposite side of the room, watching our little powwow: the ex-girlfriend, the genius professor, and the suspiciously familiar face. We must have all noticed him, because without realizing it, our group turned stone-cold sober—like actual murderers.

"Let's move fast," I said.

◻◻◻◻

The French ambassador's balcony curved like a parabola. It was a shallow curve, with Renault Cohen standing at the vertex. He was alone, facing the zoo-size backyard. His hands were clasped firmly on the rail, and his eyes gazed out at nothing in particular.

"Now what do we do?" I asked.

Professor Mallard turned to Fiora and me. "Follow my lead, kids."

We took small footsteps behind Professor Mallard as she marched confidently up to Renault Cohen.

"Senator!" Professor Mallard exclaimed, her voice sounding less like hers and more like Benji's. "A pleasure to meet you. Cecily Mallard, Georgetown."

Renault Cohen looked flustered, but he perked up and

feigned interest. "Ah, yes. Professor Mallard. I've heard great things."

"Likewise," Professor Mallard said. She took a small step back. "I'd like to introduce you to two of my students."

"Pleasure," Renault Cohen said weakly.

Fiora perked up. "It's an honor to meet you, Senator. I am so inspired by your policies. The way you juxtapose laissez-faire values with fundamental human rights . . . I speak for many people my age when I say I consider you a role model." I pressed my lips shut to resist smiling. When Fiora picked up a persona, she couldn't be stopped. "Do you have any advice for my future career?"

A freaking force to be reckoned with.

"Go make money," Renault Cohen muttered.

We stood there in awe. Senator Renault Cohen, a man whose job was to bullshit the general public about the country's "optimistic prospects" and "tradition of integrity," to inspire us towards public service . . . told Fiora to make some goddamn dough.

Before anyone could save the conversation, Fiora nudged me.

"Shit," I whispered under my breath. Benji and the doorman were standing by the balcony entrance, eyeing us like hawks.

"Excuse me," I said, shaking hands quickly with the two adults, "I just remembered Fiora and I have somewhere to be. I'll see you in class, Professor!"

We shuffled over to the far corner of the balcony.

"That jealous, whistle-blowing son of a bitch . . ." Fiora began.

"Where do we go?" I said, glancing over the ledge. I imagined our adventure reaching a new high—er, low. "Do we jump?"

"Hell no!" Fiora said, shooting down my crazy with a sour look. "We leave through the balcony entrance. There are at least six doors."

Fiora offered me her hand. I took it, clenched it, nerves shooting through our arms and bunching up in our sweaty palms. We moved slowly toward the farthest door from Benji. He and the doorman started creeping in our direction.

"Run," Fiora whispered.

We bolted through the door—narrowly missing Benji and his henchman. Fiora took the lead, pulling me past partygoers and keeping me from ricocheting off the walls as we raced down the never-ending hallway. I didn't catch a single expression, but the other guests had to be at least a little pissed off at the two kids causing a ruckus and the men chasing—hold on, were they still chasing us? Didn't matter; we kept running anyway. The amount of collision and crashing—*whack! thud!*—all that cacophony led me to believe that the string quartet *must* have been replaced by a percussion ensemble. Or maybe it was really us making all that noise, because then we stumbled down the spiral stairs, and I slipped on the marble floor in the foyer like a doofus and his banana peel. "Saaket!" Fiora yelled my name with so much life that I froze and smiled at her for a split second—I really froze!—before getting up.

We ran for two blocks until the mansion was out of sight. Fiora looked back, panting, and she nodded at me. We made a full stop at the corner of Kalorama and Connecticut.

I hunched over my knees; Fiora leaned on my back. I could practically hear her heart beating out of her chest, a million beats per second. I wondered if she could feel the sweat on my back, even with two layers of tux in between.

I pushed back to signal that I was ready to get up. Fiora and I stood face-to-face, breathless, until somehow our huffing and puffing turned into pure, insane, unruly laughter. It had gotten dark outside, and Fiora's dress was kind of messed up, but her smile lit up the entire street corner.

We walked down Connecticut to Fiora's apartment, where I had left my bag. I changed out of the tuxedo and put on a ratty T-shirt and corduroys. Fiora took a shower. When she stepped out in her towel, I was flooded with hormones. *Make a move*, I told myself. *Make a move, make a move, make a move.* But then I remembered our fight in the rain. How we had come so far with tonight's adventure. I didn't want to ruin that.

I spent the night on Fiora's couch and dozed off thinking about the universe. How it's indefinitely incomplete—like us. How the best ideas, events, people, and lives don't need to wrap up nicely to mean something.

CHAPTER 30

I WOKE UP the next morning feeling equal parts displaced and refreshed. Fiora wasn't up yet, so I left her a note. *I'll be at Kramerbooks if you want to say goodbye.* I grabbed my things and took off. It was time to go home.

I found a pay phone just off Dupont Circle. I dropped three quarters into the coin slot and dialed a familiar number.

"Hello?" he answered. I could hear him smacking his lips through the phone, probably from an extra snack he had pocketed from the airplane.

"Hey, Dad."

Silence. The static from the phone grew louder, like it would electrify my ear. You only ever notice phone static when you're desperately waiting for a reply. When both sides are holding their breath.

"Are you angry?" I asked. My voice cracked. The pay phone smelled deceptively sterile, like it had been cleaned by . . .

"I'm not angry," he said. "Are you all right?"

I closed my eyes. I didn't shut them. Voluntary, passive closure.

"Can you pick me up?" I asked.

This silence was more bearable. It sounded like a nod.

"Of course. Where are you?"

I twisted the phone cord around my pointer finger—three loops. It felt cold and scaly, constricting against my skin, so I unraveled it all at once.

"DC," I said. "Dupont Circle."

"I'll be there in a few hours," he said hurriedly. "Where will you be?"

"There's a bookstore called Kramerbooks, on Connecticut and—"

"Wait for me there."

"Okay," I said.

"I love you," he said.

I nodded. "*Meedoonam*," I said. *I know.*

□◻□◻

Growing up in a strict house, I used to imagine running away all the time. I thought it would be scrappy—a raggedy sack over my shoulder, maybe a few bucks in my pocket. Hitchhiking along the highway until a trucker pulled over and picked me up and . . . I don't know. My imagination never made it that far.

In reality, I got it good. Better than good. Most of the time in life, you expect things to be one way and they fall short. Not this. I felt like I cheated the systemless system of teenage rebellion—running away on a bogus whim and coming out of it with real experiences. Sure, I lost a few hundred bucks and a summer internship, but I felt richer than ever.

❑❐❑❐

When I hung up the pay phone, I knew there was one more adult I needed to talk to before I could properly leave DC.

❑❐❑❐

Cecily Mallard leaned back in her armchair, hoisting her legs over her desk. Her feet came crashing down on the keyboard. *Asdjklffffffffffffff.*

"I'm sorry if we put you in an awkward position last night," I said.

Professor Mallard cracked up.

"That was the most fun I've had at one of those events in a long time," she said, beaming. "Really. I should be thanking you. I was . . . I was such an intellectual goofball!"

I smiled meekly. "Well, at least it was fun, then. I'm just

disappointed we weren't able to do anything for Trent."

"Why would you say that?"

Professor Mallard handed me a card.

CECILY MALLARD

Professor, Georgetown University

"I'm confused," I said. "You already gave me your card."

"This one's not for you," she said. "Senator Cohen has a reelection coming up, and he mentioned he's hiring staffers for the campaign. I told him I might know someone for the job." Professor Mallard gave the tiniest smile, out of the corner of her lips. The delicate motion was enough to fill the room with infinite warmth. "Ask your friend to email me his résumé, and I'll see what I can do."

I was dumbfounded. "What— I can't believe— How?"

"After you and Fiora scrambled, I grew curious," she said. "I was puzzled by the senator's antisocial behavior. I felt there was something gnawing at his conscience. We spoke for a while, and I learned that his father had passed away just last week."

"Wow."

Professor Mallard took a deep breath. "My father passed away recently, too, Scott. He had a heart attack this spring. It's been hard, these last few months." She took a deep breath. "We never had the best relationship. I was too uptight; he wanted me to loosen up."

I clenched my hands. I didn't know what to say.

"Regardless," she continued, "Renault Cohen and I connected. We had a deep discussion about dealing with loss. It was even therapeutic to some extent. We plan to keep in touch, but in the meantime, I hope this can be helpful to your friend . . ."

"Trent," I said.

I looked down at my hands—fingers interlaced over and under each other. My thumbs pushed so hard into my knuckles, I could feel the nerves shooting up my arms and down my chest and all the way through my scrawny legs. I imagined those nerves reaching my feet, reinforcing my toes, helping me walk taller. More balanced.

I released the pressure and looked up, nodding.

"This is going to mean so much to Trent," I said. "Thank you."

Professor Mallard gave me one last Growing-Up Smile. Two steps forward, one back. Five forward, twelve back. Left, right, diagonal, down, across, and right back around the block. We're all just trying to keep moving. Sometimes we know where we're going and sometimes we get lost. But as long as we move, we grow.

❑❑❑❑

I rushed over to Kramerbooks, praying that I hadn't missed Fiora. Not only did I want to say goodbye, but I wanted to give her the good news about Trent. I waited impatiently by the nonfiction section, flipping through the same Steve Jobs biography I had started reading more than three weeks ago. I could hardly get through a page. Whenever the front door jingled, I shot my head around, hoping it would be Fiora. She never showed up.

But someone else did.

"Trent?" I said. "What are you doing here?"

He flinched. Trent was dressed nicely—a striped button-down shirt tucked into green khaki pants. "I'm supposed to meet Fiora. I've got a job interview at eleven, but she asked me to stop here for a second—"

We both realized at the same time what was happening.

"Classic Fiora," he said, grinning.

Fiora must have set this up so I could apologize to Trent and leave DC guilt-free. She didn't know I had something even better. I fumbled through my front pocket for the business card. It wasn't there. Back right pocket. Right.

"Here," I said, handing it to him.

"Cecily Mallard." He read the card out loud, like he was reading from a phone book. "Professor, comma, Georgetown University. Thanks?"

"She said to email her your résumé," I said. "She's going to pass it along to Renault Cohen. He's hiring for his reelection campaign and—"

Trent's face made approximately seven different expressions: puzzled, concerned, shocked, elated, hesitant, more puzzled . . . and finally, the kind of happy that can only lead to a massive bear hug, which was exactly what happened.

"I honestly don't know what to say," he whispered.

It hit me during our drawn-out embrace that Trent and I had never hugged before. If you asked me, I would have assumed we had. Hugging symbolizes support—and by that logic, Trent had been squeezing the bejesus out of me since day one.

We broke the hug mutually. Trent noticed my backpack.

"So you're leaving?"

I nodded. "My dad's gonna be here any minute."

Trent put his hand on my shoulder. "We'll miss you, man. Fiora and me. It's been a crazy couple of weeks." He smiled. "You learned a thing or two here, yeah?"

"Hah. Maybe."

"Sure you did," Trent said. "It's like liquor. You can struggle and drink it straight, or you can make yourself a mixed drink. Life works better with other people around. Always go for the fruity cocktail."

Those words defined Trent—his spirit—in so many ways.

◻◻◻◻

I could try describing the next eighteen pages of the Steve Jobs biography, or the twelve more times I heard the front door jingle, or the conversation I had with an employee who asked if I was actually going to buy a book. I could try describing those events, but the only one that mattered was the thirteenth time I heard the door jingle. I knew it was my dad. My mind went numb like a foot afflicted by pins and needles. My body acted on autopilot.

I didn't turn around for that last jingle. I kept my head buried in the biography, until before I knew it, I found my entire self buried in my dad's tight embrace.

He hasn't shaved in weeks, I noticed, his beard digging unapologetically into my cheek.

How could he already be tearing up? I thought.

Is my mom waiting in the car? I wondered.

I kept clinging on to my dad. We'd never hugged like this before—the kind of embrace that mended all that had been broken. I might have been biased, but if I could describe the hug in one word, it would be gritty.

He led me to the car without saying a word. I glanced over my shoulder and caught one last look at Dupont Circle. The fountain peeked out from behind the tall trees, gushing pristinely over the crowd of people—real people—with different wants and desires who had found themselves blissfully in the same place. Suddenly I felt absolved. I had turned the page on another chapter.

Ten minutes into the car ride, Dad spoke up:

"I'm trying to understand . . ." His voice trailed off.

I stared at my hands in my lap, running my thumb back

and forth across my palm like a windshield wiper.

"I didn't want to do the internship with Dr. Mehta," I said, almost toneless. "I came to DC to meet Professor Mallard instead, and—"

My dad braked the car abruptly at a red light, and I jumped in my seat. One of the cars behind us honked.

"The grit professor?"

"Yes," I said slowly, carefully. "I've been doing research for her book. On important figures who . . . did gritty things. Against all odds."

He didn't say anything. I felt him chewing the bits of information I had fed him, contemplating his next question. His next reaction, whether it would be rage or confusion or some morsel of fatherly, growing-up wisdom. Whether he would dole out the appropriate punishment now or later.

"I wish you had told us you were going to do this," he said, surrendering.

"What?"

My dad gripped the steering wheel tighter, his eyes bulging at the road. The words were stuck somewhere between his tongue and his lips. This was not our usual spar. We both knew I had messed up, but it felt different from all the other times I had messed up with mediocre grades or abandoned extracurriculars. There was no rubric for this one.

"I wish you hadn't lied to us." His eyes swept across the dashboard. I caught a twinkle at the end of their path, when he patted the side of my arm. "You're young. You're figuring your life out, and . . . I won't always be there to push you. But even as you take control of your future, even as you become your own man—please, *please*, think about your parents." He breathed slowly and said, "I'm glad you're safe."

That was it; he didn't say anything more. I slid lower into the tattered cushion to get comfortable, and I smiled.

⊔⊓⊔⊓

How could I begin to process the end?

I stared out past the dashboard at the endless highway: cars whizzing toward the same half-asphalt, half-sky view. There were sedans and minivans and large trucks with handlebar-mustached drivers. We even passed a Greyhound bus.

I'd never been good at finishing things. But adventures like this one stay with you; they're never really done. It's like the universe. I can't guarantee humankind will go on *forever*, but it's going somewhere. Baby steps, growth. Because completion isn't a prerequisite for growth. Momentum is.

I stared out past the dashboard and reflected on the sum of my actions. We never reflect on sums, just pieces. Those pieces—an online grit quiz, the impulsive girl you sit next to on the bus—they add up to so much more than you could have expected.

Dad pulled into the garage, the car *thump-thump*ing as we rolled up the driveway, just like I remembered. He stepped out of the car to get something from the trunk. I lingered in the passenger seat.

I didn't come out of DC with a career plan. But I came out grittier. I had to embrace my shortcomings, because they were what landed me there in the first place. I had to embrace my upbringing, my constant stream of thoughts. The same shortcomings would lead to my next great adventure.

Failure is inevitable. Productive, even. But it doesn't have to hijack my confidence.

I stepped out of the car feeling invincible. I could not imagine a circumstance where things didn't work out.

At least, for now.

EPILOGUE

EXACTLY A YEAR has passed and I still can't write about it. There's a Microsoft Word file on our PC called "DC.docx" and the word count has stayed zero for 365 days.

I stare at the blank page, hypnotized by the blinking cursor on the first line. Without realizing it, I fire up a browser and type "f-a-" into the URL bar and—holy shit!—now I'm on Facebook. I scroll through a stream of statuses and photos. I click on a link for a list of "12 Adorably Frightened Puppies." Then I click to YouTube, where I watch a corgi slipping around a perfectly greased floor. I discover more videos of awesome stunts, awful accidents, and awe-inspiring miracles. I tell myself it should be called AweTube.

Some links demand to be clicked, and some stories demand to be told. Not mine. Not yet. It's still going—still indefinitely incomplete.

I rip myself away from the PC and move to the window. I can see Dad pulling into the driveway. He steps out of the car, carefully balancing a cluster of balloons, grocery bags, and two wrapped boxes. I knock on the window and he jumps, almost losing the balloons. He looks up and smiles, shouting: *"Tavaloooodet mobarak!" Happy birthday.*

I am eighteen now. I press my forehead against the glass and close my eyes, remembering my seventeenth birthday. It was the day I came home from DC. Mom greeted me in the kitchen with a hurricane of emotions: crying, hugging, screaming, but most of all, demanding answers. My dad helped calm her down. He asked me to go up to my room so they could talk. An hour later, they called me back into the kitchen. The lights were off, and Mom brought out a glowing Iranian cake, the kind decorated with glazed fruit.

"Tavalodet mobarak," they cheered softly.

I had completely forgotten about my birthday. We sang in both Farsi and English. I blew out the candles and opened gifts from their trip: sour-cherry *lavashak*, a backgammon set, and a camel-bone box from Esfahan. Then I opened up to them about my journey. I told Mom and Dad how I quit my internship and left home in search of grit. Mom shook her head and *tsk*ed repeatedly. She was angrier than I'd ever seen her. Dad, however, couldn't help but grin as I described my persistence with Cecily Mallard. I found out later he had another reason to smile—Baba Bozorg's health was finally improving.

My parents grounded me for the rest of that summer, and I spent most of my time cranking out research for Professor Mallard. I wrote at least a hundred new reports on entrepreneurs, athletes, artists, scientists—important figures from every conceivable field. Even when Professor Mallard told me that her editor didn't think my reports added anything to her book, I kept at it. These were the stories I wanted to write.

Professor Mallard published her book in the spring: *True Grit*. It became an instant bestseller. She didn't use any of my research, but there was a familiar anecdote among the pages about a "teenage boy who barged into my office one summer, desperate to get gritty." Apparently, he had it in him all along.

Jack and I both got into Georgetown. We're going to be roommates in the fall. I like to think my stories from DC influenced his decision, but it's also the best program for aspiring diplomats, so who knows. Kevin's staying behind in Philly, but don't feel bad, because the lucky bastard got a full ride to Penn. We already have plans to visit him over fall break.

I'm thinking of studying history or psychology at Georgetown. It's not what my parents had in mind, but Dad says there's a career called "management consulting," and it could set me up well for that. We're compromising.

Trent is on the campaign trail for Renault Cohen's reelection. We keep in touch on Facebook. He's pulling long hours and knocking on thousands of doors, but it seems to be paying off. He was already promoted to assistant director of field strategy. If all goes well in November, he should end up with his dream job on Capitol Hill.

Fiora and I lost touch. After DC we became Facebook friends and were messaging for a few weeks until she deleted her profile. Trent says she practically fell off the face of the planet. She took off for Europe and never came back for the school year. I imagine she must have found her own adventure.

I solve a crossword puzzle a day now. There's an app called Daily Crossword Challenge, and the puzzles are perfect for beginners like me. They take five, maybe seven minutes to solve. It's one of the only times in my day when I'm 100 percent focused.

My parents call me downstairs, and we celebrate my eighteenth birthday together. They give me two presents: a laptop and a set of notebooks, both for college. After we finish, I run up to my room. I crack open one of the notebooks to the first page, hoping I might have better luck writing about my time in DC by hand.

I don't write. I theme-storm.

Then I draw.

I draw out a grid, fifteen squares down by fifteen across.

Across

1. Ace or queen, e.g.
5. Annual sports honors
10. Addams Family cousin
13. "In a galaxy far, far _____"
14. Steal
16. Slangy eating sound, when repeated
17. Sweaty basement that's home to BYHG and WWJB
19. "Just so you know . . ."
20. Prefix for cycle and athlete
21. It's mostly made of nitrogen
22. Scott and Saaket
24. "No idea," in slang
25. Hold on tight
28. Happiness
30. Word in brackets calling attention to a typo
32. Longest lasting of China's dynasties
34. Luxury brand Christian _____
35. Actress who played Arwen in Lord of the Rings films
38. Modern place to buy games from Apple
40. DC bar with "Angry Hour"
43. Big sale
44. Neither here ___ there
45. Type of bed in Hanover Hostel
46. First letter of the Hebrew alphabet
48. Doctors: Abbr.
51. They carry lightsabers
53. Adjust to new settings
56. Baseball ref
58. Step on the accelerator
60. Mowgli's slithery friend in The Jungle Book
61. Topic of the internship I quit last summer, slang
62. Nonprofit URL ending
63. DC store with Steve Jobs biography
67. Animated 2011 film set in Brazil
68. They say "aloha" here
69. Leg joint
70. When a plane is scheduled to take off, for short
71. Geeks and dorks, but smart
72. Don't catch these in bed

Down

1. Thorny desert plants
2. Accolades
3. Wise baboon in The Lion King
4. You might do this to your hair
5. Online shopping
6. Iranian city of poets and literature
7. ___ the tail on the donkey
8. So far
9. Pet reindeer in Frozen
10. Lower in status
11. Classic Disney movie with the characters Slink and Rex
12. "Ew, I didn't need to know that"
15. What you might study for at the last minute
18. Cul-de-___ (where I live)
23. Important type of 15-Down
26. Screwed or ripped off
27. Cops, in slang
29. Empire that dissolved in 1806: Abbr.
31. First thing you do when you start your 9-to-5
33. Once _____ a time
36. Outside doctor evaluation: Abbr.
37. Spanish word for "cow"
39. ___-mo replay
40. Cecily Mallard's latest bestseller
41. Vishnu or Shiva, for example
42. Toni Morrison novel first published in 1973
43. Popular sandwich with jam: Abbr.
47. I used Carlos Zambrano's to get into 17-Across
49. DC circle
50. Type of salmon
52. Turban-wearing Punjabi man
54. The City of Light
55. You open a new one for Facebook
57. Models strike these at photo shoots
59. Common Vietnamese surname
62. Valuable mineral
64. Jaw-dropping wonder
65. Ruin
66. Gives a thumbs-up

Answer Key:

■	■	1 T	2 O	3 P
■	4 F	O	M	O
5 A	U	D	I	T
6 G	R	I	T	■
7 E	Y	E	■	■

1 C	2 A	3 R	4 D	■	5 E	6 S	7 P	8 Y	9 S	■	■	10 I	11 T	12 T
13 A	W	A	Y	■	14 T	H	I	E	V	15 E	■	16 N	O	M
17 C	A	F	E	18 S	A	I	N	T	E	X	■	19 F	Y	I
20 T	R	I	■	21 A	I	R	■	■	22 N	A	23 M	E	S	■
24 I	D	K	■	25 C	L	A	26 S	27 P	■	28 M	I	R	T	29 H
■	30 S	I	31 C	■	■	32 Z	H	O	33 U	■	34 D	I	O	R
■	■	■	35 L	36 I	37 V	■	38 A	P	P	39 S	T	O	R	E
■	40 T	41 H	O	M	A	42 S	F	O	O	L	E	R	Y	■
43 P	R	I	C	E	C	U	T	■	44 N	O	R	■	■	■
45 B	U	N	K	■	46 A	L	E	47 F	■	■	48 M	49 D	50 S	■
51 J	E	D	I	52 S	■	53 A	D	A	54 P	55 T	■	56 U	M	57 P
■	58 G	U	N	I	59 T	■	■	60 K	A	A	■	61 P	O	O
62 O	R	G	■	63 K	R	64 A	65 M	E	R	B	66 O	O	K	S
67 R	I	O	■	68 H	A	W	A	I	I	■	69 K	N	E	E
70 E	T	D	■	■	71 N	E	R	D	S	■	72 S	T	D	S

Acknowledgments

I'm going to tell you a story. Just one more. You thought I was done with storytelling, didn't you? Well sit back down, because this is my book, and it's not over until I say it is.

A few years ago, I read an article titled "Thank You to the Author's Many, Many Important Friends: How the Acknowledgments Page Became the Place to Drop Names." At the time it sounded like the silliest thing. Why would you need to thank hundreds of people, wasting extra pages and your readers' precious time, when you could just thank your editor, your agent, and your mom? I figured authors must be a weird breed of self-righteous humans. Or that it was a scheme to sell more books. Yes, that had to be it. If you publicly thank a million people, they'll all talk about your book and you will in turn sell millions of books.

This was before I'd started writing *Down and Across*. Before I spent late nights in coffee shops and hung out in YA circles and called myself a writer. Now that I'm on the other side, holy crap. A few pages isn't nearly enough.

So here's my serpentine list of thank yous—and apologies in advance to Penguin for these unexpected pages. You asked for one book and now you're getting another.

First, Tina Wexler. I'm so grateful to have you as my agent. You've been my biggest cheerleader and champion, and these pages wouldn't exist without you. Thank you for your brilliant feedback, your brainstorming sessions, your ability to put out fires with class, and your pep talks and emails. Those long-distance phone calls from Helsinki were so worth it.

Alex Ulyett, you are the sharpest Ravenclaw I know. You deserve a genius award just for your editorial letters. I can't thank you enough for connecting with Scott, Fiora, and Trent, and for taking this story to the next level.

A special shout-out to Angela Duckworth. You are the real deal. Thank you for your inspirational TED talk and for being even friendlier in real life than Cecily Mallard.

It took a lot of editing to whip this book into shape. Huge thanks to my good friends who read early drafts and provided invaluable feedback: Joey Jachowski, Emma Stein, Isabelle Fisher, Brian McCormick, and Josh Dillon. Nicole Bleuel, who pitched my book so well to a bookseller in Helsinki that he actually thought she was my literary agent. Nava Ahmadi, my teen editor, who put awesome YA books in my hands. Lauryn Chamberlain for her slay warnings and 14/10s.

Eliot Schrefer, your editorial letter not only meant so much to me but taught me how to tell better stories. I still owe you that scotch.

Finn Vigeland, my forever roomie (Rumi!) and cruciverbalist-in-chief. You inspired (Finnspired) this novel's downs and acrosses and answered all my crossword questions. That last puzzle would have been a major disaster (Major Disaster!) without your help. Wordplay forever.

ADAM SILVERA. You deserve all caps. Damn, sometimes I feel like I owe this career to you. Thank you for aggressively hand-selling me *Simon vs. the Homo Sapiens Agenda* at the Strand, for your friendship, and for your dope blurb.

The entire team at Penguin! Ken Wright and Lily Yengle, for your tremendous support. Elyse Marshall (you are *so* not an Elaine). Maggie Edkins for this perfect cover. Venessa Carson, Rachel Wease, and the rest of the schools and libraries team. Colleen Conway, Jill Bailey, and all the wonderful sales reps. Mariam Quraishi, Samira Iravani, and any other designer who helped produce this book. The folks over at Listening Library for the audio version. And Jen Loja, Divya Sawhney, and Markus Dohle for running the show. I'm so thankful for this publishing family.

Emile Holmewood, aka "BloodBros," many thanks for the original cover. Isometric never looked sexier.

Oftentimes, the smallest interaction or encounter will inspire a character for me. Shout-out to Jeanette, who checked me into my hostel in the Scottish Highlands—I'm sure you're actually a lovely person and nothing like the Jeanette on these pages. Mimi, the photographer I sat next to and talked to for hours on a bus ride between Boston and New York. Even the tall, drunk man who tried to beat me up at four in the morning in Hong Kong.

Sofia Vassilieva and Fiora MacPherson, who embody the best of Fiora Buchanan.

Greyfriars Kirkyard in Edinburgh for providing some excellent last names.

And while we're talking about locations—I have to thank all the coffee shops and cafes where I wrote this book, both in New York City and around the world. There are far too many to name, so of course I'm going to try: Third Rail Coffee (your baristas will forever be too cool for me), Lilia Caffé (your baristas are extremely friendly), Think Coffee (thank you for not having WiFi), Dream Baby (my home away from home), Ground Support, Starbucks, Toby's Estate, Brew Lab, Apero . . . I could go on, but now that I think of it, the owner of Blue Bottle Coffee probably isn't reading my book, let alone the acknowledgments.

Down and Across is a bit of a love letter to DC, which has so much more going on than just politics. Places like Kramerbooks, Tonic, and Dupont Circle are very much real, and you should visit them the next time you're in town!

Much love to my New York writing crew: Kheryn Callender, Emily Pan, Jeremy West, Jeffrey West, Lexi Wangler, Cristina Arreola, Karen Bao, Kim Small, Sarah Smetana. Patrice Caldwell, has anyone actually read it yet? And psst, Laura Sebastian, more up-state writing retreats please.

Arthur Levine and David Levithan, for being pals. Marty Mayberry for her fantastic feedback on my query letter, and the Sun vs. Snow organizers for a really fun query contest.

Speaking of fun, can we talk about the crossword puzzle community? I knew from the moment Finn brought me to Lollapuzzoola in 2014 that I was writing about a very special group of people. Thanks in particular to Sam Ezersky and Will Shortz for your kind words about the book.

Thanks to the Yext community, who kept me energized and happy while I wrote *Down and Across* on nights and weekends.

Jon Torre and Amanda Mui, it was an honor being your first "artist in residence" in Helsinki.

Khaled Hosseini, David Arnold, and Jasmine Warga, thanks so much for your kind words about *Down and Across*, and for your stories that have inspired me. Becky Albertalli and Angie Thomas, let's go to Harry Potter World again!

To every teacher, librarian, and bookseller out there—thank you. You're doing the real work.

To my family. Maman, Baba, Neeki, Arman, and Nava—I could fill every book in the world with my love and gratitude for you, and it still wouldn't be enough. Merci.

And to you, kind reader. Thank you for picking up this book. I hope you connected with Scott and his journey, and I hope you figure out how to be gritty. Maybe you already are. Or maybe, like it did for me, it'll click when you least expect it.